# EGO
## maniac

D1113103

# VI KEELAND

Copyright © 2016 by Vi Keeland
ISBN: 978-1682309810

**EGOMANIAC**

Edited by: Jessica Royer Ocken
Cover model: Clément Becq
Photographer: Fred Goudon - www.fredgoudon.com
Cover designer: Sommer Stein, Perfect Pear Creative
Proofreading and Interior Formatting by Elaine York,
Allusion Graphics, LLC/Publishing & Book Formatting

SOMETIMES WHAT
YOU'RE LOOKING FOR
COMES WHEN YOU'RE
NOT LOOKING AT ALL.

-UNKNOWN

# CHAPTER ONE

## DREW

*I hate New Year's Eve.*

Two hours in traffic to make it not even the nine miles home from LaGuardia. It was after ten o'clock at night. Why weren't all these people at a party by now? Whatever tension two weeks in Hawaii had relieved was already back to coiling tighter and tighter inside me as the town car inched its way uptown.

I tried not to think about all the work I was coming back to—the endless string of other people's problems to compound my own:

*She cheated.*

*He cheated.*

*Get me full custody of the kids.*

*She can't have the house in Vail.*

*All she wants is my money.*

*She hasn't given me a blowjob in three years.* Listen, asshole, you're fifty, bald, pompous, and shaped like an egg. She's twenty-three, hot, and has tits so young they almost reach up to her chin. You want to fix this marriage? Come home with ten Gs in fresh, crisp bills, and tell her to get on her knees. You'll get your blowjob. She'll get her spending money. Let's not pretend it was ever more than it really was. That doesn't work for you? Unlike your soon-to-be ex-wife, I'll take a check. Make that out to Drew M. Jagger, Attorney at Law.

I rubbed the back of my neck, feeling slightly claustrophobic in the back of the Uber, and looked out the window. An old lady with a walker passed us.

"I'll get out here," I barked at the driver.

"But you have luggage?"

I was already exiting the back of the car. "Pop the trunk. It's not like we're moving anyway."

Traffic was at a dead stop, and it was only two blocks to my building. Tossing a hundred-dollar tip at the driver, I grabbed my suitcase from the trunk and took in a deep breath of Manhattan.

I loved this city as much as I hated it.

575 Park Avenue was a restored pre-war on the southeast corner of Sixty-Third Street—it was an address that gave people preconceived notions about you. Someone with my last name had occupied the building since before the place was converted into overpriced co-ops. Which is why my office was allowed to remain on the ground floor when other commercial tenants were tossed out years ago. I also lived on the top floor.

"Welcome back, Mr. Jagger." The uniformed doorman greeted me as he swung open the lobby door.

"Thanks, Ed. I miss anything while I was gone?"

"Nah. Same old, same old. Peeked in on your construction the other day, though. Looking good."

"They use the service entrance down Sixty-Third like they were supposed to?"

Ed nodded. "Sure did. Barely heard them the last few days."

I dropped my luggage inside my apartment, then headed back downstairs in the elevator to check things out. For the last two weeks, while I was screwing off in Honolulu, my office space had been getting a total renovation. Cracks in the high, plastered ceilings were to be patched and painted, and new floors installed to replace the old, worn parquet.

Thick plastic remained taped over all of the interior doorways when I walked in. The little furniture I hadn't put in storage was also still covered with tarps. *Shit. They aren't done yet.* The contractor had assured me there would only be finish work left by the time I returned. I was right to be skeptical.

Flicking on the lights, I was happy to find the lobby completely done, though. Finally, a New Year's Eve with no horrible surprises for a change.

I took a quick look around, pleased with what I found, and was just about to leave when I noticed a light streaming from under the door of a small file room at the end of the hallway.

Thinking nothing of it, I headed to turn it off.

Now, I'm six foot two and a half, two hundred and five pounds, and maybe it was just my frame of mind, my not expecting to see anyone, but when I opened the door to the file room, finding her there scared the living crap out of me.

She screamed.

I took a step back through the door.

She got up, stood on the chair, and began yelling at me, waving her cell phone in the air.

"I'll call the police!" Her fingers shook as she dialed nine, then one, and hovered over the last one. "Get out now, and I won't call!"

I could have lunged for her, and the phone would have been out of her hand before she realized she hadn't dialed the final digit. But she looked terrified, so I retreated another step and put my hands up in surrender.

"I'm not going to hurt you." I used my best soothing, calm voice. "You don't need to call the police. This is my office."

"Do I look stupid to you? You just broke into *my* office."

"*Your* office? I think you took a wrong turn at the corner of Crazy and Nutjob."

She wobbled atop the chair, holding both arms out to regain her balance, and then...her skirt fell to her feet.

"Get out!" She crouched down and grabbed her skirt, tugging it up to her waist as she turned her back to me.

"Do you take medication, ma'am?"

"*Medication? Ma'am?* Are you joking?"

"You know what?" I motioned to the phone she was still holding. "Why don't you push that last one and get the police over here. They can drive you back to whatever loony bin you escaped from."

Her eyes widened.

For a crazy person—now that I was really looking—she was pretty damn cute. Fiery red hair piled on top of her head seemed to match her firecracker personality. Although from the looks of her blazing blue eyes, I was glad I'd held off on telling her that.

She pushed one and proceeded to report the crime of entering one's own office. "I'd like to report a robbery."

"Robbery?" I arched an eyebrow and looked around. A lone folding chair and crappy metal folding table were the only furniture in the entire space. "What exactly am I stealing? Your winning personality?"

She amended her complaint to the police. "A breaking and entering. I'd like to report a breaking and entering at 575

Park Avenue." She paused and listened. "No, I don't think he's armed. But he's big. *Really big*. At least six feet. Maybe bigger."

I smirked. "And strong. Don't forget to tell them I'm strong, too. Want me to flex for you? And maybe you should tell them I have green eyes. Wouldn't want the police to confuse me with all the other *really big* thieves hanging out *in my office.*"

After she hung up, she stayed standing on the chair, still glaring at me.

"Was there also a mouse?" I asked.

"A mouse?"

"Considering you jumped up on that chair." I chuckled.

"You find this funny?"

"Oddly, I do. And I have no fucking idea why. It should annoy the crap out of me that I come home from a two-week vacation and find a squatter in my office."

"Squatter? I'm no squatter. This is my office. I moved in a week ago."

She bobbled again while standing on her chair.

"Why don't you get down? You're going to fall off that thing and get hurt."

"How do I know you're not going to hurt me when I get down?"

I shook my head and contained my laugh. "Sweetheart, look at the size of me. Look at the size of you. Standing on that chair isn't doing jack shit to keep you safe. If I wanted to hurt you, you'd be out cold on the floor already."

"I take Krav Maga classes twice a week."

"Twice a week? Really? Thanks for the warning."

"You don't have to ridicule me. Maybe I *could* hurt you. For an intruder, you're really kind of rude, you know."

"Get down."

After a full minute stare-off, she climbed off the chair.

"See? You're as safe on the ground as you were up there."

"What do you want from here?"

"You didn't call the police, did you? You almost had me there for a second."

"I didn't. But I can."

"Now why would you go and do that? So they can arrest you for breaking and entering?"

She pointed down at her makeshift desk. For the first time, I noticed papers all over the place. "I told you. This is my office. I'm working late tonight because the construction crew was so loud today that I couldn't get done what I needed to. Why would anyone break and enter *to work* at ten-thirty at night on New Year's Eve?"

Construction crew? *My construction crew?* Something was going on here. "You were here with the construction crew today?"

"Yes."

I scratched my chin, half believing her. "What's the foreman's name?"

"Tommy."

*Shit.* She was telling the truth. Well, at least some of it had to be the truth. "You said you moved in a week ago?"

"That's right."

"And you rented the space from whom, exactly?"

"John Cougar."

Both my brows shot up this time. "John Cougar? Did he drop the Mellencamp, by chance?"

"How should I know?"

This wasn't sounding good. "And you paid this John Cougar?"

"Of course. That's how renting an office suite works. Two months' security, first and last month's rent."

I shut my eyes and shook my head. "Shit."

"What?"

"You got conned. How much did all of that cost you? Two months' security, first and last month? Four months in total?"

"Ten thousand dollars."

"Please tell me you didn't pay cash."

Something finally clicked, and the color drained from her pretty face. "He said his bank was closed in the evening, and he couldn't give me the keys until my check cleared. If I gave him cash, I could move in right away."

"You paid John Cougar *forty thousand dollars* in cash?"

"No!"

"Thank God."

"I paid him ten thousand in cash."

"I thought you said you paid four months."

"I did. It was twenty-five hundred a month."

That did it. Of all the crazy shit I'd heard so far, thinking she could get space on Park Avenue for twenty-five hundred a month took the cake. I broke out in a fit of laughter.

"What's so funny?"

"You're not from New York, are you?"

"No. I just moved here from Oklahoma. What does that have to do with anything?"

I took a step closer. "I hate to break the news to you, Oklahoma, but you got ripped off. This is my office. I've been here for three years. My father the thirty before that. I was on vacation the last two weeks and had the office remodeled while I was gone. Someone named after a singer scammed you into giving him *cash* to rent an office he had no right to rent. Doorman's name is Ed. Walk through the main building entrance, and he'll verify everything I just said."

"That can't be."

"What do you do that you need office space?"

"I'm a psychologist."

I held out my hand. "I'm an attorney. Let me see your contract."

Her face fell. "He hasn't brought it by yet. He said the landlord was in Brazil on vacation, and I could move in, and he would come back on the first to collect the rent and bring me the contract to sign."

"You've been scammed."

"But I paid him ten thousand dollars!"

"Which is another thing that should have tipped you off. You couldn't rent a closet on Park Avenue for twenty-five hundred a month. Didn't you find it strange that you were getting a place like this for next to nothing?"

"I thought I was getting a deal."

I shook my head. "You got a deal alright. A raw deal."

She covered her mouth. "I think I'm going to be sick."

# CHAPTER TWO

## EMERIE

I felt like such a damn idiot.

A light knock came on the bathroom door. "You okay in there?"

"I'm fine." Embarrassed. Stupid. Naïve. *Flat broke.* But fine.

I washed my face and stared at myself in the mirror. What the hell was I going to do now? My phone line was finally being installed this week, and my stationery was being delivered. *My beautiful stationery.* With the pretty logo and fancy new Park Avenue address. *Ugh.* Another two hundred and fifty dollars wasted. I hung my head and stared down at the sink, unable to look at my dumb face any more.

Eventually, I cracked open the bathroom door and stepped out. The rightful tenant leaned against the wall, waiting for me. Of course, he had to be gorgeous. Because I couldn't just mortify myself in front of an ugly man. *No, definitely not.*

"You sure you're okay?"

I avoided eye contact. "I'm not. But I will be." I hesitated before continuing. "Is it okay if I go back into my office...I mean...*your* office...and clean up my stuff?"

"Of course. Take your time."

There wasn't too much to pack. All of my furniture was also being delivered this week. As were the files from my storage unit. I was going to have to cancel that, too. Where the hell was I going to put everything? My apartment wasn't much bigger than the file room I'd been sitting in.

As I was packing the last of my things into the box I'd brought them in, the rightful tenant came to stand in the doorway. I spoke before he could.

"I'm so sorry—for falling for the scam, for threatening to call the cops on you."

"Don't forget threatening harm with your mad Krav Maga skills."

I looked up and found him smirking. It was a good look. *Too good.* His handsome face made me nervous, albeit not the kind of nervous I felt compelled to stand on a chair and call the police over. No, this man's smile was cocky and hit me in the knees—amongst other places.

"I do take Krav Maga, you know."

"Good for you. You scared me a little when I walked in. I bet you can kick some little-girl butt."

I froze mid-packing. "Little-girl butt? My instructor is a man."

He folded his arms across his chest. His *wide, thick chest.* "How long have you been taking lessons?"

"Almost three months."

"You are not going to take down a man of my size with three months of Krav Maga training."

Maybe it was the late hour, or the realization that I'd been conned out of my life savings and had no office to meet patients in, but my sanity snapped. I lunged at the poor, unsuspecting man. I literally hopped up on my chair, jumped onto the folding table, and dove at him. *Dove at him.*

Even though I'd caught him by surprise, he had me completely restrained in less than a heartbeat. I wasn't even sure what the move he'd done was. Somehow he'd managed to spin me around so my back was to his front and my arms were pinned behind me between us.

It pissed me off that he wasn't even winded when he spoke. His breath tickled my neck as he held me in place, and his voice was low and measured. "What was that?"

"I was trying to show you my moves."

I felt his body shake behind me, although there was no sound.

"Are you laughing at me? *Again?*"

He laughed through his answer. "No."

"I have moves. I swear. I'm just all sorts of off tonight because of everything that happened."

He still hadn't released me. Instead, he leaned forward, putting his head over my shoulder, and spoke. "If we're showing off moves, I'd be happy to demonstrate some of mine, too."

Every hair on my body reached for the sky while goosebumps prickled my skin. "Umm...I...I..."

He released his hold, and it took me a minute to find my bearings. Rather then face him with the blush I felt on my face, I kept my back to him as I gathered the last of my things and pulled my charger from the wall.

"I have deliveries scheduled and a phone line being installed Tuesday." My shoulders slumped again. "I paid double for the storage company to deliver this week, too. I'll cancel everything first thing in the morning, but just in case they show up...if you're here, if you wouldn't mind turning them away."

"Of course."

"Thank you." I lifted my box and had no choice but to face him.

He walked around the table to where I was standing and took it out of my hands before leading me to the reception area. Everything else in the space was dark, but the light from what I'd thought was my file room illuminated the hall enough that we could see each other. We stopped in front of the service door I'd been using for the last week. It dawned on me that the fake real estate agent probably had me using that entrance to avoid getting caught too quickly. He'd told me not to use the main Park Avenue entrance because the building didn't want dust tracked through on our shoes during the construction. I'd bought everything that scammer had said.

"Got a name, Oklahoma? Or should I just call you squatter?"

"Emerie. Emerie Rose."

"Pretty name. Rose your last name or middle?"

"Last."

He shifted the box he was carrying from two hands to one and extended the free one to me. "Drew. Drew Michael."

I squinted. "Middle or last?"

His smile lit up the dimness as I placed my hand in his. The man didn't have dimples. He had mouth cleavage.

"Middle. Jagger's my last name."

"Nice to meet you, Drew Jagger."

He didn't let go of my hand. "Really? Nice to meet me? You're way more polite than I would be under the circumstances."

"You're right. At this point, I might be wishing you were really a burglar after all."

"Do you have a car? It's late, and this box is pretty heavy."

"It's fine. I'll just grab a cab."

He nodded. "Better be careful getting in and out. That skirt seems to have a mind of its own."

That time, not even the dark could hide the blush. "With all the mortification I've suffered tonight, you couldn't let me just have that one? Pretend it never happened?"

Drew smirked. "It's impossible to pretend I didn't see *that* ass."

I was thin, but my ass was a little on the large side. I'd always been self conscious of it. "What's that supposed to mean?"

"It was a compliment."

"Oh."

"Why did your skirt fall down, anyway? Did you lose weight recently or something?"

At that point, nothing could embarrass me any more than I'd already done to myself, so I laughed as I told him the truth. "I had a big burger for dinner, and my skirt was tight so I unzipped it. The door was locked. I didn't think anyone would be coming in."

"A woman who eats big burgers and looks like that? Don't let the other New York women know. They'll put you back on a bus to Oklahoma." He winked. And God, was I pathetic that I felt the pitter-patter of my heart speed up.

We walked outside, and Drew waited with me, holding my box until a cab pulled up at the curb. He leaned on the top of the door after I climbed in.

"New Year's Eve always sucks. Tomorrow will be better. Why don't you stay in bed, order another big burger, and try to get some rest. I'll meet you at the police station the day after tomorrow. 19th Precinct over on 67th Street. Say eight a.m.? New Year's Day will be crazy at the station—still processing drunken idiots from the night before."

I hadn't even thought of the police. I guess I did need to file a report.

"You don't have to come with me. I've already intruded enough on you."

Drew shrugged. "They'll want my statement for their report anyway. Plus, I'm friendly with a few of the guys. It'll get you in and out faster."

"Okay."

He rapped his knuckles on the top of the cab twice and leaned in to speak to the driver. "Take good care of her. She's had a shitty night."

Once we pulled away into traffic, everything that had happened over the last hour hit me. My adrenaline had spiked, and I started to free-fall down.

*I've been scammed out of my life savings.*

*I no longer have an office.*

*I've given all of my patients my new address.*

My head spun.

*Where will I go?*

*What will I do for a security deposit even if I find someplace new on short notice?*

Feeling nauseous again, I leaned my head back against the leather seat and shut my eyes, taking a few deep breaths. Oddly, the first thing that popped into my head was the handsome, dark-haired man with the full lips leaning against my office doorway. *His* office doorway. And with that image in my mind—in the midst of my spiral down and a massive anxiety attack—I couldn't stop the small smile that curled my lips.

# CHAPTER THREE

## DREW

I twisted the dial on my watch. *Twenty minutes late.* She was sexy, and that one little soft spot that remained in my heart actually felt bad for how she'd been conned. But *twenty minutes*? I billed at $675 an hour. I'd just lost $225 standing in front of the damn police station. I took one last look up the block and was about to head back down to my office when a flash of color turned the corner.

Green. I'd always been fond of green. What's not to like? Money, grass, those frogs with the bulging eyes that I loved to chase as a kid—but today *fond* was promoted to *favorite* as I watched Emerie's tits bounce up and down in her sweater. For a little thing, she had some rack—went nicely with that curvy ass.

"I'm so sorry I'm late." Her coat was open and her pale cheeks pink as she panted from her sprint up the block. She looked different than she had the other night. Her long, wavy hair was down, and sunlight picked up little flecks of gold in its copper color. She attempted to tame it as she spoke. "I took the wrong train."

"I was just about to leave." I looked down at my watch and caught tiny droplets of sweat beading between her cleavage. Clearing my throat, I padded how long I'd been waiting. "Thirty-five minutes. That'll be $350."

"What?"

I shrugged and kept my face stoic. "I bill at $675 an hour. You made me waste more than a half-hour of my time. So that'll be $350."

"I can't afford to pay you. I'm broke, remember?" She held up her hands in exasperation. "Swindled into renting your fancy office. I shouldn't have to pay you that kind of money just because I overslept."

"Relax. I'm screwing with you." I paused. "Wait. I thought you took the wrong train?"

She bit her lip, looking guilty, and pointed to the door of the police station. "We should go inside. I've kept you waiting long enough."

I shook my head. "You lied to me."

Emerie sighed. "I'm sorry. I overslept. I couldn't fall asleep again last night. This all still feels like a bad dream to me."

I nodded and uncharacteristically let her off the hook. "Come on. Let's see if there's a chance in hell they can catch this guy."

Inside the police station, the desk sergeant was talking on the phone when we walked in. He smiled and held up two fingers. After he finished telling the caller that stolen supermarket circulars would be a matter for the US Postal Inspector and not the NYPD, he extended his hand, leaning over the counter.

"Drew Jagger. What brings you down to the dregs? Slummin' today?"

I smiled and clasped his hand. "Something like that. How's it going, Frank?"

"Never been happier. Go home at night, don't take my shoes off at the door, leave the seat up in the bathroom after I take a piss, and use paper plates so I don't have to wash jack shit. The single life is good, my friend."

I turned to Emerie. "This is Sergeant Frank Caruso. He keeps me in business the way he goes through wives. Frank, this is Emerie Rose. She needs to file a police report. Any chance Mahoney is on today? Maybe he can help her out."

"He's out for a few weeks. Twisted his ankle chasing a perp on a B&E. But I'll take a look at who's in the bullpen and get someone good. What's up? Domestic issue? Husband giving her a hard time?"

"Nothing like that. Emerie's not a regular client. She leased space in my building a few weeks ago."

Frank whistled. "Space on Park Avenue. Pretty and rich. You single, honey?"

"Don't you ever learn your lesson, old man?"

"What? I've only tried ugly and broke. Maybe that's my problem."

"Pretty sure that ain't your problem."

Frank waved me off. "What seems to be the issue? Landlord giving her a hard time or something?"

"She leased my place for $2,500 a month. Paid $10,000 up front. Problem is, she didn't lease it from the landlord. Got scammed by someone posing as a leasing agent while I was out of town and my office was getting renovated."

"$2,500 a month. For your building?"

"She's from Oklahoma."

He looked to Emerie. "No Monopoly in Oklahoma? Couldn't figure out that Park Place was five times the price of Baltic?"

I cut Sergeant Wise Ass off before he made Emerie feel worse than she already did. After all, I'd ridiculed her judgment the other night when she'd surprised me with a welcome home I wasn't expecting. Enough was enough. Frank gave her some paperwork to start filling out and showed us to a private room to wait. On our way, I stopped to talk to an old friend, and Emerie was nearly done with the forms when I joined her.

I shut the door behind me, and she looked up and asked, "Do you do criminal work?"

"No. Just matrimonial."

"Every cop seems to know you."

"My buddy used to work in this precinct. Some of my first clients were cops. You're a friend of a brother in blue, and do a good job for one, you get the business of the entire precinct and then some. They're a loyal bunch. At least to each other. Highest occupational divorce rate in the city, though."

A minute later, a detective I'd never met came in and took Emerie's statement, then mine. When he finished, he said he was done with me, if I wanted to go.

I had no idea why I was still hanging around a half-hour later as Emerie flipped through her second thick book of mug shots.

She turned the page and sighed. "I can't believe how many criminals look like everyday people."

"Would make it more difficult for you to hand over ten thousand in cash if the guy *looked* like a criminal, wouldn't it?"

"I suppose."

I scratched my chin. "What did you carry that kind of cash in anyway? A brown paper bag filled with hundreds?"

"No." Her tone was defensive, but she didn't offer anything more. So I stared at her, waiting. She rolled her eyes. "Fine. But it wasn't a brown paper bag. It was white. And said Wendy's on it."

I raised my brow. "Wendy's? The fast food place? Really got a thing for burgers, huh?"

"I put the burger I'd just picked up for lunch in my purse and carried the cash in it because I didn't want to let it out of my hands on the subway. I figured it was more likely someone might try to steal my pocketbook than my lunch."

She had a point. "Good thinking for a girl from Oklahoma."

She squinted at me. "I'm from Oklahoma City, not farm land. You think I'm naïve just because I'm not from New York, that I make bad decisions."

I couldn't help myself. "You did give a fake real estate agent ten grand in a Wendy's bag."

It looked like smoke was about to blow from her ears. Luckily, a knock at the door prevented me from getting chewed out Oklahoma-style again. Frank popped his head in. "Got a second, counselor?"

"Sure thing."

Frank opened the door wide, waited for me to walk through, and shut it behind us before he spoke. "We got a little problem, Drew."

He had his sergeant face on as he pointed to the closed door Emerie sat behind. "Standard operating procedure is to run the complainant."

"Yeah, so?"

"Oklahoma there, she popped. Got an outstanding warrant."

"You're shitting me?"

"Wish I was. New computer system makes us record the reason we run the name. Detective who took her statement had already entered in that she was here in the stationhouse. Not like the old days. Everything is traceable now. She's gonna have to take care of the warrant. I'm off in an hour. I'll take the collar and drive her over to the courthouse to answer the charges so we don't have to put her in cuffs, if you want. It's an appearance ticket. I'm sure she can enter a plea and take care of it easy enough."

"What's the charge?"

Frank smirked. "Indecent exposure."

———

"So tell me the whole story, from the beginning." We sat on a bench outside of the courtroom, waiting for the afternoon warrant session to begin.

Emerie hung her head. "Do I have to?"

I lied. "You're going to have to tell your story to the judge, so as your attorney, I need to hear it first."

She'd no doubt be pissed when she realized an appearance ticket didn't require recounting the events in question. We would walk in, plead guilty, pay a fine, and be out the door in an hour. But my entire day was wasted, so I deserved a little fun. Plus, I liked the fiery side of her personality. She was even sexier pissed off.

"Okay. Well, I was here in New York for the summer visiting my grandmother. And I met this guy. We went out a few times, were getting close, and this one particular August night it was really hot and muggy. I'd just graduated high school and never did anything even remotely wild back home. So when he suggested we go skinny dipping in the public pool, I thought, *Why not? No one will ever know.*"

"Go on."

"We went to the Y on Eighty-Second Street that has an outdoor pool and hopped the fence. It was so dark when we got undressed, I didn't even think the guy would be able to see me."

"So you undressed? What color were your bra and underwear?" *Seriously?* I was a sick fuck asking these types of questions. But in my twisted imagination, I saw her in a little white thong and matching lacy bra.

She looked momentarily panicked. "Do you really need to know all this? It was ten years ago."

"I should. The more details the better. It'll show the judge you remember the night well, and he'll think you're remorseful."

Emerie nibbled on her thumbnail in deep thought. "White! They were white."

*Nice.* "G-string or briefs?"

Her cheeks turned pink, and she covered her face with her hands. "G-string. God, this is so embarrassing."

"It'll make things easier to flesh it out now."

"Okay."

"Did you undress yourself or did this guy undress you?"

"I undressed myself."

"Okay. What happened next? Tell me all the details. Don't leave anything out. You might not think it's relevant, but it could help your case."

She nodded. "After I got undressed, I left my clothes in a pile near the fence we'd climbed. Jared—that's the guy I was with—he took off his clothes, left them next to mine, went to the high-dive board, and cannonballed in."

"Then what?"

"Then the police came."

"You weren't even in the water yet? No fooling around in the pool or anything?"

"Nope. I never even made it into the pool. Right after Jared came up for air, the sirens were flashing."

I felt like I got ripped off. All that build-up and that's it? Not even any groping? Before I could ask her any more questions, a court officer rattled off a list of names. I heard him call Rose, so I guided Emerie to where he was standing outside of the courtroom with a clipboard.

"Room 132, down the hall to your right. The ADA will meet you there to discuss your case before you see the judge. Wait outside. She'll call your name when it's your turn."

Knowing where the room was, I walked Emerie down the hall, and we took a seat on the bench outside. She was quiet for a minute before she spoke. Her voice had a little shake to it, like she was fighting back crying.

"I'm so sorry about all of this, Drew. I probably owe you five thousand dollars for all of your time, and I can't even afford to pay you five hundred."

"Don't worry about it."

She reached out and touched my arm. I'd had my hand on her back as we walked and also helped her out of the back of the police car Sergeant Caruso drove us over in, but it was the first time she'd touched me. I liked it. *Damn it.* I didn't know her well, but I knew enough to know Oklahoma was not the type of woman you screwed and screwed over. I needed to get this over with and get out of here.

"I mean it. I'm really sorry, and I can't thank you enough for coming with me today. I'd be a wreck if I didn't have you here. I'll pay you back somehow."

*I can think of a few ways.* "It's fine. Really. Don't worry about it. This is all going to go smoothly, and we'll be out of here in twenty minutes."

Just then, a voice called from behind the door. "*Rose. Docket number 18493094. Counsel for Rose?*"

I assumed it was the ADA. I didn't do much criminal work, just the occasional traffic ticket or domestic violence charge for an existing high-net-worth divorce client. But the woman's voice was vaguely familiar, although I couldn't place it.

Until I opened the door.

Suddenly it was eminently clear why the yell had sounded familiar.

I'd heard it before.

The last time, she'd been screaming my name as I plowed into her from behind in the office bathroom of a rival law firm.

Of all the lawyers in New York County, Kierra Albright had to be our ADA.

Maybe *smooth* wasn't exactly the right word for how things were about to go.

# CHAPTER FOUR

## DREW

*Fuck.*

"I don't understand. What's going on?" Emerie's voice was full of panic.

And I couldn't blame her. Everyone knows cobras, tigers, and sharks are dangerous. But the bottlenose dolphin? So sweet looking and loveable, their whistle plays harmony when you pet them on the top of the head. But accidentally injure one and they *will* attack. It's true. My hobby, other than fucking and working, is watching the National Geographic channel.

Kierra Albright is a bottlenose dolphin. She'd just recommended thirty days in jail to the judge, rather than the fine she'd told us she would offer less than a half-hour ago.

"Give me a minute. Take a seat in the galley, and I'll come get you in a few. I need to have a word with the ADA. Alone."

Emerie nodded, even though she looked like she was on the verge of tears, and I took a moment to let her compose herself. Then I opened the gate that separates the spectators from the players in the courtroom and led her to an empty row in the back. As I started to walk away, I saw a tear roll down her face, and it stopped me in my tracks.

Without thinking, I lifted her chin so our eyes met. "Trust me. You're going home tonight. Okay? *Just trust me.*"

My voice startled Kierra in the ladies' room across from the courtroom.

"What the hell was that all about?" I locked the door as she turned to face me.

"You can't come in here."

"If anyone asks, I'm identifying with my feminine side today."

"You're an asshole."

"*I'm* an asshole? What the hell was with all that 'Nice to see you, Drew,' crap? 'I'll recommend a fifty-dollar fine, and you'll be out of here in time to play golf.'"

She turned away from me and walked to the mirror. Slipping a lipstick from her suit jacket pocket, she leaned in and lined her lips in blood red, saying nothing until she was done. Then she gave me the widest, brightest smile I'd ever seen.

"Figured your new plaything needed to get used to being told one thing and then having another happen when she least expects it."

"She's not my plaything. She's a…friend I'm helping out."

"I saw the way you looked at her, the way you had your hand on her back. If you aren't screwing her already, you will be soon. Maybe she needs a night in county lockup because you can't handle yourself in the courtroom. Might sour her to your charm. Come to think of it, I'm doing the woman a service. She should thank me."

"You're out of your mind if you think I'm going to let you get away with this. Emerie has nothing to do with what went down between the two of us. I'll ask Judge Hawkins to recuse himself if I have to."

"Recuse himself? On what grounds?"

"On the grounds that your father plays golf with him every Friday, and you yourself have told me he gives you whatever you want. Did you forget how much you liked to talk shop after I fucked you?"

"You wouldn't dare."

I had been standing at a distance—ten feet away in front of the locked door—but I walked slowly to where she was standing, getting nice and close.

"Try me."

She held my stare for a long moment. "Fine. But let's do this the way adversaries are supposed to. Not threatening below the belt. We'll make a deal."

I shook my head. "What do you want, Kierra?"

"You want your client home tonight. I want something in return."

"Fine. What do you want?"

Her tongue glossed over her top lip like she was starving and looking at a juicy steak. "You. And not in a bathroom or the back seat of an Uber. I want you—a proper date where you take me out and wine me and dine me before you sixty-nine me."

⌣

"Oh my God. I can't thank you enough."

"Let's just pay the fine and get out of here."

As I sped her out of the courtroom, Emerie seemed to interpret my rush to be about her taking up too much of my day. But it wasn't that at all. I'd almost made it out when Kierra called after us.

"Drew, do you have a moment?"

"Not now. I need to be somewhere." *Anywhere but here.*

I kept my hand on Emerie's back and continued moving, but my client had other ideas. She stopped walking.

"We need to go," I said.

"Let me at least thank the ADA."

"That's not necessary. The city of New York thanks her every other Friday when they hand her a paycheck."

Emerie's eyes scolded me. "I'm not being rude, just because you are." With that, she turned and waited for Kierra to catch up.

She extended her hand. "Thank you so much for everything. I was a wreck this morning when I thought I might be taken into custody."

Kierra looked at Emerie's hand and snubbed her. She turned her body my direction and spoke to me while responding. "Don't thank me. Thank your attorney."

"Yes, I'll do that."

"But don't thank him too much. I don't want him worn out." Kierra turned on her heel and waved goodbye over her shoulder. "I'll call you for our appointment, Drew."

Emerie looked at me. "That was odd."

"She must be off her meds. Come on, let's get you out of here."

By the time we paid the fine and picked up copies of Emerie's warrant clearance, it was nearly four o'clock.

Out on the court steps, she turned to me. "I hope you're not anti public displays of affection, because I need to give you a hug."

I actually wasn't much of a public affection person at all, but hey—I wasn't getting paid for this wasted day, so I might as well get something out of this. Those tits pushed up against me were definitely better than nothing—might even be better than a full day at six seventy-five an hour.

"If you insist."

The smile she shot me was pretty damn close to as perfect as I'd ever seen. Then came the hug. It was a long one—those tits and that tiny, lithe body enveloped me into more than a courtesy hug. She even smelled good.

When she pulled back, she kept her hands on my arms. "I'm going to pay you back for today. Even if it takes me years."

"Don't worry about it."

"No, I mean it."

We spent a few minutes more talking, exchanged numbers in case any deliveries showed up for her, and said goodbye. She was heading uptown, and I was heading down, so we parted in opposite directions. After I took a few steps, I looked back over my shoulder and watched the sway of her ass. She looked just as good going as she did coming.

That made me think... I bet she looked even more incredible when she was *coming*. Just as I was about to turn back around, Emerie turned in my direction, and she caught me watching her walk away. She smiled big and gave a last wave before turning the corner and disappearing out of sight.

I wanted her to pay me back for today, alright.

And I could think of several ways I'd like to collect.

# CHAPTER FIVE

# EMERIE

I lifted my buzzing cell to my ear, catching the time as I did. Almost eleven p.m.—late for anyone to call.

"Hello?"

"Emerie?"

*That voice.* I didn't have to ask who it was. In person, his voice was deep and raspy, but it was downright gravelly on the phone.

"Drew? Is everything okay?"

"Yeah. Why?"

"Because it's sort of late."

I heard the phone move around and then, "Shit. Sorry. I had no idea. I just looked at the time. I thought it was maybe nine."

"Time flies when you spend most of the day in court with criminals, doesn't it?"

"Guess so. I went back home, started to catch up on some work, then stopped in my office. I must've lost track of time."

"I came back home, had a few glasses of wine, and felt sorry for myself some more. Your evening sounds way more productive. Are you still in the office?"

"Yeah. That's what made me call you. I'm sitting here

thinking that when you find a new office, it's going to look very nice."

*What an odd thing to say.* "Thank you. But what makes you say that?"

"Glass and dark wood. I like it. I would have taken you for something more girly, though."

"What are you—oh, no. They delivered my office furniture today?"

"They did."

"How? How did they even get in when you were with me all day?"

"My contractor was here finishing up, and I hadn't had a chance to tell him what went down yet. He thought he was doing you a favor by letting them in."

I banged my head against my kitchen counter, then kept my forehead pressed to it to stop from bludgeoning myself. I couldn't catch the groan that came from my mouth, though.

"I'm sorry. I'll deal with it right away. First thing in the morning."

"Take your time. My stuff is still in storage. I can keep it here for a while."

"Thank you. I'm so sorry. I'll get on the phone first thing in the morning and make them come back and get it. Then I'll come wait at your office so you don't have to deal with it, if that's okay."

"Of course."

"I'm sorry."

"Stop saying you're sorry, Emerie. Ex-cons are hardened. They don't apologize. I'll see you in the morning."

I laughed, because it kept me from crying.

"Hello?" I knocked on the half-opened door and listened to my voice echo back to me. The door pushed open, and I was surprised to find the lobby area still empty. I thought my furniture would have been dropped here.

In the distance, I heard a voice, but couldn't make it out. I stepped inside and yelled a little louder. "Hello? Drew?"

Rapid footsteps clanked against the new marble flooring, each step growing louder until Drew appeared from the hallway. He had his cellphone up to his ear and held up a finger as he continued with his call.

"We don't want the house in Breckenridge. My client hates the cold. She can keep it, but it will be the only property she's leaving this marriage with." A pause, then, "No, I'm not nuts. After I hang up, I'm going to send you some photos of the Breckenridge property. I think they'll convince you that Mrs. Hollister *really enjoys* that house."

Just then, a FedEx deliveryman appeared with a hand truck full of boxes. Drew moved the phone from his ear to speak to him. "Give me one minute."

Deciding the least I could do was help him out, I signed for the delivery and asked the nice delivery man to stack the boxes on top of the plastic-covered reception counter. Drew mouthed *thank you* and continued his call.

While he was semi-yelling at whoever was on the other end of the conversation, I took a minute to check him out. He wore what I assumed by the fit was a very expensive suit. The sleeve on the arm holding the cell was pushed back, revealing a big, expensive-looking watch. His shoes were shiny and his shirt crisply pressed. His hair was dark and too long for a man who shined his shoes, and his skin was tanned from his recent vacation, which made his very light green eyes stand out even brighter.

But it was his lips that were impossible not to stare at—so full and perfectly shaped. *He really is beautiful.* I wasn't sure I'd ever thought of a man as beautiful before. Handsome, yes. Hot, even. But *beautiful* fit the bill to describe Drew Jagger— no other word did him justice.

He finished up his call. "Seriously, Max, how many cases have you been on the other side of the table staring at my pretty face? You don't know when I'm not bluffing by now? Look at the photos, then let me know your answer on the offer. I think you'll find it more than fair after things are put in perspective for you. Her twenty-year-old ski instructor was teaching her a new kind of snowplow. Offer's on the table for forty-eight hours. Then I have to make another phone call to you, which means my client gets another bill and your offer goes down by a fuck of a lot."

Drew pushed a button on his phone and looked up at me, about to speak, when it started to buzz in his hand. "*Shit.*" He sighed, eyes flicking to his phone again and back to me. "Sorry. I need to take this, too."

A Poland Spring delivery guy wheeling big jugs of water knocked at the front door. I looked at Drew. "I got it. Go take your call."

Over the next fifteen minutes that Drew was on the phone, I turned away a solicitor, answered the ringing office phone buried under a tarp—twice—and signed for some legal documents served to the Law Offices of Drew M. Jagger. I was bluffing my way through a prospective client call when Drew reappeared.

"We'll have to thank Mr. Aiken for recommending you." I listened for a moment and then added, "Our rate is..." I caught Drew's eye. "Seven hundred an hour."

The corner of his mouth twitched.

"Sure. Why don't I make you an appointment for an initial consultation? Let me put you on hold for just a minute so I can look up Mr. Jagger's calendar."

I pressed the button and held out my hand, palm up. "Is your calendar synched on your phone?"

Drew pulled his phone from his pocket and handed it to me. "It is."

Opening his mobile Outlook calendar, I scanned for the next opening. There was nothing for a solid month. "Can you move your dinner with someone named Monica from six to eight, and I'll book Mr. Patterson for four-thirty next Wednesday? He said it's urgent. He may need a restraining order to protect his assets like you did for Mr. Aiken."

"Done."

I reconnected the call. "How about four-thirty next Wednesday, the eighth? That's perfect? Great. And our standard retainer is—" I looked to Drew, and he held up ten fingers. "Twelve thousand...Okay, thank you. We look forward to seeing you then. Goodbye."

Drew looked amused as I hung up. "Did I raise my hourly rates from six seventy-five to seven hundred?"

"No. That extra twenty-five dollars is mine. For every hour you bill him, you can take it off of what I owe you. I figured out that my bill for eight hours yesterday is fifty-four hundred dollars—I pay the standard rate, of course, not Mr. Patterson's inflated rate—so if you could bill Mr. Patterson for a few hundred hours, that would be great."

Drew chuckled. "There's the spitfire who attacked me with her mad Krav Maga skills a few nights ago. Your lack of tenacity had me concerned yesterday."

"I was arrested and almost thrown in jail."

"I'm heartbroken. You had such little faith that I would get you off?"

"That woman was out for my blood at first yesterday. What did you say to her to get her to change her tune anyway?"

"We made a deal."

I squinted. "What did you have to give her in return for lightening up on me?"

Drew looked me in the eyes. "Nothing important."

The office phone began to ring again behind me. "Do you want me to..."

He waved me off. "The answering service will pick it up. Come on, I'll show you your furniture."

"I thought it would be in the lobby."

"Tom thought he was helping, so he had them set it up in my office."

I followed Drew down the hall, and he opened the door to the large office next to the file room I'd been working in. The other day when I was here, it hadn't been done—moldings and trim still needed to be hung, and everything was covered by tarps. The contractor must have worked all day yesterday to get it finished.

"Wow. It looks beautiful in here. Except..." I thought better of sharing my thought and shook my head. "Nothing. It looks beautiful."

"Except what? What were you going to say?"

"The office is beautiful. It really is—tall ceilings, wide crown moldings, except...everything is white. Why didn't you paint any color? It's kind of boring all white."

He shrugged. "I like things simple. Black and white."

I snorted. "Good thing you came back when you did, then. I'd already picked out a bright yellow for your office. Copy room was going to be red."

My beautiful desk actually did look amazing in his giant office, even with the boring white paint. The top was a thick tempered glass, and the bottom had dark mahogany legs shaped like a workhorse. I wasn't generally a modern furniture person, but the desk was so beautiful and serene-looking that I had to have it.

"The furniture company wouldn't give me a time, but they're supposed to come today to pick it back up. They wanted to charge me a forty-percent restocking and pickup fee. Took me an hour on the phone with a manager to explain they'd violated their own delivery contract by letting an unauthorized person take delivery."

"You're good on the phone."

"I worked as a customer service rep for a printer company through college. I remember what made me really listen and bend the rules for a customer after a long day of complaint calls."

Drew's cell phone began to ring again. He looked down at it, then decided not to answer.

"Take it. I'll get out of your way. God knows I've taken up enough of your time. And you seem really busy."

"It's okay. I don't need to answer it."

"Is it just you in this big space all alone?"

"I normally have a paralegal and a secretary. But my secretary went out on a few months of medical leave two weeks ago, and my paralegal decided to go to law school out of state."

"Sounds like you're going to be pretty busy."

His cell phone rang again, and this time he said he needed to take the call. He told me to make myself at home, but...there wasn't really anything to do. Drew went into the file room and sat down at the table I'd been using as my desk, and I went back to the lobby. After removing the rest of the plastic from the reception desk, I found some cleaning supplies in the bathroom and wiped it down before setting up my laptop.

In between catching up on emails, I answered the office phone and took messages.

When Drew came back out an hour later, he looked annoyed. "My cell phone died. Could I borrow yours for a few minutes? My cordless is in storage with the rest of my crap, and I was almost done hammering out a settlement. I don't want to give the attorney time to reconsider all the stupid things he just agreed to."

I lifted my phone. "By all means."

Drew took a few steps away and stopped. "What's the password?"

"Ummm. Fuck."

"You don't want me to know your password?"

"No. My password is fuck."

Drew chuckled. "Girl after my own heart." Then he typed it in and was gone again.

By the time noon rolled around, my stomach was growling since I woke up late and hadn't eaten any breakfast. But I couldn't leave the office and chance missing the furniture delivery company again. When I heard Drew take a break from talking on the phone, I ventured to the file room.

"Do you usually order lunch? I'm afraid to go out and miss the delivery."

"Sometimes. What are you in the mood for?"

I shrugged. "I don't care. I'm not picky."

"How about Indian food? Curry House is a few blocks away and delivers quick."

I scrunched up my nose.

"You don't like Indian food?"

"Not really."

"Okay. How about Chinese?"

"Too much MSG."

"Sushi?"

"I'm allergic to fish."

"Mexican?"

"Too heavy for lunch."

"You do understand what the phrase *I'm not picky* means, right?"

I narrowed my eyes at him. "Of course. You're just picking weird stuff."

"What would you like to eat, Emerie?"

"Pizza?"

He nodded. "Pizza it is. See? *I'm* not picky."

After we finished lunch, Drew took his phone from the charger. Then he reached for mine. "Can I look at your pictures?"

"My phone pictures? Why?"

"Best way to get to know someone is to look at their cell phone pictures when they least expect it."

"I'm not even sure what I have on there."

"That's the point. If you have a chance to clean up your pictures, I won't be seeing the real you. I'll be seeing what you want me to see."

I tried to remember if there was anything embarrassing or incriminating on the phone as Drew slid it from my side of the table to his with a smirk on his face. At the last second, I covered his hand with mine, stopping him.

"Wait. I want to look at yours if you're going to look at mine. And you better have some embarrassing things on there, because I'm pretty sure I do."

"By all means. I don't embarrass easily." Drew slid his phone across the folding table.

I watched as he keyed in the password and began to swipe through my photos. After a moment he paused, and his eyebrows rose. "This one tells me a lot about you."

I reached for the phone, but he pulled it back too fast. "What? What photo is it?"

Drew turned the phone so the screen faced me. *Oh, God.* How embarrassing. It was a close-up of me last week while I was working. I'd had a full day of telephone therapy sessions, and my speakerphone had decided to stop working bright and early on that Monday morning. I didn't have time to run out and get a new office phone, and by early afternoon I was frustrated with not being able to multitask because one hand had to hold the phone to my ear. So I'd gotten creative. I'd taken two large, orange rubber bands and put them around the phone and my head—effectively banding the phone in place so I didn't have to hold it anymore. One of the rubber bands ran across my forehead, slightly above my eyebrows and pushed my brow down, giving me an odd, scrunched face. The other rubber band wrapped around my chin, causing the skin to pucker into a very crooked chin dimple that I didn't normally have.

"My speaker phone died, and I had a lot of telephone calls that day. I needed to be able to use my hands."

He chuckled. "Inventive. There hasn't been a good iPhone update since Steve Jobs died. You might want to look into selling them your new technology."

I crumpled up my napkin and threw it at his face. "Shut up."

He swiped a few more times and then stopped. This time, I couldn't make out what he was thinking.

"What? What did you stall on?"

He stared at the photo for a long moment and swallowed before again turning it to face me. It was a full-length photo taken the night I went to a wedding with Baldwin. It was, without a doubt, the best I'd ever looked in a photo. I'd had my hair and makeup professionally done, and the dress I wore fit me like a glove. It was simple—black and sleeveless with a daring, low-cut V that showed off my cleavage and curves. The dress was more risqué than I would normally wear, and I'd been feeling confident and pretty. Although that lasted only about fifteen minutes after Baldwin took that photo, right up until I answered the door to his apartment and realized he was bringing *a date* to the wedding we'd both been invited to. And that date wasn't me.

Remembering the sadness I'd felt that night, I said, "Wedding."

Drew nodded and stared at the photo again before looking back up to me. "You look gorgeous. Sexy as hell."

I felt the blush creep up my face. I hated having fair skin for this exact reason. "Thank you."

He swiped a few more times and turned the cell back to me. "Boyfriend?"

That one had been taken a few minutes after Baldwin told me how beautiful I looked and took that full-length photo of me. His arm was wrapped around my waist, and I was smiling and gazing at him as he took the selfie. His date had rung the doorbell right after that shot. The rest of the night was all forced smiles.

"No."

"Ex-boyfriend?"

"No."

He looked down again and back up at me. "There's a story here, isn't there?"

"How do you know?"

"Your face. The way you're looking at him."

It's pretty sad that a virtual stranger was able to see my feelings after ten seconds of looking at a photo of us, yet Baldwin never was. I could have lied, but for some reason I didn't.

"We met in undergrad school. He was the TA for my psychology class while working on his doctorate. He's one of my closest friends. I actually live in the apartment next to him."

"It didn't work out?"

"We never tried. He doesn't feel the same way about me."

Drew looked like he was going to say more, but just nodded and resumed his picture snooping. By the time he was done, he really had learned a lot about me. He'd seen photos of my two little sisters, including some selfies we'd taken with the dog before I moved to New York. He knew about my feelings for Baldwin, and he was aware of how creative I could be in my need to multitask.

When he slid the phone back to me on the table, I asked, "So...you said checking out each other's photos would tell us a lot about the other person. What did my photos tell you about me?"

"Family oriented, brokenhearted, and a little bit of a nutjob."

I wanted to be offended at that last part, but it was hard when he was completely on point. Although I wasn't going to admit he was right. Instead, I reached for his cell.

"Password?"

He smirked. "Suck."

"Get out of here. You just changed yours."

He shook his head. "Nope. It's one of my favorite words for a multitude of reasons. *You suck* is grumbled under my breath at people at least once a day. And, of course, who doesn't love a good suck?"

"You're a perv."

"Says the woman whose password is *fuck*."

"I made my password *fuck* because I could never remember what my password was, and every time I entered the wrong one, I would grumble *fuck*. Baldwin suggested I just make it *fuck* the last time I was locked out of my own phone."

"Baldwin?"

Our eyes caught. "The guy in the photo."

Drew nodded.

For some reason, talking about Baldwin to Drew made me feel uncomfortable, so I changed the subject. Typing *suck* into his iPhone, I said, "Let's see what I learn about you, counselor."

Drew clasped his hands behind his head and sat back in his chair, watching me. "Have at it."

I found the photos icon and opened it. Seeing nothing, I went to the camera app and opened it. Nothing was there either.

"You have no photos? I thought this was an exercise to learn about each other."

"It was."

"And what exactly did I just learn about you with a camera full of nothing?"

"You learned I don't play fair."

# CHAPTER SIX

## DREW

What an ass.

Me. Not the shapely one I was just caught staring at. Although...*what an ass.*

Emerie had been leaning over the reception desk to reach for my ringing office phone when she caught me leering at her succulent rear end. The polite thing would have been to look away, pretend I wasn't checking her out. But what did I do? I winked.

Again. *What an ass.*

And now, Emerie stared at me as she continued to talk on the phone. Things went one of two ways when a woman caught you red-handed ogling her. She flirted back, or...

Emerie hung up the phone and walked down the hall toward me with purpose. Her face was impassive, so I wasn't sure what to expect.

She stopped at the doorway and crossed her arms over her chest. "Were you just checking out my ass?"

So this was heading the *other* way, where the object of the ogle calls you out on your shit. I mimicked her stance, folding my arms across my chest, too.

"Do you want me to lie?"

"No."

"It's a great ass."

Her cheeks flushed. "*You're* an ass, you know that?"

"Then I must be a great ass. Because it takes one to know one."

Her stoic face cracked, and she laughed. I liked that she was more amused than annoyed. "Do women tend to find your behavior attractive?"

I shrugged. "I'm handsome and rich. Women tend to find that attractive. You'd be surprised how much I can get away with."

"You are *so* full of yourself."

"Maybe, but it's true." I came out from where I'd been standing behind my desk, leaving only about a foot or two between us. "Tell the truth. If I was short, bald, broke, and toothless with a hump on my back, you'd have told me off after catching me looking at your ass."

Her mouth opened, and she looked adorable trying to come up with a retort even though her face had already told me I was right.

"You're an egomaniac."

"Maybe. But an attractive one."

Emerie rolled her eyes and huffed, but I caught a slight smirk on her face right before her hips sashayed out of my office.

*What an ass.*

The rest of the afternoon, I was tied up on the phone. Even though I'd cleared my calendar of office consults until next week, word had gotten out that I was back, and all of my miserable clients wanted to update me on their spouses' latest maneuvers. I worked in an ugly-ass business, but I was damn good at my job. Revenge was what they wanted, and every time I dealt a blow to a wife who deserved it, I mentally got even with my own ex, Alexa, all over again. I probably needed a therapist, but vicarious revenge was cheaper and far more satisfying.

I'd just hung up with a client who wanted a restraining order to keep his estranged wife from burning his porn stash when I overheard Emerie talking on the phone from the reception area. The empty office space carried her voice, and I couldn't help but listen.

"Queens? That's the closest you can get me to midtown for under fifteen hundred a month? What if I went smaller? No reception area, just a simple office in a building somewhere?" She paused for a minute. "What's so funny? Yes, I did think you were quoting me space where more than one person can fit." Another pause. "No, I'm not from New York. But...but... You know what? Forget it. I'll call another agent."

"Trouble finding a place?" I said from behind her.

Emerie spun around. The look on her face was pure exasperation.

"What am I doing in New York?"

"You tell me."

She sighed. "Long story. I—" My office phone rang, and she held up a finger and reached for it before I could even attempt to.

"Drew Jagger's office...Who, may I ask, is calling?...Mr. London..."

She looked to me, and I held up two hands in the universal no-way sign. She continued smoothly.

"Mr. Jagger is in with a client right now. He also has an appointment immediately following this one that is already waiting. Can I take a detailed message for you?"

She was quiet for a minute as she held the phone away from her ear and raised her brows. I could hear that blowhard

Hal London even standing two feet away. When he took a breath, she politely managed to get him off the phone.

"Did you get all that?" she asked me.

"I did. Guy's an asshole. I would almost rather represent his cheating bitch of a wife. He keeps me on the phone for an hour every chance he gets. It's his dime, but I still don't want to talk to him. You managed to get him off pretty quick."

"Try pouring on the sweet extra thick. That always throws people off."

"I'll have to keep that in mind."

Emerie looked at her watch. "It's almost four o'clock. I can't believe the furniture company isn't here yet. I'm sorry, I've been here all day."

"No problem. I'll just add it to your rent bill."

She smiled. "Fine. But then I'm charging you for my secretarial services. I'm not cheap."

A dirty flash of Emerie playing secretary with me as her boss popped into my head, and the words tumbled out before I could stop them. "I'd pay a lot for your services."

She blushed, but then pushed back. "You must be a dick to work for, between your big ego and pervy comments. Good thing you're a lawyer for when you get sued."

"Did you just call me a dick?"

She bit her plump lip. "I did."

I chuckled. "You figured that out pretty quick."

An alarm on her phone began to buzz. She turned it off. "I have a four o'clock call with a patient I have to take. I'm going to step outside to take it. That way I don't miss the furniture company either."

"Why don't you use my office? Might as well get some use out of that desk before they take it back. I'm hard on furniture. I didn't want to ding it and screw up your returning it. More privacy to talk to your patient."

"I don't want to miss the furniture company."

"I'll keep a lookout."

She hesitated. "You don't mind?"

I shook my head. "Nope. Go ahead. I'll play secretary for you now."

It didn't take much to convince her. I watched her walk down the hall—correct that, I watched her ass walk down the hall. When she reached my office she stopped and looked back over her shoulder, catching me once again. So I winked. I'm nothing if not consistent.

It was a little after four-thirty when the furniture company finally showed up. Emerie was still in my office, so I knocked on the half-closed door to get her attention. She was writing in a notebook while talking with a headset on. She'd piled her long, copper hair in a messy bun on top of her head, and when she looked up, it was the first time I'd seen her wearing glasses. They were dark frames, rectangular in shape, and screamed *fuck-me librarian*.

At least that's what I heard when I looked at them. I stared for a minute, getting caught in my own fantasy as she finished up her call.

Her brows drew down as she said goodbye and slipped off her headset. "Is everything okay?"

*Were her eyes always that blue?* The black spectacles must have made the color pop even more than her fair skin already had. "Uh, yeah. The furniture company is here."

She looked at me funny, but then walked out to the lobby. After she signed some paperwork, the workmen followed her to my office. They wrapped the desk in moving blankets and taped them in place.

Emerie sighed, looking on. "It's a beautiful desk."

I watched her watching them ready it for moving. "Gorgeous."

In the last three days, she'd realized she'd been swindled for ten grand, gotten arrested, and found out her dream office belonged to someone else. Yet this was the first time I'd seen her truly saddened. It looked like she'd reached her limit. When I saw her eyes well with tears, I felt it in my chest. It affected me more than I could explain. And obviously it affected more than just my chest, it affected...

My sanity.

Because the *bad idea* I heard myself suggesting certainly wouldn't have come out of my mouth had I not had a momentary lapse in sanity.

"Stay. You and your desk should stay. I have plenty of space here."

# CHAPTER SEVEN

## DREW
*New Year's Eve, Eight years ago*

Some of the best times in life come from bad ideas.

The tall blonde with long legs that stretched like a ladder to heaven? She was definitely a bad idea. I'd been keeping tabs on her all night. She'd come with two friends—all three of them looked barely eighteen. Some local who was a friend of a friend of one of my fraternity brothers had brought them with him. The local had his eye on the blonde, and sometimes his hands, but she seemed to have more interest in getting to know Sigma Alpha guys than him.

I should have been studying for the LSAT. Should have left Atlanta and gone home for break like I normally did. But since it was our last semester in the house, all the seniors in my frat decided to stay for the winter break. One party led into another for ten straight days. And tonight, since it was New Year's Eve, it was an odd crowd. Most of the students were back home, which made room for the locals. And Daisy Duke and her long legs screamed Georgia peach.

Our eyes caught as I took a swig from my beer. She smiled wide, and I had a sudden craving to eat some fruit. She came to me; I didn't even have to get up.

"Is this seat taken?" Momentarily confused, I looked to my right and then my left. I was sitting in a recliner in the corner of the living room, watching the party around me. The closest seat was on the other side of the room.

"You're welcome to sit anywhere you want."

She did just that, plopping her shapely ass down on my lap. "I noticed you looking at me."

"You're a hard person to miss."

"So are you. You're the best-looking guy at this party."

"Is that so?" I took another draw on my beer, and Little Miss Longlegs took it from my hand when I was done. She brought it to her lips and sucked down half the bottle. Finishing, she made a loud *ahhh* sound.

"What's your name, legs?"

"Alexa. What's yours?"

"Drew." I took the beer back and finished it off. "Who's the guy you came here with?"

"Oh, that's just Levi."

"Not a boyfriend or anything?"

She shook her head. "Nope. He's just Levi. He lives in Douglasville, not too far from me. He's good with cars. Sometimes he fixes mine."

Just then, Levi tagged Alexa from the doorway. He didn't look happy to find her sitting on my lap.

I lifted my chin in his direction. "You sure Levi doesn't think you're more than just friends? Looks like he's a little pissed off right now."

She had been sitting with her legs across my lap, but she shifted to face me and swung one over to straddle my hips, effectively blocking my view of her scowling mechanic. "Now you can't see him."

I clasped my hands behind her back. "My view just got a whole lot better."

It was less than an hour later when she asked me to show her my room. Of course, I obliged. I'm nothing if not accommodating to beautiful women. I'd been living at college going on four years now. Some women were straightforward about what they wanted. I was busy and not looking for a relationship, and I appreciated a woman who didn't play games, got straight to the point.

Alexa's fingers were at the zipper of my shorts before I closed the bedroom door. I pushed her up against it to block out the party, and it also slammed shut—two birds, one stone.

"You're applying to law school next year?" she asked as I felt up her tits. It should have set off an alarm since I hadn't mentioned my plans for the future. But...she had great tits. And killer legs. Those were currently wrapped around my waist. I'd also been drinking since the afternoon.

"Yeah. I'll probably stay at Emory. My father and grandfather are legacy."

After that, we brought in the new year with a bang.

Great memories.

Bad idea.

# CHAPTER EIGHT

# DREW

"You what?" Roman Olivet stared at me like I'd just told him I killed Queen Elizabeth. He shook his head. "Bad idea, man."

I looked down at my scotch, swirling the amber liquid in my glass for a minute before bringing it to my lips. "She's going to help me while Tess is out for three months in exchange for rent. It'll give her a chance to find a place she can afford and get back on her feet."

Roman sucked back his beer. "I asked you to rent me space two years ago, and you told me you couldn't share space with anyone."

"I can't. This is temporary."

He squinted at me. "She's hot, isn't she?"

"What's that got to do with anything?"

"You're such a dick."

"What the hell? Emerie said the same thing."

Roman's eyebrows jumped. "She called you a dick, and you're letting her share office space with you? She must have some ass."

I tried to maintain my stoic face, but Roman and I have been friends forever. He caught the slight tick at the corner of my lip.

He shook his head and laughed. "A good ass is your kryptonite, my friend."

To be honest, I was still trying to figure out what the hell had come over me a few hours ago. Not only did I invite this woman—yes, she had a spectacular ass—to move into my office, but I'd had to *convince her* to take me up on my offer. I repeat, I talked her into moving into my Park Avenue office—the space I loathed sharing with anyone—for free.

I tossed back the rest of my scotch and held up my hand to call for a refill.

"What kind of law does she practice?"

"She's not a lawyer. She's a psychologist."

"A shrink? You're going to have a bunch of crazy people walking around your office?"

I hadn't exactly thought of that. What if her patients were psychotic with a variety of multiple personality disorders? Or ex-cons who slit the throats of old ladies but escaped hefty prison sentences because they were insane? *I'm going to be murdered because of a great ass. No ass is worth that.*

Then again...how sane are my own clients? Seventy-one-year-old Ferdinand Armonk, who is worth a hundred-million dollars, was arrested last year for assaulting his twenty-three-year-old bride with his cane because he caught her tongue between his physical therapist's legs. *This* is the crazy I deal with on an everyday basis already.

I shrugged. "Her crazy can't be much worse than my crazy."

Candice Armonk had her husband arrested for hitting her with a cane and was trying to get half his net worth out of the divorce. Roman wasn't just my best friend, he was also my private investigator and had worked the Armonk case. He'd found an old girl-on-girl porno Candice did at eighteen while she still lived in France. It was titled *Candy Caned*—she got off on women caning her, but apparently her husband giving her one whack that didn't leave a mark was worth fifty mil. When she came to my office with her lawyer for a settlement conference, she'd refused to sit in the conference room with Ferdinand until I put the cane outside of the building.

The bartender brought my new drink and I sipped. "Crazy will fit right in."

After a morning conference across town, I walked into my office and found Emerie pacing back and forth in my spare office wearing a headset as she talked on the phone. Her back was to me as I turned up the hallway, which gave me a chance to take my time checking her out. She had on a black fitted skirt that hugged her in all the right places and a white silky blouse. When she heard my footsteps, she turned, and I noticed her feet were bare. The bright red polish on her toes matched her smiling lips. An odd tightness in my chest had me smiling back while wondering if I needed to take a Prilosec or something. I waved and walked into my office, which was filled with my office furniture—though I hadn't arranged for it to be redelivered yet.

Ten minutes later, Emerie knocked lightly on my door even though it was open. Her shoes were back on—red heels covering her red toes. *Nice.*

"Good morning."

"Morning." I nodded.

She lifted a pad and took a pencil from behind her ear. "You had a busy morning. Six calls: Jasper Mason, Marlin Appleton, Michael Goddman, Kurt Whaler, Alan Green, and

Arnold Schwartz. I wrote down the messages on a message book I found in your supply closet. Hope you don't mind me helping myself."

I waved a hand. "By all means, help yourself. I don't know where anything is without Tess around anyway."

She ripped the messages from the carbon copy message book and put them on my desk. "Here you go."

"Thank you. By the way, did you have something to do with getting my furniture back from storage?"

"Oh. Yes. I hope you don't mind. The storage company called this morning and wanted to schedule the delivery for today, so I took the first appointment he had available. The contractor was here cleaning up when I got in this morning, and said he was done with anything that would make a mess. He's going to send one of his guys by later to do the last few things like hang the light switch covers and put the sign back up in the lobby. The boxes with your personal items from your office are on the floor. I was going to go through them and set it up for you, but thought that might be overstepping."

"I wouldn't have minded. But thank you. Thanks for taking care of all that this morning. I thought I was walking in to sit on the folding chair and table again. This is a nice surprise."

"No problem." She looked down at her watch. "I have a video conference in a few minutes, but I'm open from twelve-thirty to two today if you want help setting up your office. I can order in and make it a working lunch, if you want."

"That would be great. I have a call that should end before twelve-thirty."

"What do you feel like for lunch?"

"Surprise me."

"Anything I want?"

"Anything. Unlike you, I'm not picky."

Emerie smiled and turned to walk back to her office. I stopped her to ask a question that had been on my mind since dinner with Roman last night.

"What kind of psychologist are you? Do you specialize?"

"I do. I thought I told you. I'm a marriage counselor."

"A marriage counselor?"

"Yes, I work to save troubled marriages."

"We definitely didn't discuss that. I'd have remembered, considering I also work with troubled marriages—to dissolve them permanently."

"Is it a problem?"

I shook my head. "Shouldn't be."

*Famous last words.*

# CHAPTER NINE

## EMERIE

"Here are a few more messages."

Drew had just hung up the phone after waving me into his office. I set the bag containing our lunch on his desk and handed him the little slips of paper. He shuffled through them quickly and held one up.

"If this guy calls back—Jonathon Gates—you have my permission to hang up on him."

"Can I call him a name first?"

Drew looked amused. "What would you call him?"

"That depends. What did he do wrong?"

"He beats his wife."

"Oh, God. Okay." I twisted my lips as I thought of a good name for Mr. Gates. "I'd call him a fucking animal, and then hang up on him."

Drew chuckled. "You don't curse like a New Yorker."

"What do you mean?"

"You pronounce the entire word. F-u-c-k-i-n-g."

"How should I pronounce it?"

"Fuckin. Leave off the hard g."

"Fuckin," I repeated.

"It sounds stiff. You should practice more so it sounds natural."

I reached into the bag and pulled out the food I'd ordered. With a smile, I offered it to him. "Here's your *fuckin* lunch."

"Nice." He smiled. "Keep it up. You'll sound like Tess in no time."

"Tess?"

"My secretary who's out because she had back surgery. She's sixty and looks like Mary Poppins, but she swears like a sailor."

"I'll practice some more."

I'd ordered us sandwiches from a deli I discovered on my first day of fake tenancy. Since Drew looked like he took care of himself, I picked him out a turkey club on whole wheat with avocado and ordered myself the same, though I usually tended to eat less healthy food. Drew devoured his entire sandwich before I could finish half of mine, and I wasn't a slow eater.

Looking at his empty wrapper, I asked, "I take it you liked the sandwich?"

"Went to the gym at 5 a.m. and didn't have time to eat before an early meeting uptown. That was the first thing I'd eaten today."

"5 a.m.? You went to the gym at five in the morning?"

"I'm an early riser. From the appalled tone in your voice, I take it you're not."

"I try to be."

"How's that working out for you?"

"Not so good." I laughed. "I have trouble falling asleep at night, so mornings are tough."

"Do you exercise?"

"I started taking that Krav Maga a few times a week at

night to wear myself out, hoping it would help me sleep. It doesn't really help. But I like it anyway."

"How about those drinks with melatonin in them?"

"Tried them. Nothing."

"Sleeping pills?"

"I wind up groggy for twenty-four hours after I take anything. Even Tylenol PM wipes me out."

"Prolactin then."

"Prolactin? What's that? A vitamin or something?"

"It's a hormone you release after orgasm. Makes you sleepy. Have you tried masturbating right before bed?"

I was mid-swallow and choked on the sandwich bite. Not the sputtering, coughing, it-went-down-the-wrong-pipe cute kind of choke. No. I choked. Literally. A small chunk of bread lodged in my throat, blocking my airway. In a panic, I stood, knocking the wrapper with the rest of my turkey club and my soda to the floor, and began to point furiously to my throat.

Luckily, Drew took the hint. He ran around to my side of the desk and smacked me on the back a few times. When I remained unable to breathe, he wrapped his arms around me from behind and performed the Heimlich. On the second hard thrust, the bread blocking my airway dislodged and flew across his office. Even though the entire episode probably only lasted fifteen seconds, I bent and gasped for air as if I'd been deprived for three minutes. My heart thundered inside of my chest, the sudden adrenaline surge hitting hard.

Drew didn't let go. He kept his arms locked around me tightly, just under my chest, as I heaved in long breaths.

Eventually, when my breathing had returned to somewhat normal, he spoke in a low, hesitant voice. "You okay?"

My voice was scratchy. "I think so."

His grip around me loosened, but he didn't move away.

Instead, he rested his head on top of mine. "You scared the shit out of me."

I held my throat with one hand. "That was a terrifying feeling. I've never actually choked before." For the brief moment of my impending doom, I'd completely forgotten what had made me choke. But it quickly came back to me. "You almost killed me."

"*Killed you?* I think your brain was deprived of oxygen. I just saved your life, beautiful."

"You made me choke. Who brings up masturbating with an almost stranger while eating lunch?"

"An almost stranger? I've seen you in your underwear, bailed you out of prison, and given you a place to park your ass all day long. Pretty sure I'm your best friend in town at this point."

I whipped around and stared at him. "Maybe I don't need to masturbate anyway. Maybe I have a boyfriend who takes care of those needs."

Drew smirked. Not smiled. *Smirked.* "If that's the case, and you're still having trouble sleeping after he takes care of you at night, then dump his ass because he sucks in bed."

"And I suppose all of your women are fast asleep after you *take care of them.*"

"Damn straight. I'm like a superhero. The Prolactinator."

This man had the uncanny ability to make me laugh in the middle of an argument. I snorted as I leaned over to clean up my sandwich from the floor. "Okay, Prolactinator. How about you use your superpowers to help clean up this mess?"

After the lunch debacle was straightened, I offered to help Drew unpack his boxes. He had a cordless drill in the first one we opened, and he hung some of his fancy-framed degrees while I unwrapped things and cleaned them off.

Our conversation was light and easy until he asked me the question I always dreaded answering.

"So you never told me the other day, what brought you to New York?"

"It's a long story."

Drew looked at his watch. "I have twenty minutes until my next consult. Shoot."

For a brief moment, I considered making up a story so I didn't have to tell the truth. But then I figured, this guy has seen me at my worst—he helped me keep out of jail and witnessed firsthand that I could be sold the proverbial Brooklyn Bridge in the form of Park Avenue real estate. So I went with honesty.

"My first year of college, I wasn't sure what I wanted to major in. I took a Psychology 101 class, and the professor was amazing. But he was also a drunk who often missed classes or came in with ten minutes left in the lecture. He had a TA who was from New York but working on his doctorate at the University of Oklahoma, and he wound up teaching a lot of the course. The TA was Baldwin."

Drew dumped a pile of files into a cabinet and shut it, turning to face me. "So you moved to New York to be near this Baldwin guy? I thought you said the other day he didn't return the feelings you have?"

"He doesn't. Baldwin and I became good friends over the next four years. He had a girlfriend he lived with—an art history major who modeled on the side." I rolled my eyes thinking of Meredith—she was so full of herself. "He stayed at the college to teach after he finished his doctorate, and then decided to move back to New York to start his own practice and teach here. We kept in touch while I did my graduate work, and he pretty much helped me write my thesis over Skype for a year."

"Are we getting to sex or something good in this story soon? Because Baldwin's starting to bore the shit out of me."

Drew was next to me, opening the last box, and I shoved at his arm. "You're the one who wanted to hear the story."

"I thought it would be more interesting," he teased with a cocky smile.

"Anyway. I'll sum up so I don't put you to sleep—"

Drew interrupted. "No worries. I'm not sleepy. Didn't masturbate this morning."

"Thanks for sharing that. Do you want me to finish or not?"

"Of course. I don't know why, but I'm anxious to hear what's wrong with Baldwin."

"Why do you assume something's wrong with him?"

"Gut feeling."

"Well, you're wrong. There's nothing wrong with Baldwin. He's a great guy who's extremely intelligent and cultured."

Drew put his hands on his hips and stopped unpacking to give me his full attention. "You said he *had* a girlfriend for four years. I take it they broke up?"

"Yes. They broke up right before he left to come back to New York."

"And he didn't make a move on you, knowing you were in love with him?"

"How do you know I was in love with him?"

He looked at me like the answer was obvious. "Were you?"

"Yes. But...I didn't tell you that."

"You're easy to read."

I sighed. "Why is it so easy for you to see it, but Baldwin seems to be clueless?"

"He ain't clueless. He knows. But for one reason or another, he isn't letting you know he knows."

It was pretty amazing that Drew had zeroed in on something I'd suspected for a long time. I'd always felt like Baldwin knew about my feelings for him, even though I'd never voiced them. And part of me believed Baldwin returned some of those feelings, even though he'd never acted on them. Which is why I'd decided to make the first move—literally—and I moved to New York. Somehow I'd gotten it into my head that since he was single now, the time was right. But all I'd succeeded in doing was torturing myself, as he brought different dates home a few nights a week.

"I thought if I moved to New York, maybe it would be our time."

"He's single now?"

"He's not dating anyone seriously, no. Although it seems like he's been through half of the women in New York over the last few months. He comes home with a different woman almost every week. The newest one is Rachel." I rolled my eyes.

"You live with this guy?"

"No. I sublet the apartment next door to him while his neighbor is teaching in Africa for a year."

"Let me get this straight. He walks women by the apartment you live in and has never acknowledged that he knows how you feel about him."

"It's my fault. I've still never told him how I feel."

"It's not your fault. The guy's an asshole."

"No, he's not."

"Open your eyes, Emerie."

"You have no idea what you're talking about."

"I hope you're right. But I'd put money on not being wrong."

I could feel the anger rising in my throat and considered storming back to my office and not helping unpack the rest of his boxes, but I was getting Park Avenue space for free. So instead, I kept quiet and finished what we'd started—until I unwrapped the last item.

It was a small picture frame covered in bubble wrap. Drew had left the office to take some boxes out to the garbage compactor in the building's maintenance room. He'd just returned when I unraveled the last layer of tape. The photo was of a beautiful little boy dressed in a hockey uniform. He was probably six or seven years old, and a golden retriever licked his face as he laughed.

Smiling, I turned to face Drew. "He's adorable. Is this your little boy?"

He took the photo from my hand. His answer was curt. "No."

When our eyes met, I was about to ask another question when he cut me off. "Thanks for helping me unpack. I have to get ready for an appointment."

# CHAPTER TEN

## DREW
*New Year's Eve, Seven years ago*

I stood in the little room at the back of the church, staring outside. It was pouring, and the sky was a deep shade of somber grey. Fitting. It was how I felt.

Somber.

Which was probably not the most encouraging sign that I was making the right choice.

Roman opened the door. "There you are. How many people did your father invite? There have to be four hundred people filling the place. They started ushering them up to the balcony already."

"I have no idea. I didn't ask." The truth was, there was very little I'd asked about regarding the wedding. I'd chalked my lack of interest up to being busy studying in law school, but lately I'd realized it was more than that. I wasn't excited to be getting married.

Roman stood next to me and joined my staring out the window. He reached into the inside pocket of his tuxedo and pulled out a flask, offering it to me first. I took it because I needed it.

"Car is in the back if you want to bail," he said.

I sidelong glanced at him as I sucked a double shot of whiskey out of the flask. "I couldn't do that to her. She's having my baby, man."

"She's gonna be having your baby whether she likes it or not in two months."

"I know. But it's the right thing to do."

"Fuck the right thing."

I handed the flask back to my best man with a smirk. "You know you're in a church."

He drank from the flask. "I'm going to hell already. What's the difference?"

I laughed. At twenty-four, my best friend had already been politely *asked* to leave the NYPD. *Asked* was a polite way to say *quit or we fire you*. He wasn't exactly an angel.

"I care about Alexa. We'll make it work."

"I haven't heard the word *love* yet. Would you be marrying her if you hadn't knocked her up like an idiot after only a few months of hooking up?"

I didn't respond.

"That's what I thought. People can have a kid and not be married. It's not 1960 anymore, Mr. Cleaver."

"We'll make it work."

Roman slapped me on the back. "Your life. But keys are in my pocket if you change your mind."

"Thanks, man."

# CHAPTER ELEVEN

## EMERIE

"Just because you're physically thousands of miles away doesn't mean your hearts are. You should each take time to let the other know you're thinking of them. Let me ask you, Jeff, you mentioned that you thought of Kami today when you went for a run because you passed a lingerie store named Kami-souls. Had you mentioned that to Kami before our therapy session today? Perhaps when she brought up she feels as if you don't give her any thought?"

The screen on my forty-two-inch monitor was split—a video feed of Jeff Scott on the left and a video feed of Kami Scott on the right. The two had been married less than a year when Jeff was transferred to the west coast. Considering he was their only income, with Kami in her second year of a dental residency, it left him little choice but to relocate until he was able to find a new job closer to their home in Connecticut.

"No. I hadn't mentioned it to her before today," Jeff said. "I'm busy. She knows I think about her." His face froze on my screen for a few seconds, even though his voice kept going. He was mid speaking, and the stilled video had caught him in an odd frame. One eye was fully closed, and I could only see white on the other half-closed eye. His mouth was open, and his tongue looked stained with coffee. I needed to find better video software for my counseling sessions. God knows what I looked like on their screens at the moment.

Our forty-five-minute couples therapy session was almost up. "This week I'd like to do an exercise. At least once a day, when something reminds you of each other, let the other person know at that moment. If you're out for a jog and see something, maybe snap a picture and text it. Kami, if a patient comes in with a cold and sneezes a lot, reminding you of Jeff's propensity to sneeze six to eight times in a row, let him know. These little things can go a long way in reminding each other that your heart is never far, even if there are miles between you. Distance is only a test to see how far love travels."

I heard what sounded like a snicker outside my partially closed door. So after my session ended, I was curious and went to find Drew. He stood in the copy room, which was next to the office I was using, making photocopies.

"Did you just say something to me?" I asked, giving him the benefit of the doubt.

"Nope. My father always taught me that if I had nothing nice to say to a woman, I should keep it to myself."

I hadn't been imagining it. "You were eavesdropping on my counseling session. You *laughed* at the advice I gave my clients, didn't you?"

Drew's eyes narrowed. "I wasn't eavesdropping. You had your door open, and you're loud on the phone. You do know you don't need to yell for the person on the other end of a video conference to hear you, right?"

"I wasn't yelling."

Drew finished making his copies, slipping a pile of papers

from the feeder. "Whatever, but you might want to shut your door if you don't want me overhearing your bad advice."

My eyes grew to saucers. "Bad advice? What are you talking about? I'm a licensed psychologist who did her dissertation on overcoming barriers in relationships by opening the lines of communication in couples therapy."

Drew snickered. Again. "You're the expert then. I'll leave you to it." He walked back to his office.

He had no clue what he was talking about. My advice was solid, based on years of studying couples who *wanted* to work things out. I couldn't help myself. I followed him, standing at his doorway.

"And what advice would *you* give a couple forced to endure a long-distance relationship?"

"I'd give them more realistic advice than 'Distance is only a test to see how far love travels.' That's a load of shit. Where'd you read that one? A Hallmark card?"

My eyes bulged. "And what is *your idea* of *realistic* advice?"

"Simple. Hire a good divorce attorney. Long-distance relationships *Do. Not. Work.*"

"I take it you had one and it burned you, so you assume everyone else is going to be burned?"

"Not at all. I've never had a long-distance relationship. You know why? *They don't work.* And I know this from experience. What experience do you have in long-distance relationships?"

"I've studied couples for years. I think I have more experience than you do on the subject. "

"Is that so?" Drew went to his file cabinet and pulled out a large, rubber-banded expandable file. He slammed it down on his desk. "Morrison. Happily married fourteen years.

Divorced two years ago. Three years before the divorce, Dan Morrison took a job as a regional traveling salesman. More money—his wife wouldn't have to work anymore. Four nights a week on the road, yet Dan never missed date night with his wife on Fridays or driving forty miles on Sundays, his day off, to give his elderly father-in-law a bath. But you know what he missed? Every Tuesday, Wednesday, and Thursday when Mrs. Morrison was fucking her tennis instructor, Laire."

When I continued to glare at him, he opened another drawer and took out a second file, slapping it down on top of the Morrison file. "Loring. Happily married six years when his office relocated from New York to New Jersey. Eighty miles. Not too far. But Al Loring worked sixteen hours a day a few days a week. His bitch of a wife, Mitsy, was a light sleeper, so he would spend the nights he worked too late on the couch at his office, not wanting to wake his princess bride. Came home one night that he was supposed to crash at the office because he missed Mitsy. Found his wife on all fours in their bed with his neighbor balls deep inside of her. Neighbor has his dog and his wife now, and Al turned into an alcoholic and lost his job in New Jersey."

He reached into the same drawer and took out yet another file. "McDune. Married six years. Erin went to live in Dublin temporarily to take care of her mother who became depressed after the death of her father. Divorced Liam for a guy who looks like a leprechaun because she found her *soul mate* back in the *motherland*. So much for long distance to nurse your mother's soul."

Drew reached down to the bottom cabinet and opened it. This time, I stopped him. "Should you even be telling me any of this? Ever hear of attorney-client privilege?"

"I changed the names to protect the not-so-fucking-innocent. Believe it or not, unlike my clients' spouses, I have some ethics." He pointed to the cabinet. "Want to hear more? I think you'll really like Lieutenant O'Connor's story. It's a real tearjerker. Wife was screwing his brother while he was off in Iraq and she—"

I cut him off again. "I get your point. But what you're missing is that maybe these divorces wouldn't have happened if the couples had sought counseling. You see people when they're at their worst—people who gave up instead of fighting for their marriage."

Drew stared at me. "You really believe all marriages can be saved?"

I thought about the question for a minute before answering. "Not all. But I think most can be saved, yes. Opening the lines of communication can fix a lot of things."

Drew shook his head. "That's naïve. I also have some real estate on Park Avenue you can rent for two grand a month."

"Screw you," I hissed and stormed back to my office.

⁓

I kept my office door shut the rest of the afternoon. A knock that came at almost seven p.m. startled me as I worked on transcribing my chicken-scratch notes from today's counseling sessions. I kept an e-case file for each patient.

"Come in."

The door opened, but only slightly, just enough to fit an arm through. Which is exactly what appeared. Drew's arm, waving something white around.

*What is he waving? Are those...underwear?*

I'd been carrying around a full load of angry all afternoon after our heated argument, and it was starting to weigh me down. His gesture brought some much-needed levity.

"Come in," I said again.

He pushed the door open a few more inches. This time his head joined his white-flag-waving arm. "You're not still pissed and planning to use your mad Krav Maga skills on me, are you?"

I laughed. "I should. You deserve a good ass-whipping. But I'll hold back."

Drew smiled and opened the door the rest of the way, staying in the doorway. "I guess I owe you an apology for some things I said today?"

I sat back in my chair. "You do."

He hung his head. The action reminded me of a little boy who'd given his dog a bath—in red paint. It was cute. *He* was cute. But I was going to make him grovel anyway. His head was still slightly bowed as he looked up at me from beneath his dark lashes. "I'm sorry for today."

"What exactly are you sorry for?"

He dropped his head back down. "You're going to make this difficult, aren't you?"

"Yep."

"Fine. I'm sorry for calling you naïve."

"Anything else?"

I watched his face as the wheels spun in his head. "For listening to your conversation with your client."

"Is that it?"

"Is there supposed to be more?" He looked a little nervous for a second.

"There's more."

After thirty more seconds of thought, he snapped his fingers as if he was proud of himself. "I'm sorry for looking at your ass."

My brows drew down. "When did you look at my ass?"

He shrugged. "Every chance I get?"

I couldn't help but laugh. "Apology accepted."

His shoulders dropped a bit and he looked relieved. The man had a tough exterior. But sometimes the ones who'd had it rough wore the thickest armor.

"How about I buy you a burger at Joey's for dinner to make it up to you?" He winked. "I'll buy the biggest one they have so you can get real full and take your skirt off for me again."

# CHAPTER TWELVE

## EMERIE

"Can I ask you something personal?"

"No." Drew's response was quick.

"No?" I crinkled up my face, confused. "You know, usually when two people are sitting around talking and eating, and one of them asks the other if they can ask something personal, the other generally says yes. It's polite."

"I have a rule. Whenever someone asks if they can ask something, I say no."

"Why?"

"Because if you have to ask if you can ask, it's probably something I don't want to answer anyway."

"But how do you know if you don't even hear the question?"

Drew sat back in his chair. "What's your question, Emerie?"

"Well, now I feel like I shouldn't ask it."

He shrugged and finished off the last of his beer. "Okay. So don't."

"Did something happen to you that made you bitter about relationships?"

"Thought you didn't feel like you should ask?"

"I changed my mind."

"You're kind of a pain in the ass. You know that, right?"

"And you're kind of a bitter jerk, so I'm curious what made you that way."

Drew tried to hide it, but I saw the corner of his lip twitch toward a smile. "I'll tell you why I'm a bitter jerk, if you tell me why you're a pain in the ass."

"But I don't think I'm a pain in the ass."

"Maybe you should see a therapist, help you figure that shit out."

I crumpled up my napkin and threw it at his face. It hit him square in the nose.

"Very mature," he said.

"I don't think I'm a pain in the ass in general. I think you just bring out the ass in me."

He smirked. "It's a nice ass to bring out. Speaking of which, if you're full, I could help you unzip to get comfortable."

Jesus, he really was a smartass. "I'm never going to live down the night we met, am I?"

"Not a chance."

I sipped my merlot, not wanting to waste it, but I was so full from the humongous burger Drew had ordered me. Honestly, I couldn't wait to get home and unzip my skirt, although I wasn't about to admit that to Drew.

"So, back to my original question. Why are you so bitter about relationships?"

"I deal with divorces all day long. It's a little hard to have a positive outlook when all you see is cheating, lying, stealing, and people who started out in love getting off on hurting each other."

"So it's because of your line of work. You didn't have a bad relationship that soured you?"

Drew stared at me for a while. His thumb went to rub at the center of his bottom full bottom lip as he deliberated over his answer, and my eyes followed. *Damn, he has great lips. I bet they would devour my mouth.*

Luckily, the waitress came and interrupted my ogling.

"Can I get you anything else?" she asked.

Drew looked to me. "Some dessert or anything?"

"I'm too full."

He answered the waitress. "Just the check. Thank you."

She took our plates, and when she left, there was a minute of awkward silence. He still hadn't answered my question, and I thought maybe he was going to try to change the subject again. I was surprised when he answered.

"I'm divorced. Marriage lasted five years."

"Wow. I'm sorry."

"Not your fault."

Even though I could tell it took a lot of effort to share that much, and I knew I should probably leave well enough alone, I couldn't help myself. "Did you have a long-distance relationship?"

"Not in a physical sense, no. That bitterness today was purely from my experience in divorces. The number-one reason people wind up in my office is they don't spend time together."

"I'll admit, a lot of my counseling cases are similar. It's not always a long-distance relationship like the one you heard me talking about today, but in the majority of my counseling, the couples don't spend time together. They're either working a lot and don't make time for each other, or they're still hanging on to the separate lives they had before they were married."

"I bet our cases are very similar. Come to think of it,

maybe you can hand out my business cards, for when your counseling doesn't work."

My eyes widened. "You've got to be joking?"

A slow smile spread across his face as he brought his beer to his lips. "I am."

The waitress returned with the check, and Drew took out his wallet. I went to take out mine, and he stopped me. "Dinner's on me. It's my apology offering for being a dick today, remember?"

"Well, thank you. I hope you're a dick often," I joked. "I have ten grand to save up again."

Drew stood and walked around to my chair, pulling it out as I stood. "Oh, that won't be a problem. I'm pretty much a dick every day."

---

The lock on my apartment door was tricky. I had to wiggle it around and pull the key in and out a few times before finding the exact right spot that allowed me to turn the bolt. Baldwin must have heard my keys jingling. His apartment door, next to mine, opened.

"Hey. I knocked earlier to see if you wanted to grab some dinner, but you weren't home yet."

"Oh. I had dinner with Drew."

Baldwin took the keys from my hand. Somehow, he got the lock on the first try every time. The door opened, and he followed me inside. "Drew?"

"He's the real tenant in the office I thought I rented. The one who's letting me stay for a few months?"

Baldwin nodded. "You're dating him now, too?"

I snorted. "No. He was a jerk today and made it up to me with dinner."

"Why was he a jerk?"

I went into my bedroom to change and continued our conversation through the partially closed door.

"I guess he really wasn't a jerk. We just have very different opinions on counseling relationships. He overheard me on a call and gave me his thoughts on how my advice to my patients would work out."

After I'd slipped into some sweats and a T-shirt, I went out to the living room. Baldwin was sitting where he always sat when we hung out. I took the couch, and he sat on the oversized leather chair. Sometimes it made me feel like his patient.

"He shouldn't be listening to your counseling sessions. They're confidential."

"It was my fault. I tend to yell when I'm on those video conferences, and I left my door open."

"Maybe I should stop by the office?"

"For what?"

"I don't know. Check things out."

Baldwin was being sweet. Hearing that someone had been a jerk to me brought out his protective side. Although the thought of Baldwin vs. Drew was actually pretty comical.

The two were polar opposites. Baldwin was thin, well mannered, average height, and looked every bit the professor he was. He even wore bow ties and glasses that made him appear older than his thirty-five years. Drew was twenty-nine, tall, broad, and thick. He also cursed whenever it suited him, regardless of who was around. Even though I would never describe Drew as well mannered like Baldwin, there was something very chivalrous about him beneath the rough exterior.

"I don't think that's necessary. I'm fine. He's just a little jagged around the edges is all. Funny, I hadn't thought of it until now—his last name is Jagger...jagged. Sort of fitting."

Knowing Baldwin liked a late-evening glass of wine, I walked to the kitchen and opened the fridge, taking out the bottle I kept for him before he'd even responded to my question.

"Would you like a glass of wine?"

"Yes, thank you."

I poured it and grabbed myself a water. As I handed it to him, he said, "You're not joining me?"

I plopped down on the couch. "I'm too full. I ate a huge burger for dinner. Drew ordered me a double cheeseburger deluxe."

"He ordered for you? You're such a picky eater."

"He knew I liked burgers." I shrugged. Untwisting the cap from my water, I asked, "What did you wind up eating?"

"I had sushi from Zen's delivered."

I scrunched my nose. "Glad I missed that."

"I would have ordered something different if we were eating together."

Baldwin always deferred to me for ordering. It was one of the things I loved about him. Sushi seemed to be his go-to meal for dates, so it wasn't like he was deprived of his favorites.

"No date tonight?" I asked. Normally, I avoided the topic of his love life. It was difficult to see him with women, and hearing about them in any detail would kill me. But tonight I felt less hesitant for some reason.

"Papers to grade. You would have appreciated the answer I received from a female student."

"What was the question?"

"I asked them to give me a sound argument that Freud's psychoanalysis techniques were flawed. We've spent the last three weeks studying Grünbaum and Colby, so it should have been an easy question."

"Yes. I agree. What did you get as an answer?"

"Ms. Balick wrote, 'Freud was a man.'"

I laughed. "I think that might be a valid argument. You should probably give her some points for that."

"Cute. But I don't think so."

"You were always a tough grader."

"I always gave *you* good grades."

"I earned them." Which was true, but it got me thinking. "Have you ever given anyone points they didn't deserve? Maybe because they were pretty or you felt bad for them?"

"Never." His answer didn't surprise me. Baldwin sipped his wine. "So where do you want to go Thursday night?"

"Thursday?"

"Your birthday dinner."

"Oh. I forgot. I've been so busy lately, it totally slipped my mind that my birthday is coming up."

"Well, it didn't slip mine. I was thinking we could go to Ecru. It's a new French place on the Upper East Side. The waitlist for a reservation is three months long, but a colleague of mine is friends with the owner and said he could make sure we get in."

"That sounds great. Thank you." If I was being honest, I would have preferred to go to Joey's again for a big, greasy burger. But Baldwin was a foodie and always trying to expand my palatal horizons. On occasion, I even liked some of the fancy foods.

Baldwin stayed for a while, and we talked shop. He told me about a paper he hoped to get published, and I told him how nervous I was to meet two of my video clients in the office tomorrow. After I relocated to New York, some of my video and phone clients who were local to the area had become face-to-face clients. It was always odd meeting them that first time, but tomorrow's appointment made me particularly nervous because I suspected the husband could be physically abusing the wife.

It started to get late, and at one point I yawned and stretched. My thin T-shirt rode up and exposed some of my stomach. Baldwin's eyes zeroed in on the flesh, and I watched as he swallowed. Moments like these confused me the most. I wouldn't claim to be an expert on men, but I'd dated a decent amount myself, even had a few long-ish relationships. Generally, I could read a man's attraction to me pretty well, and in this moment, I would have sworn Baldwin was into me. It wasn't new. I'd felt it on plenty of other occasions. Which might be the reason I was still hanging on after so many years.

*Sometimes a spark turns into a fire.*

Baldwin cleared his throat and stood. "I should get going. It's late."

"Are you sure? Maybe I'll pour a glass of wine for myself if you want to have a second..."

"I have an early lecture tomorrow."

"Okay." I hid my disappointment and walked him to the door.

Baldwin said goodnight, and then stopped and turned back. For a brief second, my imagination got the best of me, and I imagined him turning around and shutting the door—deciding to stay.

Instead, he said, "I'm expecting a package tomorrow. If you see it in the hall, can you grab it for me? I won't be home until late."

"Sure. Is tomorrow night the New York Psychology Symposium you were telling me about?"

"No. That's next week. Rachel has tickets to see an off-Broadway play tomorrow."

"*Oh*. Rachel."

"You met her last week briefly at the coffee shop."

"Yes. Rachel." *Like I could forget*. She'd been wearing the dress shirt he'd worn the night before when I heard his door open and peeked through the peephole. "I'll grab anything outside your door. Have fun tomorrow night."

After he left, I washed off my makeup and brushed my teeth. Of course, even though I'd been yawning not five minutes ago, I was wide awake once I *could* go to sleep.

*Story of my life.*

I thought about my conversation with Drew earlier in the day—it seemed like it had occurred a week ago. Captain Prolactinator had suggested I masturbate before bed. But I was in no mood to think about Baldwin after hearing about his date tomorrow with Rachel.

Although...

I didn't have to visualize Baldwin, did I? A vision of Drew suddenly popped into my head. He was definitely good looking enough...

*But I shouldn't.*

I turned over and forced myself to close my eyes. An hour later, I reached over to my end table. I was desperate for some sleep after the long, draining day.

I turned on my vibrator and closed my eyes, attempting to relax to the hum.

Ten minutes later, I was sound asleep with a smile on my face.

# CHAPTER THIRTEEN

## DREW

Alexa had ruined my job for a long time. After my divorce, I found bits and pieces of my marriage in every client's bitter battle. It reminded me how much time I'd wasted, how from that first night I'd let my dick make decisions when it came to Alexa, instead of my head. Everything in my client's files became personal to me, and it was like reliving the worst nights of my life on a daily basis.

Eventually, I learned to separate things—somewhat. But I'd lost something along the way. My job became a source of money and not something I enjoyed doing. While I no longer dreaded going downstairs to my office, I also didn't look forward to it anymore.

Until today.

I was up even earlier than usual. After hitting the gym, I was in my office by seven, reviewing a case file. Henry Archer was one of the few clients I truly liked. His divorce was even amicable because he was a genuinely nice guy. I had his settlement conference today at eleven. The entire gang would be here to try to hammer out a final deal. Miraculously, I didn't despise his soon-to-be ex-wife either.

I was in the copy room when I heard Emerie come in. Her heels clanked as she came down the hall carrying a large brown box. I stopped what I was doing and walked to take it from her hands.

"Thank you. Do you know no one offered me a seat on the subway carrying that thing?"

"Most people are assholes. What the hell do you have in here? It's heavy as shit." I set the box down on her desk and opened it without asking. Inside was a glass paperweight, but it might as well have been made of lead. "This thing is ten pounds. Are you worried a hurricane is going to gust through the office and blow around all your papers?"

She swiped it from my hand. "It's an award. I earned it for a paper I wrote that was published in *Psychology Today*."

"It's a weapon. Glad you didn't have that thing when I found you in my office that first night."

"Yes, I could have put a dent in that pretty head of yours."

I smirked. "I knew it. You think I'm pretty."

I attempted to see what else was inside her box, but she swatted my hand away.

"Nosy."

"You unpacked my boxes."

"That's true. I guess you can look."

"Well, now I don't want to, since you told me I could."

"You're like a child, you know that?"

I'd left my cell phone at the copy machine and heard it ringing from down the hall. I went to answer it, but the caller had hung up. After finishing making my copies, I gathered the stack of papers and stopped by Emerie's office again.

Standing in the doorway, I teased, "You're early today. Did you take my advice on falling asleep?"

"No." Emerie's rapid answer was...too rapid. Years of running depositions had made me skilled at picking up on small clues—sometimes something ever so slight took me down a path I hadn't expected and led to something interesting. I'd picked up a scent from her two-letter word and was about to follow the trail.

"So you didn't have trouble falling asleep last night, huh?"

When she started to blush and attempted to busy herself at unpacking her box, I knew I was on to something. Curious, I walked into her office and around to the other side of her desk so I could see her face even though she was looking down and unpacking.

I ducked my head and looked up to catch her eyes. "You masturbated last night, didn't you?"

Her blush reddened. "Did *you*?" she countered.

*Deflecting.* We all know what that means. I grinned. "I did. And this morning, too. Wanna know what I was thinking about while I did it?"

"No!"

"You're not even the slightest bit curious?"

Even though she was red-faced, I loved that she pushed through it and faced me. "Don't you have any marriages to desecrate, pervert?"

"Come on. Admit it. You masturbated last night, and that's why you had such a good night's sleep and got to work on time for a change."

"Why do you care?"

"I like to be right."

"You're really a giant egomaniac."

"So I've been told."

"Will you drop the subject if I tell you the truth?"

I nodded. "I will."

She looked me directly in the eye. "I did."

"What?"

"What do you mean *what*? You know what I mean."

*Of course I do.* "I'm not sure I do. Why don't you explain what you're referring to?"

"Get out."

"Say you masturbated, and I'll get out."

"Why? So you can get off on the thought of me masturbating?"

"I thought you didn't want to hear what I was thinking about this morning when I took care of myself?"

I chuckled. Emerie was trying to be tough, but her voice told me she was more embarrassed and amused than pissed off. Feeling unusually kind, I decided to let her off the hook before I pushed my luck.

"I have a conference at ten today that will probably turn into lunch with my client afterward. There are menus in the top right drawer of the reception desk if you want to order in."

"Thank you."

"You're welcome."

I stopped just outside of her doorway. "One other thing."

"Hmm?"

"Were you thinking of me when you masturbated?"

I'd said it just to be an ass, but her sudden deer-in-the-headlights face told me I'd actually hit the nail on the head. *Well, shit. Coming to work just got even better.* A part of me (a *very* large part of me, of course) wanted to stay and push *that* interesting tidbit of information even more, but I'd suddenly turned into a twelve-year-old boy and could feel my cock swelling. Thanks to her dirty thoughts, Little Miss Oklahoma with the great ass got a reprieve after all.

"That's not the fucking problem. The problem is your inability to cook a decent meal without burning it."

Hearing that type of statement yelled wasn't new to these walls. Only this time, it wasn't coming from one of my clients.

I'd just returned to the office after a late lunch with Henry Archer, and the sound of an angry man echoed through the hall. Emerie's office door was slightly open, and I debated checking in with her, making sure everything was okay. Listening, I heard her ask the guy to settle down and then another woman began to speak. So I went back to my office to mind my own business.

Fifteen minutes later, there it was again. I was on the phone when that same guy's voice carried down the hall and straight into my office.

*"I was on the fence about marrying you in the first place. Should have called it off after you couldn't even carry our kid."*

The hair on the back of my neck rose. What he'd said was horrible. But I'd heard spouses spit vile things back and forth at each other during a divorce. Not much shocked me anymore. Yet this guy—it wasn't *what* he said but *how* he said it. His voice was laced with anger and intimidation, threatening while insulting. I hadn't even seen his face, but my gut told me he was more than just a verbal abuser. Unfortunately, I'd seen physical abusers over the years, too. There was just something about the way the scumbags yelled that set them apart from your run-of-the-mill, I-hate-you-and-want-to-injure-your-soul spouse.

I rushed the client I'd been speaking to off the phone and went to check on Emerie. Before I could reach her office, a loud crashing sound sent me running.

When I got to the door, the guy was sitting in his seat while his wife knelt on her hands and knees to clean something up. Emerie was standing.

"What's going on in here? Everything okay?"

Emerie hesitated and caught my eye when she spoke. She was trying to diffuse the situation. I saw it in her eyes, heard it in her voice.

"Mr. Dawson was a little excited and knocked over a glass award I had sitting on my desk."

The heavy paperweight she'd lugged on the subway in her box was shattered all over the floor.

"Take a walk and cool off, buddy."

The asshole's head whipped around. "Are you talking to me?"

"I am."

"Who the hell are you?"

"I'm the guy telling you to take a walk and cool off."

He stood. "And what if I don't?"

"You'll be physically removed."

"You're going to call the cops on me for breaking a piece of glass?"

"Not unless Emerie wants me to. But I will toss your ass out on the street myself."

I folded my arms across my chest and kept eye contact. Men who abused women were pussies. I'd kick his ass and enjoy every fucking minute of it.

After a few seconds, the guy looked at his wife. "I'm done with this counseling shit." Then he stormed out. I stepped aside to make room for him to pass.

Both Emerie and her client stayed quiet until we heard the front door slam closed.

"You good?" I asked.

Emerie nodded, and for the first time, the woman turned and faced me. Her cheek was purple and yellow with a fading bruise. My jaw clenched. I should have punched the fucker while I had the chance.

"He's not usually like that. It's just been tough at his job lately."

*Sure he isn't.*

Emerie and I locked eyes one more time, an unspoken exchange. We were on the same page.

"I'll let you two talk." I shut the door behind me.

For the next half hour, I worked on a case file at the empty reception desk in the lobby, not wanting that asshole husband to walk back in without my knowing. Eventually, I caught his face outside the front window. He was smoking a cigarette and waiting outside for his wife. *Smart move.*

Emerie walked Mrs. Dawson to the lobby as they spoke. "How about we talk on the phone tomorrow? Even if it's just for fifteen minutes? I'd really like to hear from you after today's session."

Her client nodded. "Okay."

"How does ten sound?"

"That's good. Bill leaves for work at eight."

Emerie nodded. "You know what? I didn't give you an appointment card for next week's session. Let me grab one for you, and I'll be right back."

After she walked away, I spoke to Mrs. Dawson. My voice was low, nonjudgmental, and cautious. "You gonna be okay?"

She briefly looked in my eyes, but quickly diverted hers to the ground. "I'll be fine. Bill isn't really a bad guy. Honestly, you just saw caught him at a bad time."

"Uh-huh."

Emerie returned and handed her client a small card. "Talk to you tomorrow?"

She nodded and left.

When the door shut, Emerie sighed loudly. "I'm so sorry about that."

"Nothing to be sorry about. You can't help that your client is an asshole. Got plenty of 'em myself."

"I think he's physically abusive to her."

"I'd tend to agree with you."

"I also don't think I'll ever hear from her again. She's going to cut me off because I confronted her about what I suspected was going on."

"You don't think she'll call tomorrow or show up at her appointment next week?"

"Nope. He's not going to let her continue. Now that I know him a little better, I'm really surprised he ever agreed to come here at all. My counseling sessions have been with just her."

"It's tough."

She sighed again. "I hope she calls you."

"Me?"

"The appointment card reminder I gave her was your business card. Figured she needed a divorce attorney more than relationship counseling."

My eyebrows jumped. "Nice."

We walked side by side down the hall.

"I could use a drink," Emerie said.

"Your office or mine?"

Emerie looked at me. "You have alcohol in the office?"

"I have a lot of shitty days."

She smiled. "My office."

"This tastes like turpentine." Emerie's entire face twisted.

I sipped. "It's twenty-five-year-old Glenmorangie. That's six-hundred-dollar-a-bottle paint thinner you're drinking there."

"For that price, they could have added some flavor."

I chuckled. I sat in a guest chair, and Emerie was behind her desk. She must have unpacked the rest of her box because there were some new personal items on display. I lifted the glass coaster-like base that had gone with the award douchebag Dawson broke.

"You're gonna need a new weapon."

"Don't think I need one with you around to threaten my clients."

"He deserved it. I should have punched him in the face like he likes to do to his wife."

"You should have. That guy was a real asshole. *A fuckin asshole.*"

She was cute working her New York accent, although it still sounded like Oklahoma doing New York.

There were two new frames on her desk, and I reached for one of them. It was a photo of an older couple.

"Help yourself," she said with sarcasm and a smile.

I looked at her face, then the couple, then back at her. "These your parents?"

"Yep."

"Who do you look like?"

"My mother, I'm told."

I studied her mother's face. They looked nothing alike. "I don't see it."

She reached over and slipped the photo from my hands. "I'm adopted. I look like my biological mother."

"Oh. Sorry."

"It's fine. It's not something I'm secretive about."

I leaned back in my chair, watching her look at the photo. There was reverence on her face when she spoke again. "I may not look like my mom, but we're a lot alike."

"Oh yeah? So she's a pain in the ass, too?"

She pretended to be offended. "I'm not a pain the ass."

"I've known you barely a week. Day one you were stealing office space and tried to kick my ass when I caught you. A few days later you started a fight because I made an innocent comment about some bad advice you were feeding a client, and today, I almost got into a fist fight because of you."

"My advice wasn't bad." She sighed. "But I guess the rest is true. I have been a pain in the ass, haven't I?"

I finished my drink and poured two fingers more into the tumbler, then topped off Emerie's glass. "You're in luck. I like pains in the asses."

We talked for a while longer. Emerie told me about her parents' hardware store back in Oklahoma and was in the middle of some story about selling supplies to a guy who was arrested for locking his wife in an underground bunker for two weeks when my office phone rang. I went to grab it, but she reached for it first.

"Mr. Jagger's office. How may I assist you?" She answered in a sexy, flirty voice.

The two drinks had loosened her up, made her playful. I liked it.

"May I ask who's calling?" She picked up a ballpoint pen and paused to listen, mindlessly rubbing the top along her bottom lip.

My eyes followed. *I bet they taste good.* I had the sudden urge to lean over the desk and bite one. *Shit.* Not a good thought.

Yet I was still staring at her lips when she looked back up at me. I should have stopped, but the way they moved when she started to speak held me captive.

"Okay, Mrs. Logan. Let me see if he's available."

*That* broke my gaze. I waved both hands in front of me, motioning to her that I wasn't available. She put the phone on hold for five seconds and then returned to the call.

"I'm sorry, Mrs. Logan. He seems to have stepped out." A pause. "No, I'm sorry. I'm not at liberty to give out Mr. Jagger's cell phone number. But I will tell him you called."

After she hung up, she said, "You know what I just realized?"

"That your voice sounds sexier after a few drinks?"

She blinked. "My voice sounds sexier?"

I gulped a mouthful of my second drink. "Yeah. You were flirting answering the phone."

"I wasn't flirting."

I shrugged. "Whatever. I liked it. What were you going to say you realized?"

"I don't even remember now. I think those two little drinks went right to my head."

"And your lips," I grumbled.

"What?"

"Nothing."

"Oh! I remember what I was going to say." She pointed a finger at me. "I've taken at least twenty phone calls in three days and saw a ton of appointments on your calendar. That was the first *Mrs.* that called. You don't have any clients named Jane, Jessica, or Julie."

"That's because I only take male clients."

"What?" She looked at me like I'd just told her the sky was purple.

"Male clients. You know, they're like women, except with less drama and bigger di—" I quieted mid-word, hearing the front door open. "Are you expecting someone?"

"No. Why?"

"I just heard the front door open." I stood and walked to the hallway. "Hello?"

A guy I'd never seen before popped his head around the corner from the lobby. "Hi. I'm looking for Emerie Rose?"

I squinted. "Who are you?" I was concerned that the Dawson douchebag had come back to start trouble. But this guy looked like the last trouble he saw was when the kids picked on him in elementary school.

I turned back to Emerie, who was already heading toward me. She joined me in the doorway.

"Baldwin? I thought that was your voice. What are you doing here?"

"Thought I would surprise you."

The guy raised flowers I hadn't noticed at his side; their color matched his crooked bow tie. They were lame—looked like he bought them at the Chinese market down the block for $7.99.

"That's so sweet."

Emerie stepped out of the doorway where we were nice and close and walked to the guy, giving him a hug and kiss. For some reason, I stayed put, watching it all.

After she took the flowers, she remembered I was behind her. "Baldwin, this is Drew. Drew, Baldwin is the friend I told you about the other day."

I was confused, and she read it on my face.

"My TA in college. Remember, I told you all about him?"

*Really? That guy?* "Oh. Yeah." I extended my hand. "Nice to meet you. Drew Jagger."

"Likewise. Baldwin Marcum."

There was an odd, awkward silence before Emerie broke it. "Isn't the office beautiful?"

"Very nice."

"Are you on your way to meet Rachel?"

"The show isn't for another hour and a half. So I thought I'd check in on you."

Baldwin was still looking around the office when he spotted the bottle of Glenmorangie and two empty glasses on Emerie's desk.

He looked at her. "Is that scotch? At five in the afternoon?"

Emerie either didn't catch the disdain in his voice or was good at ignoring it. "We had a rough day," she said.

"I see."

"Care for a glass?" I asked, certain he would decline after the sixty-second assessment I'd made. "It's twenty-five and smooth."

"No, thank you."

I'd seen enough. "I have work to catch up on. Nice to meet you, Baldwin."

He nodded.

An hour later, I was packing up my office when I heard the two of them laughing. The earlier events of the day still had testosterone pumping through my veins. Which was probably why, out of nowhere, I had the urge to punch the guy. An outlet was needed. *Angry fucking. I need to get laid.*

I knocked lightly on Emerie's door before pushing it open. "I'm going to head out. You should try that sleeping technique I told you about again tonight so you're on time again tomorrow."

Emerie's eyes widened as she attempted to hide her smirk. "Yes. Maybe I'll do just that."

Baldwin watched our exchange closely.

I waved and nodded. "You have a good night."

I made it one step before Emerie called to me. "Drew."

I turned back. "Yeah?"

She rang her hands together. "Thank you for today. I didn't say it, but I appreciate everything you did."

"Anytime, Oklahoma." I rapped my knuckles against her office doorframe. "Don't stay too late, okay?"

"I won't. I'm going to head out in a few minutes. Baldwin has plans tonight, so I'll walk out with him."

"Want me to wait? We can grab a burger at Joey's again?"

Emerie started to respond when Mr. Bowtie interrupted. "Actually, I've had a last-minute change of plans. Why don't I take you for some dinner?"

"You're not going to the show with Rachel?"

"We can see it another time. I wasn't aware you'd had a bad day. You can tell me all about it at dinner."

Emerie looked to me, conflicted. I made the choice easier for her. Who was I to interrupt the happy couple?

"You two have a good night then."

I might have been full of myself.   After all, I'd been told on more than one occasion lately that my ego was pretty big, but I could have sworn Emerie's little friend's change of plans had something to do with me.

# CHAPTER FOURTEEN

## DREW
*New Year's Eve, Five years ago*

"Happy anniversary."

Alexa sat on the couch flipping through a *People* magazine. I bent to kiss her cheek, then leaned down farther to touch my lips to my almost-two-year-old son's forehead where he slept with his head on her lap. He was drooling. A big pool of spit puddled on my wife's thigh.

I pointed to it and joked, "A few years ago, making you wet on New Year's Eve meant something very different."

She sighed. "I wish we could go out. This is the first New Year's I've been home since I was a kid."

New Year's Eve was a huge holiday to my wife. She looked forward to it like a kid waiting for Santa. And yesterday, someone had told Alexa there was no Santa. We'd planned on going out tonight—a party in downtown Atlanta thrown by a friend of hers I didn't really care for—but the sitter canceled on us. Alexa was devastated. I was secretly glad. Today was the first day off I'd had in a month, and staying home and watching movies—maybe ringing in the new year inside of my wife—was as much excitement as I was in the mood for.

But Alexa had been sulking for twenty-four hours. She

was still having a hard time adjusting to the new lifestyle motherhood had brought. It was understandable. After all, she was only twenty-two, and all of her friends were partying like carefree twenty-two-year-olds.

I had hoped she'd make some new friends at the Mommy and Me class she joined last month—perhaps friends who were married, had a child, and didn't think drinking responsibly meant not spilling your shot of Goldschläger.

"Why don't you go out? I'll stay home with Beck tonight."

Her eyes lit up. "Really?"

Not exactly how I thought we'd spend our anniversary, but Alexa needed it.

"Sure. I'm wiped out. Me and my little buddy will hang. We don't get to spend enough time alone anyway."

Alexa gently lifted Beck's head from her lap, rested it on a throw pillow, and sprung up to give me a big hug.

"I can't wait to wear the dress I bought. Lauren and Allison are going to be so jealous I can afford to shop at Neiman Marcus now."

I forced a smile. "I can't wait to help you out of it when you get home."

~~~~~

We'd dropped Alexa off at her friend Lauren's last night, and I offered to pick her up, but she insisted she'd take a cab home so I didn't have to wake the baby. Turned out, that wasn't a problem. The baby was wide awake—considering it was eight o'clock in the morning, and my wife still hadn't come home.

Beck sat in his high chair, sucking on Cheerios, and made a loud quacking noise to get my attention while I was pouring my second cup of coffee. Filling my cheeks with air, I forced it out and quacked back at him as I sat. He looked momentarily startled at the sound, and for a second, I thought he was going to cry. But then he let out a loud giggle, which made me laugh right back.

"You like that, buddy, huh?" I leaned closer to him and filled my cheeks again. "Quack. Quack."

My son studied my face as if I were an alien, then broke out in a giggle fit. After the third or fourth time, he caught on, and I watched as *he* tried to make the same sound. His little cheeks would fill, but only a rush of air with some spit would come out of his mouth. No quack. It didn't discourage him.

After every one of his attempts, I'd make the sound, and he'd watch intently and try again. At one point, it was his turn, and I thought it might finally be his shining moment. He sucked in a big mouthful of air and then...held his breath. His chubby cheeks started to turn red, and his face was so intent. That's my boy. *If at first you don't succeed, work harder.* I had a proud dad moment there. My boy was going to be a hard worker.

He did the red-face-holding-his-breath thing a few times and then started giggling again. It was my turn. So I leaned in close to quack, and when I sucked in the air, I realized during that last round he hadn't been working on his quack. He was shitting in his diaper.

We both laughed for ten minutes as I changed him. Although I think he was laughing at me and not with me.

Shortly after, the little shit machine conked out. I stared at him in wonderment for a while. This wasn't exactly how I'd seen my life as I looked forward three years ago, but I wouldn't change it for the world. My son was everything to me.

By the time ten o'clock rolled around, being annoyed

because Alexa hadn't come home yet started to morph into worry. What if something had happened to her? I swiped my phone from the kitchen counter and checked my texts. Still nothing. So I dialed her phone. It went right to voicemail.

The living room window in our third-floor condo faced Broad Street, a quiet, tree-lined block on the outskirts of Atlanta. Most of the world had been out partying last night, so the street was particularly quiet this morning. Which was why I couldn't miss the bright yellow, souped-up Dodge Charger with the number nine painted on the side coming around the corner. Even though the windows were closed, I could hear the roar of no muffler and the screech as the driver took the turn too fast.

*What an asshole.* That corner was a big blind spot. Alexa could have been crossing the street with the stroller, and that idiot wouldn't have seen them until it was too late. I shook my head and watched the car from the window as it rolled to a stop a few buildings over. It sat idling loudly for a few minutes. Then I watched as the passenger-side door opened, and a killer pair of legs peeked out.

I was married, not dead. Looking was okay.

Then the woman exited the car, and I realized looking was definitely okay.

Because the woman getting out of a street racecar a few buildings away from where we lived *was my wife.*

# CHAPTER FIFTEEN

## EMERIE

I arrived at the office before Drew. When he walked in at almost ten, I greeted him with sarcasm. "Wake up late? Perhaps I can recommend something that might help you sleep."

I'd expected a comeback worthy of blushing. But I wasn't even sure he'd heard me.

"Morning." He disappeared into his office and immediately got on the phone and into what sounded like a heated argument. After I heard him hang up, I gave him a few minutes to settle and then took the morning's messages to his office.

Drew was standing behind his desk looking out the window and sipping a tall coffee. He looked a million miles away. I was just about to ask if everything was okay when he turned, and I got my answer. He hadn't shaved, his normally crisp shirt looked like he'd slept in it, and he had dark circles under his usually bright eyes.

"You look terrible."

He forced a half smile. "Thanks."

"Is everything okay?"

He rubbed the back of his neck for a minute and then nodded. "Just some personal shit. I'll be fine."

"Do you want to talk about it? I'm a good listener."

"Talking is the last thing I need. Spent two hours on the phone last night. I'm done talking."

"Alright. Well...what else can I do? What do you need?"

Even though he looked like he'd been through hell, a glimpse of Drew shone through. He arched a brow in response.

"Somehow I doubt you need *me* for that."

He grinned. "Definitely would have helped me fall asleep last night."

We talked for a few minutes, and then I pointed to my office. "I have a video conference in a few minutes, so I won't be able to answer the phones for an hour. After that, I'm good until a late-afternoon conference here in the office."

"No problem. I got the phones."

"Thanks." I went to turn away, then remembered what I'd wanted to ask him this morning before he arrived. "Would you mind if I hang a small whiteboard on my office door? I have those glue sticky things to put it up with, so it won't ruin the door."

"Help yourself."

After putting yet another call through to Drew, I managed to hang the whiteboard level on my door before my video call. My plan was to write a thought-provoking statement on it each day, as I'd always done on my website when my counseling was strictly video conferences and telephone calls. Now that people visited, I wanted to continue the practice.

Since my appointment hadn't rung on my computer yet, I grabbed my reading glasses, went to the journal where I kept relationship thoughts and quotes, and thumbed through until I found one I liked. I printed it neatly on the whiteboard.

**Blowing out someone else's candle doesn't make yours shine brighter.**

**Today I will make my spouse shine by _____.**

I stepped back and smiled, rereading my quote. *God, I love helping people.*

⌒

"Rifle though her mail. I don't give a shit how you find out. I need to know if she's shacking up with the guy before tomorrow at two."

I hadn't seen Drew since this morning, although I heard him loud and clear as I rinsed out my coffee mug in the small kitchen next to his office.

"Roman, I'll give you five grand if you get an intimate photo of them together. Drop off a picnic basket at the front door if you have to—just get them out in public looking cozy." Drew's voice boomed through the hall, followed by a hearty laugh. And then, "Yeah, right. Blow me, big guy...Later."

While I was drying my coffee mug, Drew came into the kitchen.

"I couldn't help but overhear part of your conversation."

"Oh yeah? Which part?"

I smiled. "Most of it. I take it you and your private investigator are close?"

Drew grabbed a water bottle from the refrigerator and twisted the cap off. "Roman's been my best friend since I stole his girlfriend in sixth grade."

"You stole his girlfriend and that made you friends?"

"Yep. He'd given her the chicken pox, which she then passed to me. Roman and I both got bad cases and were out of school for two weeks. We wound up playing video games at his place for ten days straight."

"What happened to your girlfriend? She didn't come between you?"

"Roman and I made a pact. We'd never go for the same girl again. I dumped her the day we got back, and Roman and I have been buddies ever since."

"Oddly, that's kind of sweet."

Drew laughed. "That's us. Roman's the guy who goes through a woman's garbage at the curb in the middle of the night to find used condoms, and I'm the guy who slips what he's found to opposing counsel in the middle of a divorce trial. We're both *sweet*."

I scrunched my nose. "Is that a true story? It's disgusting. Physically and morally."

"How can you say that without knowing what my client was put through? Revenge can be very sweet."

"What part of revenge is sweet? Where you *both* feel horrible after the revenge is complete instead of just one of you?"

Drew took a long draw on his water and leaned one hip against the counter. "I forgot you're the eternal relationship optimist. Speaking of which, how was your date last night?"

"Date?"

"With Mr. Bowtie."

"Oh. Dinner was nice. But I wouldn't exactly call it a date."

"No action at the end of the night, huh?"

"Not that it's any of your business, but no. Nothing happened between us physically. We had a nice dinner and talked a lot about work. Baldwin's been trying to get me an adjunct position at NYU where he teaches. I don't think I would ever want to be full academia, but I'd love to teach part time and see patients part time. Anyway, after dinner we said goodbye at my door."

"What's the deal with that guy? Is he in or is he out?"

"I don't know. He sends me mixed signals. Like last night. He was supposed to be going out with Rachel—a woman he's been seeing—and then he shows up here unannounced, changes his mind, and takes me out to dinner last minute."

"Did you ever talk to him about how you feel?"

"It's never been the right time."

Drew pulled his head back. "The right time? What was wrong with last night?"

"He's seeing someone."

"So?"

"I don't want to interfere in his relationship."

"I didn't say to fuck the guy. Tell him how you feel."

"Is that what you would do?"

Drew snickered. "Actually, normally I fuck my dates and don't discuss my feelings. But that's not your style."

I sighed. "I wish that was my style."

He wiggled his eyebrows. "I can help with that, if you want to give something new a try."

"How generous of you."

"Oh, I'd be plenty generous. Trust me."

My heart fluttered a little at the sight of Drew's wicked grin. I shook my head. "Is this what my life's come to? I'm a couples counselor, and I'm getting my own relationship advice from a divorce lawyer."

"You're an idealist. I'm a realist."

I straightened my shoulders. "And what exactly is your relationship status, if you're such an expert?"

"I have lots of relationships."

"You mean sexual relationships?"

"Yes. I like sex. In fact, I fucking love sex. It's the other shit I don't like."

"You mean the relationship part?"

"I mean the part where two people get together and start to rely on each other, share a life even, and then one of them fucks the other one over."

"Not every relationship turns out that way."

"In every relationship, one person ends up screwing the other at some point. Unless you keep it to *just* screwing. Then there are no false expectations."

"I think your divorce and line of work have tainted your outlook."

He shrugged. "Tainted works for me."

---

Sarah and Ben Aster were a prime example of the reason I loved couples counseling. I'd started seeing Sarah after their son was born and realized quickly that their relationship problems were much more than the added stress of having a new baby. The couple had only been together for four months when Sarah became pregnant, which led to a quickie wedding and having the normal honeymoon-marriage period cut short by the arrival of a baby.

After such a whirlwind, the couple had finally begun settling into their lives, only to discover that their hopes and dreams were very different. Ben wanted a houseful of children, a home in the suburbs with a big backyard, and Sarah to stay at home. His wife, on the other hand, wanted to stay in their tiny apartment on the Upper East Side, go back to work, and hire a nanny.

The funny thing is, they both insisted they'd told the other how they saw their future—and I believe they did. The problem lay in their communication. So even though over the last few months they'd found a way to compromise on their living arrangements by looking for a house in Brooklyn with a small yard and short commute to Manhattan, they still needed to work on communication. Which led me to this week's exercise.

I'd asked both Sarah and Ben to bring a list of five things they wanted to accomplish over the next year. Today we'd spent most of our hour going through Sarah's list. She would read Ben one of her planned accomplishments, and he would have to explain back to her what that plan meant. It was amazing how a couple that had been married for eighteen months could still misinterpret things.

"I want to take a trip down to South Carolina to see my best friend, Beth," Sarah said.

I looked to Ben. "Okay. Tell me what Sarah just said."

"Well, she wants to go to South Carolina to visit her single friend, Beth."

"Yes. Well, Sarah hadn't mentioned that Beth was single, but it sounds like you heard something important to you. Why is the fact that Beth is single significant?"

"She wants to get away. I get that, and she deserves a break. But she wants to go down and spend time with Beth to recapture what she had before we were together—the single, carefree life. Then she'll come back and resent us."

Sarah then told him the things she missed about not having her best friend near her anymore and how she would like to spend her time while visiting. It was clear that what she wanted and what he'd interpreted her trip to mean were very different. But after fifteen minutes of talking it out, she'd put his mind at ease. Communication and trust were getting better each week with these two, and at the end of our session, I suggested that we begin every-other-week sessions rather than weekly.

"You know what I just realized?" Sarah said as Ben helped her put on her coat.

"What's that?"

"After our video conference sessions end, there's always a cute little quote on your home page that I read—something that reminds me to do something nice for Ben. We're not going to have those anymore."

I smiled. "Actually, we are. The quotes are still updated on my website, but I'll also be writing them on my door. It was open when you came in, so you probably didn't notice it. But you should read today's on your way out."

Sarah stopped Ben, and together they read the whiteboard after they opened the door. Sarah looked back at me with an odd expression, while Ben smiled from ear to ear.

After they were gone, I grabbed my reading glasses and went to the door, wondering if perhaps I'd spelled something wrong.

I hadn't, but apparently Drew thought it would be funny to adjust my quote. While I'd written:

**Blowing out someone else's candle doesn't make you shine brighter.**

**Today I will make my spouse shine by _____.**

The board on my door now read:

**Blowing someone else makes his day shine brighter.**

**Today I will make my spouse shine by <u>blowing him</u>.**

*I'm going to kill Drew.*

# CHAPTER SIXTEEN

## DREW

"You are such an asshole!"

"Steve, let me call you back. I think there's an argument that needs refereeing in the conference room next to me." I hung up the phone just as Emerie marched into my office to continue her rant. "That type of stuff might be funny with your all-male clients who hire people to dig in their wives' garbage, but it's not to mine!"

"What the hell is up your ass?" She looked seriously pissed. But...she also had those glasses on while she was yelling at me. *Something about those damn glasses.* And I hadn't noticed it this morning, but that skirt was a bit on the tight side. Red looked good on her.

She tilted her head. "What are you doing?"

"What? What am I doing?"

"You're checking me out. I just watched you do it. I came in here to yell at you for being an asshole, and you're checking me out." She threw her hands up in the air.

"I was admiring your outfit. That's different than checking you out."

"Oh, really?" Her hands went to her hips. "How is it different?"

"How is it different?"

"Don't repeat the question so you can stall for time to make up an answer. How are admiring my outfit and checking me out different?"

There was only one way out of this. "I like you in your glasses."

"My glasses?"

"Yeah. Your glasses. Are they just for reading?"

She was quiet while she assessed my level of bullshit. Eventually she shook her head. "You think you can diffuse what you've done with a compliment, don't you?"

*I'm hoping.* "I think you're a little crazy."

"*I'm* crazy?" Her voice rose.

I sat back in my chair, amused. She was fun to play with. Took my mind off other things. "I didn't think redheads could pull off wearing red."

She looked down at her skirt and back to me, momentarily perplexed, but then she squinted. "Stop that."

"What?"

"Trying to soften me by saying nice things."

"You don't like compliments?"

"When they're real, yes. I like them. But when they're bullshit to distract me? No, I don't like them at all."

"I don't give out bullshit compliments."

She gave me a face that said she wasn't buying it. "So you really like my reading glasses?"

"Gives you that sexy librarian look."

She shook her head. "And my red skirt?"

"To be honest, I don't give a shit about the color. But it's tight. And hugs all the right places."

Emerie's cheeks started to pink. It made me wonder how her creamy skin would look after I sucked on it a bit.

"Don't play with my whiteboard! My clients read it. I'm lucky they're in a good place, or they would be doubting my professionalism after your little stunt."

"Yes, ma'am." I lifted two fingers to my forehead in a mock salute.

"Thank you."

She turned to walk out. I couldn't resist. "Bet the guy gets a blowjob tonight."

"That would make one of you then."

For a change, I was leaving the office at six o'clock. "Want to join me and Roman for a beer over at Fat Cat's?"

Emerie sat at her desk looking in a small mirror as she lined her lips in a bright red that matched her skirt. Following her hand as it curved into the bow of her top lip, it dawned on me that against the backdrop of the stark white office walls, she looked liked a splat of colorful living art on a canvas.

*What the fuck, Jagger? Living art?*

"Thanks, but I have plans tonight."

"Hot date?"

"Baldwin is taking me to a French restaurant."

Tension mixed with a healthy dose of unexpected jealousy rumbled in my stomach. "French food, huh? Not much of a fan."

"Me either. But Baldwin loves escargot."

"Snails," I scoffed, then mumbled "Figures."

"What's that?"

"Nothing." What I really wanted to say was that snails reminded me of slugs. And eating that shit would be cannibalism for Mr. Bowtie. The guy was a *slug*. But instead, I went with, "You have a good night."

# CHAPTER SEVENTEEN

## DREW

"What's your favorite position?"

Emily climbed onto my lap, straddling me. "I like this one."

I'd have to send Roman a bottle of Gran Patrón Platinum for his brilliant idea tonight. We'd met for drinks at our usual bar, but then he insisted we go next door to Maya to try their empanadas—the guy had an obsession with Mexican food. Emily DeLuca and her friend Allison were already there, enjoying margaritas at the bar. Emily was an attorney at a firm across town where I often referred estate planning work. We'd flirted a few times, and there was a spark, but for me, spark never trumped sparkle on a certain finger on the left hand. And the huge rock she wore was pretty hard to miss.

It was also hard to notice it was missing tonight, especially since she'd wiggled the fingers on her left hand at me right before asking if she could buy me a drink. Even with that obvious gesture, I still confirmed her breakup before we left together. No matter how hot or ready a woman was, I didn't touch cheaters.

Emily ground down on my growing cock, and I reached around under her bunched-up skirt to grab a handful of ass. Then I pulled on the lacy fabric running up the crack to increase the friction on the front. She moaned, so I pulled harder.

*Christ, I love G-strings.*

She reached for my shirt and started to work the buttons while I sucked on her neck. "I knew the first time I met you that we'd be good together. I hope you have a full box of condoms. Because after I ride you, I want to be on all fours while you take me from behind."

The thought of Emily ass-up was exactly what I needed. Especially since I'd spent the last week fantasizing about another woman's ass—one I should not be thinking about. Although, the repeated visual of Emerie's creamy, round ass with my pink handprint on it as I hammered into her from behind was a new go-to favorite fantasy of mine. I dreamed of finishing inside of her and then cupping my cum as it dripped out to rub into my handprint on her skin like a salve.

My eyes were shut, and I had to press them tighter to ward off the visual of another woman. Because thinking of one woman while another rides you is a complete dick thing to do, even for me.

Emily lifted enough to slide her hand between us and cupped my cock, giving it a good squeeze. "I want you now." She began to frantically unbuckle my pants, which had me reaching for my wallet. And then remembering there was no condom in there. *Fuck.*

"Any chance you have a condom?" I asked, biting on her earlobe.

Her voice was strained. "No. And I screwed up my birth control this month, so please tell me you have one *somewhere* in this apartment."

*Shit.* I didn't. I'd finished off the big box in my nightstand last month and never got around to replacing it. Then I'd used the emergency one I kept in the back of my wallet in Hawaii.

But...I had a few down in my office in the top right-hand drawer. At least I didn't have to go outside and freeze my balls off. I groaned as I pulled back. Cupping Emily's face, I said, "I need two minutes. I'm sorry. Condoms are in my office downstairs."

"Want me to come with you? I wouldn't object to a little desk sex. Plus, it will save time."

Smart girl. But...probably not a good idea to bring her to a place where we'd be surrounded by shit that reminded me of the woman I was trying to keep *out* of my head.

I gave her a chaste kiss and lifted her off of me. "Stay put. My office is on the first floor. There's twenty-four-hour security down there. I don't want to have to cover your mouth when you scream my name."

The damn elevator took forever to make its way up to my floor, so I took the opportunity to at least buckle my pants before running into Ted, the night doorman. What I should have done was put on shoes. The marble-tiled floor was like an ice cube, and I didn't want my body temperature cooling down.

Inside my office, I made a point of not looking at Emerie's closed door as I walked up the hallway. I didn't need anything else to remind me of her. Definitely not the whiteboard where she wrote sappy relationship crap and then stormed into my office looking all sexy and angry. *Nope. Not going to look.* Like a two year old, I held my hand up to block my peripheral view of the office across from mine as I opened my door.

Rummaging through my desk, I found three loose condoms in the drawer. *Thank fuck.* I shoved them in my pocket and started back down the hall toward the lobby. I'd almost cleared the hallway when I heard a sound.

*I should look.*

*Fuck that.* Let someone break in and steal whatever they want. I'd deal with it tomorrow. I had more important things waiting for me upstairs.

Then I heard it again. It almost...sounded like a sniffle.

Was Emerie still here? I tried to keep going, but I knew I'd never be able to focus if I thought she could be hurt or something. What if she fell on her way out and was bleeding all over the floor in her closed office? I jogged back to her door and opened it.

"Drew! You scared the shit out of me." Emerie jumped in her seat and clutched her chest.

"What are you still doing here? I thought you had a hot date with Mr. Escargot?"

"So did I."

Upon closer inspection, I could see that she'd been crying. She had a tissue wadded up in her hand, and her pale skin was blotchy. "What did he do?" I had the sudden urge to choke the little dweeb with his own bowtie.

She sniffled. "Nothing, really. He just canceled our dinner plans."

"What happened?"

"Today's my birthday, and—"

"It's your birthday? Why didn't you say anything?"

"Birthdays have never been a big deal for me. I celebrated Gotcha Day growing up like most people celebrate birthdays."

"Gotcha Day?"

"The day my parents brought me home from the adoption agency. They always said everyone had a birthday, but the day they *got me* was the best present they ever received. So they started to celebrate Gotcha Day with me instead of their own birthdays. It just sort of stuck, and birthdays are just a number for me."

"That's really incredible. But you still should have told me it was your birthday." It didn't escape me that Emerie barely acknowledged her birthday, while my ex-wife thought her birthday was a national holiday. That had always annoyed the shit out of me even before things got really bad.

She shrugged. "Anyway, I'm just being a big baby. Baldwin made reservations at this popular French restaurant where it's impossible to get a table, and I was supposed to meet him at eight."

"What happened?"

"He texted me and said Rachel was pissed that he blew her off to take me to dinner the other night, and when he'd mentioned he was taking me out again, she got annoyed, so he had to cancel tonight."

The guy was a total asshole. He was definitely stringing Emerie along. There was no doubt in my mind after everything she'd told me and then seeing how he reacted the other night when I'd suggested she and I grab a bite to eat. He was territorial about her in more than a friendly way. Yet he wanted to have his cake and eat it, too.

"I know you have feelings for him. But the guy seems like an asshole to me."

"I just need to let go and move on."

"I think that's a good idea."

"I should go out and celebrate my birthday myself—pick someone up in a bar and bring him home with me."

"That's not a good idea."

She sighed. "I know. I'm just not a random-hookup type of girl. I've tried it, and I hate myself for weeks after. It's not worth it."

*Thank God.* The thought of her bringing some random guy home to hook up with made me physically sick. Speaking of which…my random hookup was upstairs waiting.

"What are you going to do tonight?" I asked.

"I'm just going to finish up this file and then head home. I'm tired anyway."

"Okay. Don't stay too long. We'll celebrate tomorrow. I'll take you to Joey's for lunch."

Emerie forced a sad smile. "That sounds good." Her eyes dropped to my feet. "No shoes?"

"I just ran down quick."

"You're working late and forget something?"

"No...I...uh...have company."

"Oh." Her face, which was already sad, looked like I'd just told her a puppy had died. This time, she couldn't even force a smile. "Don't let me keep you. I'll be out of here shortly anyway."

I said goodnight but felt like complete shit walking away. Why did I feel like two hundred pounds of added weight was sitting on my shoulders as I rode the elevator back upstairs? It wasn't me who had screwed her over. I hadn't even known it was her birthday.

I walked back into my apartment, completely lost in thought, only to be greeted by Emily. She was standing in the doorway that led to my living room, wearing nothing but those sexy-as-shit skinny-heeled shoes and her black lace G-string.

*Nothing like a pair of perky D cups to cheer you up when you're feeling down.*

She tilted her head and crossed her legs at the ankles. The shoes were definitely staying on. I could almost feel them digging into my back already. "Like what you see?"

I responded without words, stalking over and lifting her up, guiding her legs to wrap around my waist. "You can ride me later. Right now, I'm going to fuck you on my kitchen table. You okay with that, Emerie?"

She chuckled. "Emily. I think all the blood is rushing south and messing with your ability to speak."

*Fuck.* I'd called her Emerie and hadn't even noticed.

"That must be it." I walked us to the table and spread her out so I could quickly unbuckle my pants, but when I looked back up at her smiling face, I saw Emerie.

*Emerie.*

Not Emily who I was just about to fuck.

I blinked a few times, and my eyes came into focus. Chestnut hair, dark Italian skin, big brown eyes. The two looked nothing alike. Hovering over her, I held off on taking down my underwear to clear my head and get back in the moment. Then I took her mouth again, and we were kissing.

But I couldn't shake the image of Emerie crying alone at her desk. Her big blue eyes red, fair skin blotched, sad about some asshole who was probably eating escargot and would wake her up with shaking walls at two in the morning.

*Fuck.*

*Fuck.*

"Fuuuuckkk." I stood up and dragged my hand through my hair, wanting to yank it out in frustration.

"What? What's wrong?"

I pulled up my pants as I responded. "It's a client. She called while I was downstairs, and I blew her off. But I need to go work on something."

"Are you kidding me? Now?"

"I'm sorry, Emerie."

"Emily." She covered her breasts as she sat up on the table.

"Emily. Yes. Sorry. My mind is elsewhere." Like on Eme*rie*, instead of Em*ily*, where it should be.

"It's fine," she said.

I could tell it wasn't. Of course, I didn't blame her one bit. I'd be pissed as hell if a woman pulled the crap I'd just pulled on her. But there was nothing I could do about it. Except apologize.

"I'm really sorry. It's time-sensitive, or I wouldn't do this."

"I understand."

She got herself dressed, and less than five minutes after I'd walked into my apartment with a smoking hot naked woman waiting for me, I was walking her to the elevator.

The ride down was uncomfortable. In the lobby, she kissed me on the cheek and walked out without looking back. I should have felt badly, but instead, all I felt was anxious, wondering if Emerie was still here.

*She'd better not be gone already.*

# CHAPTER EIGHTEEN

## DREW

"Jesus Christ!" Emerie was just behind the front door to the office when I whipped it open. If she'd taken another step, I probably would've slammed her in the face.

She clutched at her chest. "Are you trying to give me a heart attack?"

"Good. You're still here."

"I was just getting ready to leave. What's the matter? Is everything okay?"

"Everything is fine. But I'm taking you out for your birthday."

"You don't have to do that."

"I know I don't. But I want to."

She squinted. "I thought you had company."

"Got rid of her."

"Why?"

"Why what?"

"Why did you ditch your date?" The confusion on her face melted as a realization of some sort seemed to hit her. "Oh."

My brows drew down. "Oh what?"

"You're *done* with your date."

"I was far from *done*," I grumbled, then nodded my head toward the street. "Come on. You deserve a nice night out on your birthday. That dumb putz has no idea what he's missing. Let's go get shitfaced."

She smiled from ear to ear. "That sounds awesome."

———

"I'm never getting my balls in."

"Maybe that's why you're so uptight. You haven't been laid in so long, you forgot it's not the balls that go inside." I smirked at Emerie as the five ball rolled into the left corner pocket. It was our first game of pool, and I'd just banked in my fifth ball in a row. She was right. I might clear the table before she chalked up her stick.

She narrowed her eyes. "How do you know how long it's been since I've gotten laid?"

"You're wound a little tight."

I expected her to go off on me, but instead she surprised me. *Literally.* Just as I was about to take my sixth shot, she yelled, "Watch it!" My hand veered mid-shot, and the two ball landed nowhere near the pocket I'd intended.

She sported a smug smile, all proud of herself.

"Is that how we're going to play this?"

"What? I'm so uptight, I can't help myself. Sometimes words get bottled up, and they just pop out of my mouth like a cork from champagne."

"Your shot." I extended my hand toward the felt. As she positioned herself, I rounded the table, moving closer until I stood directly behind her. She attempted to pretend it didn't bother her, but eventually she turned around.

"What are you doing?"

"I'm watching you take the shot."

"From behind?"

I grinned. "It gives me the best view."

"Go back to where you were standing." She waved her hand to the other side of the pool table. "I think your view is clearer from over there."

She bent again, attempting to line up her shot. My eyes dropped to her amazing ass. "That depends on what I'm looking at."

When she finally took the shot, her cue scraped along the felt and completely missed the ball.

"I thought you knew how to play."

"I do."

"Doesn't look that way."

"You're making me nervous standing behind me."

I leaned down next to her and showed her how to position her hand to cradle the stick so it would at least be easier to connect with the ball. After she got the hang of it, I went back to the other side of the table. My intentions that time had been truly altruistic—at least until her shirt gapped open, and I was staring straight down at her tits.

I couldn't bring myself to move. She must have been wearing one of those bras that only holds half a breast, because all I could see were two perfectly round globes of luscious, creamy skin with just a hint of something black and lacy.

*Great tits to go with a spectacular ass.*

I brought my beer to my lips as I waited for her to take her shot, but kept right on gawking over the bottle as I took a long draw. The only thing that eventually distracted me was watching her slide the stick back and forth between her fingers.

Then I imagined my cock was the stick.

Forcing my eyes shut as she finally took her shot, I emptied the contents of my Stella. Emerie managed to connect with the ball this time, only she sank one of my balls instead of her own. She was so excited, I didn't have the heart to tell her.

"Does that mean I go again?"

"Sure does. I'm gonna grab another beer. You want one?"

"Yes, but not another beer. They make me too full."

"Okay? What do you want?"

"Surprise me. I'll drink whatever you give me."

I *definitely* needed to walk away for a minute.

The line at the bar was two deep, but I was a regular here. Roman and I met at Fat Cat every weekend to play pool and talk shop. So when Tiny—the bartender who had to be nearly seven feet tall—saw me, he took my order ahead of most people.

"I'll take another Stella and one of those." I pointed to a margarita.

Tiny cracked a smile. "Roman getting in touch with his feminine side tonight?"

"Nah. He's probably home getting in touch with himself. I'm here with..." What the hell was she? She wasn't a date. Wasn't a co-worker even though we worked in the same office. I couldn't even call her an employee. Searching for a word, I settled on the simplest one: "a woman."

Emerie was most definitely a woman.

While I waited, I thought about the fact that I'd never once even considered taking a date here—again, not that tonight was a date. But this was the kind of place you came to hang out and be yourself. Yet I hadn't thought twice about bringing Emerie here. It was nice to spend time with a woman who I knew would be comfortable in an underground pool hall slash dive bar. It was a bonus that she was sexy as shit.

I was only gone a few minutes, but when I returned to the pool table, there was a guy talking to Emerie. A pang of good ol' male jealousy sprang to life inside of me. Resisting the urge to tell him to beat it, I opted to make the guy feel uncomfortable until he slithered away.

I walked up and stood next to Emerie. Handing her the drink as I looked at the snake, I said, "Here you go. Who's your friend?"

"This is Will. He offered to show me some pointers."

"Oh yeah?"

Will was holding a drink in his left hand. The finger he'd slipped his wedding ring off of still had the indent in it. I waited until our eyes locked, then I let mine lead his down to his finger. "We have the table for another twenty minutes. You and your wife want next game when we're finished?"

Nothing like a little silent man-to-man conversation.

He nodded to the bar. "Maybe another time. My friends are waiting for me."

*Nice talking to you, Will.*

After that, Emerie and I finished our game and went to sit at a table in a quieter area of the bar. She drank that first margarita pretty quick, and the waitress had just delivered a second. Her mood had changed from down about the asshole with a bowtie to alcohol-assisted upbeat.

"So what was your favorite birthday present you ever received?" she asked.

"Me? I don't know. Growing up my father bought me lots of shit. A car for my seventeenth birthday, I guess."

"That's boring." She took a sip of her margarita, and a line of salt stuck to her lip.

"You have..." I pointed to my mouth where the salt was on hers. "Salt."

She reached up and swiped her lip, but the wrong side.

I chuckled and reached across the table. "I got it."

Without giving it a second thought, I brought the salt from her lips to mine and sucked it off my thumb. Maybe I was deluding myself, big ego and all, but I swear her lips parted, and if I'd leaned in, I would have heard a little gasp.

*Fuck. I bet she's really responsive in bed.*

I cleared my throat. "What about you? Best present you ever received?"

"My parents gave me a gift certificate for Lasik surgery when I turned eighteen."

"Lasik? But you wear glasses."

"Oh, I didn't keep the gift. I went down to the doctor's office and explained that my parents had made a mistake, and I didn't want the surgery."

"So you didn't want the surgery, but it was the best present you ever received?"

She sipped her margarita again. Unfortunately, no salt left behind this time. I thought about pretending there was, but she started to speak again too quickly.

"Oh, no, I wanted to get the surgery. In second grade, Missy Robinson called me Grandma because I needed different glasses to see the board and to read. The name stuck throughout elementary school. I hated my glasses. For a long time, I wouldn't wear them, even though I had to squint and constantly got headaches."

"What am I missing? Your parents got you something you really wanted, so you returned it?"

"My parents couldn't afford the surgery. It was six thousand dollars, and my dad was driving around in a twenty-year-old car. But it was the nicest present I could ever have asked for."

Add *sweet* to a great rack, highly fuckable ass, and smart mouth. *That smart mouth is also quite fuckable, I might add.*

"What about now? If you could have anything you wanted for your birthday today, what would it be?"

Her finger tapped at her lip while she thought. "A bath."

"A bath? Like one of those spa treatment mud things or something?"

"Nope. Just a good soak in a nice tub. My apartment only has a shower, and I really miss taking a bath. I used to take one every Saturday morning—put in my headphones and soak until I was shriveled. It's my happy place."

I took a long draw from my beer, watching her again. "You're easy to please."

She shrugged. "How about you? If today was your birthday and you could pick one present, what would it be?"

I swallowed my immediate thought. *Beck.* Not wanting to bring down Emerie's mood on her birthday, I gave her my second pick for a present. "A blowjob would be nice."

Emerie was mid-sip and sprayed her margarita all over me when she laughed.

I wiped my face with a napkin. "Well, now I've had the salt and the margarita."

She giggled. "I'm sorry."

It was after two in the morning by the time we stumbled to Emerie's apartment. I'd insisted on walking her home. I had a buzz going, but I thought she might be closer to drunk.

"Shhh...." She held a finger up to her mouth to tell me to keep it down, yet she was the one being loud. Pointing to the apartment next door as she fished in her purse for keys, she added, "That's Baldwinny's apartment."

Yep. She was drunk.

I took the keys from her hand. "Might do him some good to hear you with another man."

Emerie stepped aside so I could unlock the door for her. Letting out a big sigh, she leaned her head on my arm while I screwed with the lock. The damn thing seemed to be stuck.

"He wouldn't be jealous," she slurred. "He doesn't want me."

I jiggled the keys in the lock a few more times and the bolt clanked open. "Well, then he's an idiot."

I pushed the door open and held out the keys to her. On the handoff, she bobbled them and giggled some more when we banged heads reaching down to pick them up from the floor. Over the sound of her laughter, I heard the door next to her apartment open. Emerie didn't seem to.

When Baldwin stepped into the hall and looked at us, I suddenly felt very territorial. With her back to him, Emerie was still unaware that we had an audience. She smiled up at me with those big blue eyes, and something came over me. I leaned in and gave her a soft kiss on the lips—a toe in the water to take the temperature.

That little kiss was all testosterone, me being a dick to the asshole next door. Pissing on the fire hydrant, so to speak. But when I pulled my head back and saw her eyes dilated and lips parting for more, my next move had nothing to do with who was watching.

It was sheer desire. I lost it. My mouth crashed down on hers again, and her lips parted for me. My tongue slid in, and I took my first long stroke inside. It was salty and peppered with tequila, but it was the most delicious thing I'd ever tasted. And suddenly, I was starving.

I pulled her flush against me and wrapped my arms around her tight. There was no guy who she was in love with watching—it was just me and Emerie. Everything else disappeared as I deepened the kiss, and she eagerly pushed her tits up against my chest. The sound she made when my hand went to her phenomenal ass encouraged me to keep going. I wanted nothing more than to push her up against her door and grind my swelling cock against her. And I might have given in and done it, had the asshole next door not put a damper on the moment.

Baldwin cleared his throat. Hearing the sound, Emerie pulled away and turned to find that the man she was in love with had just watched this entire thing. She looked startled, and I hated that there was already a look of regret in her eyes. I didn't have the heart to make her feel any more shaken than she already was.

Cupping her cheeks, I leaned in and whispered in her ear, "Maybe that will wake him up." Then I kissed her cheek. "See you at the office, birthday girl."

# CHAPTER NINETEEN

## DREW
*New Year's Eve, Four years ago*

"Who the fuck are these people?" Roman was sitting on the balcony of my apartment in the dark, smoking a hand-rolled cigarette, when I snuck out to escape for a few minutes.

"Maybe you'd know if you were inside instead of out here." I took the seat beside him and stared out into the sea of lights that was New York City. "It's fucking freezing."

"Did you see the tits on that blonde with the blue sweater?"

"That's Sage. One of Alexa's new friends."

"She ain't the brightest bulb. I was joking around and told her I could tell her age by feeling her up."

"Don't tell me she let you grope her?"

The end of Roman's cigarette illuminated bright red as he took a long drag. "Yep. After I copped a good feel, she asked me when she was born." He blew out a string of smoke rings. "I told her yesterday and came to sit out here."

I chuckled. Fucking Roman. He either got smacked or lucky, and sometimes I wondered which one he actually liked better. "Yeah. Alexa has a knack for picking choice friends."

"Looks like she's settled into New York okay, at least."

From the outside, at least tonight, it would appear that way. This was certainly better than her going out alone last year, followed by a huge fight to kick off the new year when I'd questioned her about the guy who'd driven her home. This year, our home was filled with all of the friends she'd made over the last four months since we moved to New York from Atlanta. But the truth was, she still bitched daily about leaving her friends behind.

"She's made some friends. Mostly from the acting class she's taking and the gym. I was hoping she'd find friends who have more in common with her—maybe some of the ladies from Mommy and Me, but she says they're all sweater-wearing, stuffy bitches."

"If those sweaters are anything like the blonde's, I might be borrowing your kid to take a Mommy and Me class."

We were both quiet for a few minutes, enjoying the peace of a clear night. Roman's voice was serious when he spoke again. "How's AJ doing?"

AJ was my father's nickname, short for Andrew Jagger. Neither of us used our given name—I was always Drew, and he was always AJ. "Not good. It's spread to a lung now. Looks like they're going to have to remove a piece."

"Fuck. I'm sorry, friend. AJ's too damn young for this shit."

Four months ago my father had gone to the doctor for an annual physical and his blood work revealed his liver enzymes were off. Two days later he was diagnosed with liver cancer. Even though the statistics weren't on his side—a fifteen percent five-year survival rate from diagnosis—he was optimistic. He'd endured months of high-dose chemo that made him sick as a dog, only to be told the day after he finished the last round that the cancer had metastasized to his lung.

"Yeah. I'm glad I could be here for him. He's got a shitload of friends and business associates, but without a wife taking care of him, I needed to be back in New York."

"I was beginning to think you weren't coming back."

"I think that was Alexa's plan."

I'd always intended to come back to New York to work with my father in his practice. After I passed the bar, Alexa had begged me to stay in Atlanta one more year. It meant having to take a second bar exam, but I was trying to make her happy while she was adjusting to motherhood. So we agreed to stay in Atlanta for one year. One turned into two, and until my dad got sick, I think it was Alexa's plan to keep asking for one more year.

"She's adjusting. She likes the shopping and has decided to take some acting classes. Apparently that's something she's always wanted to do, but never mentioned until she signed up for the first class." I shrugged. "Whatever, it keeps her happy."

Roman looked at me. "What about you? She keep you happy?"

"She's a good mother."

"So is my mother. But that doesn't mean I want to fuck her and spend the rest of my life hanging out with her."

"You have a unique way of looking at shit."

"I'm banging a yoga instructor; she's into all that introspective crap."

"I'm sure that's why you're with her. Not because she can lift her leg over her own shoulder."

"The only time she shuts the hell up and stops trying to enlighten me with useless wisdom is when I have her legs over her shoulders. My dick acts like a stopper in a bathtub full of wisdom quotes."

I chuckled and stood, smacking my friend on the back. "Come on, let's go back to the party. I'm freezing my balls off, and I want to check on Beck. It's getting pretty loud in there."

Navigating through the growing party, I made my way to my little boy's room. So damn sweet—he even smiled in his sleep. Okay, so maybe it was a twitch, but his mouth relaxed and then jumped to a grin every few seconds. He must have been dreaming about his racecars and grapes, his two favorite things the last few months. I pulled the cover up to his chin and ran my fingers over his soft cheeks. God, I'd never dreamed I could love anyone in the world so much. My heart clenched in my chest momentarily as I wondered if my own father had looked at me the same way twenty-some-odd years ago. I needed my dad to get better. I wanted him to get to know my son and guide me to be the kind of father he was to me.

I wasn't a religious guy—the last time I'd been in church was my shotgun wedding to Alexa. And before that, probably a funeral. But a small cross hung over my son's crib. I looked at it every day, but never really saw it as more than a decoration.

*It couldn't hurt to try.*

Standing beside Beck's crib, I said a small prayer for God to watch over my father and my son.

We'd been back in New York for four months, and that cross had hung on the wall next to his crib the entire time. But when I opened the door to go back to the party, the thing fell to the ground.

I hoped that wasn't a sign.

# CHAPTER TWENTY

## EMERIE

My head felt like I'd been run over by a car full of pissed-off AA members. I was so thirsty, my mouth had been overtaken by a desert, yet every sip of water made me queasy. *Jesus. No wonder I don't drink very often.*

The only good thing about this hangover was that I was so busy feeling like crap, I didn't have the capacity to think about last night.

Drew.

That kiss.

*That kiss.*

Baldwin.

Holding my breath, I walked into the office even later than my normal late. I didn't have a session until the afternoon, but I was behind on typing my notes into patient files.

The thought of facing Drew suddenly made my hangover nausea seem like just a warm up for the real thing. I was relieved when I turned the corner into the hallway to see his door was shut. The awkwardness with him was inevitable, but it would be easier when I felt better. Putting it off as long as possible seemed ideal at the moment.

Inside my office, I hung my coat on the rack behind the door and popped my laptop into the docking station. It wasn't until I sat down at my desk and reached to flip on my monitor that I saw the note. It was Drew's handwriting:

*All day deposition in Jersey. Won't be back until tonight. Need you to do me a favor and go upstairs to my apartment. I left a note with instructions in the kitchen. Penthouse East. Keycard for the elevator and door key are in your top drawer. Thanks, D.*

That was odd. I attempted to settle in and answer a few emails, but curiosity wasn't going to wait long. Taking the key and elevator card from my desk, I headed out to the lobby after less than five minutes. On the ride up, I watched the lights illuminate in a daze. I knew Drew lived in the building, but he'd never mentioned it was the penthouse. What could he need me to do in his apartment? Did he have a cat?

The shiny silver elevator doors slid open when I reached the top floor. Stepping off, there were only two doors, PW and PE. Unlike my apartment, the Penthouse East lock turned easily. Drew had written that he wouldn't be back until tonight, yet I felt compelled to call out as I cracked the door open.

"Hello?... Hello? Anyone home?"

The apartment was quiet. No furry little creatures greeted me at the door either. I closed it behind me and went in search of the kitchen.

*Holy shit.*

Drew Jagger's apartment was stunning.

Mouth hanging open, I walked right past the sleek kitchen, down two steps into the sunken living room and went to the wall of glass. Floor-to-ceiling windows framed a view of Central Park that could have been plucked out of a movie. After taking in the scenery for a few minutes, I unglued my eyes and went back to the kitchen. On the granite countertop was a note:

*Down the hall, first door on the right.*

What the?

There was only one hall. My palms were sweaty when I reached for the doorknob. Why was I so nervous?

I had no idea what to expect, so I pushed the door open ever so slowly. Only to find...an empty bathroom? I was still holding the note from the kitchen in my hand, so I rechecked the directions. *First door on the right.* Assuming he must have made a mistake, I was just about to shut the door when I saw a sticky on the mirror above the sink. I flicked on the light and took a good look around the room before reading it. It was one hell of a nice bathroom. Bigger than the bedroom in my apartment. Turning to meet my reflection, I pulled the sticky note from the mirror.

*Bag on counter. Got you some girly bath stuff. Remote to tub jets in bag, too. Happy belated birthday. Enjoy your day. P.S. Motrin in medicine cabinet.*

Unexpectedly, my eyes welled up with tears. The hard-ass destroyer of relationships had a soft side.

My skin was getting pruney. I'd actually dozed off for twenty minutes soaking in the tranquil tub and listening to Norah Jones. Drew had picked up bath salts, lavender bubble bath, and two small lavender candles. The odd feeling I had stripping out of my clothes and drawing a bath in an unfamiliar home quickly faded when I stepped into the warm water.

I'd been in the tub for more than a half hour, and the water was starting to chill, yet I still wanted to try out the whirlpool jets. I opened the drain for a minute, then added some scalding water to warm the bath back up. Grabbing the tiny remote, I pushed a couple of buttons, and the tub whirled to life.

*Mmmm, that feels heavenly.*

I increased the pressure of the jets on my back and covered the one at my feet with the arch of my right foot, simulating a foot massage.

It really felt like a massage. When was the last time anyone actually gave me a massage? A man? It had been a long time. *Too long.* Which was probably why when I shut my eyes to enjoy the sensation, I began thinking what that sensation would feel like *other places* on my body.

And that brought my mind right back to Drew.

That kiss.

*That kiss.*

Sigh. I hadn't realized Baldwin had walked into the hallway, and Drew was only doing it to make him jealous. It had felt so real. So filled with desire. The way he pressed his body up against mine so hard, holding me so tight, I thought it was hunger fueling the kiss. And even though I'd been startled by it at first, my body had reacted immediately. Which was why when I realized he'd only done it because Baldwin was watching, to make him jealous, I was flooded with so many mixed emotions.

Today I was also confused for another reason. I seemed to be more concerned about things turning weird between me and Drew than I was about what Baldwin would think.

Since I had the man on the brain, I decided to send Drew a text. I wasn't even sure if he was a texter—I'd never really seen him pay attention to his phone other than to answer it.

**Emerie:** *This might be my new favorite birthday present ever. Thank you.*

My pathetic heart sped up when I saw dots start jumping.

**Drew:** *Topping a gift to slice open your eyeballs, which you returned? You're damn easy to please.*

I laughed. I also moved my foot to uncover the jet and spread my legs to feel the water pressure.

**Emerie:** *It was really sweet of you. This bathtub is heavenly.*

**Drew:** *Is? Are you texting me from the tub right now?*

**Emerie:** *I am.*

**Drew:** *You can't tell me shit like that. I'm in the middle of a deposition, and now I'm going to be distracted picturing you naked in my tub.*

I started to type a response, then stopped. Drew was picturing me naked. Tiny goosebumps broke out over my body, even though I was blanketed with warm water. I knew he was teasing me, yet there was still something exciting about it, and I wanted to play back.

**Emerie:** *Do you like what you're picturing?*

**Drew:** *I just had to adjust my pants under the table. What do you think?*

I think...I liked the thought of Drew Jagger getting a hard-on thinking about me. My body was reacting to his texts the same way it had reacted to his kiss last night. I attempted to think of something sexy to type back, but before I could come up with something witty, the little dots were jumping again.

**Drew:** *How did things go with Professor Putz last night after I left?*

At the mention of Baldwin, the same *other* feeling I'd had last night hit me like a bucket of cold water: a reminder that Drew was just being his normal crass self. Yet again I'd thought he was serious for a minute.

**Emerie:** *Not much to tell.*

For some reason, I left off that Baldwin had asked if he could take me out tonight to make up for canceling on me.

The texts from Drew had been coming in rapid succession, but he went silent for a few minutes. Eventually, the dots started again.

**Drew:** *Have fun. Gotta get back to my case.*

I didn't hear from him again after that. I soaked a few more minutes in the bath, and then went back down to the office. My afternoon appointments were uneventful, and the rest of the day blew by while I caught up on updating case files. Baldwin texted to say he'd made reservations for seven at someplace I wouldn't attempt to pronounce, so I left the office at five-thirty to freshen up before dinner.

I changed out of the skirt and blouse I'd worn to the office and into a little black dress. It wasn't necessary to look up the restaurant where we were going; I knew it would be fancy. Unlike Drew, Baldwin didn't go to underground pool hall bars or eat greasy burgers from Joey's. The funny thing was, I really had no desire to go to some uppity place tonight. As I fastened small, pearl drop earrings to my ears, I became annoyed with myself for pretending I wanted to be at those places with Baldwin. The truth of the matter was, I had pretended to like some of the same things as him just to have a reason to spend time together.

When Baldwin knocked promptly as seven, I still wasn't feeling like myself. My normal excitement had been replaced by annoyance. I was annoyed he'd blown me off last night in favor of the latest woman he was screwing, and I was annoyed I'd been pretending to like things for him when he clearly didn't go out of his way for me. I opened the door and invited him in so I could grab my phone from the charger and change purses. While I was in the bedroom, I heard a cell phone ring from the living room and then Baldwin's voice say hello.

I listened to one side of the conversation as I returned to the living room.

"Probably about eleven."

I walked to the kitchen and opened the purse I'd used today to go to work and began to transfer a few things to my small black clutch.

"Okay, yes. It'll be late, but we can discuss it then."

I scrolled through my messages while Baldwin finished up his conversation. A text had come in from Drew about ten minutes ago.

**Drew: *On way back. You still at the office? Have to write a motion when I get back, going to be a long night for me. Ordering Chinese for delivery. You want something?***

I started to text back and then stopped when Baldwin hung up and asked, "You ready?"

"Sure." I picked up my new purse and went to the closet to get my coat. Baldwin—always the gentleman—took my coat and stood behind me to help put it on. "You have to work after dinner?"

"Hmmm?"

"The phone call. I overheard you say you would talk to someone later."

"Oh. That was Rachel. We both have work events this weekend, and she wants me to attend hers with her after mine. I told her I'd discuss it when I get there later this evening."

The little bubble of anger that had been threatening finally broke inside of me. Oddly, I wasn't really angry at Baldwin. I was pissed at myself. I turned to face him.

"You know what? I'm sorry to do this last minute, but I've had a headache all day, and it's just getting worse. I'm afraid I won't be very good company tonight."

Baldwin was taken aback, his brow furrowed. "You don't want to go to dinner?"

"Not tonight. I'm sorry. Can I take a rain check?" I hadn't intended to, but I realized immediately after I said it that Baldwin had used the same phrase on me when he canceled last night. *Can I take a rain check?*

After he left, I remembered I hadn't sent Drew the text I'd began typing out. My finger hovered over the *I'm already gone, but thank you for asking* message until it started to erase the words.

Screw it.

I typed something without allowing myself to rethink it.

**Emerie: *I'll take a moo shu pork.***

# CHAPTER TWENTY-ONE

## DREW

"Looks like I picked the wrong day to be out of the office."

Emerie had slipped off her coat, revealing a slinky little black dress. She smiled. *Damn.* I'd spent the cab ride home last night convincing myself that kiss was for her own good. I was helping her. It wasn't because she was beautiful and smart and couldn't play pool for shit, yet didn't complain once when I brought her to a pool hall. It was because Professor Putz needed a little incentive to make his move. I'd almost convinced myself, too.

But it had been eating at me all day. What if I'd spurred the dope to finally act and then primed the pump for him, too? Emerie had melted into me with that kiss. I felt her body surrender, heard that little sound she made, and knew she felt it like I did. The engine was all fired up and ready to run. *For that fucker.*

My deposition should have wrapped in four hours today. Yet it took me almost twice that because of my lack of focus. Then tonight, I called Yvette and canceled the date we'd made a month ago. *Yvette, the flight attendant who didn't want a commitment and hummed a sweet tune while she gave a blowjob.* The woman was bachelor gold.

"I was supposed to go out and had a change of plans," Emerie said.

I nodded. "Come eat. Your moo shu is getting cold."

She sat in one of the guest chairs on the opposite side of the desk. "This looks like a lot of food. Is someone else joining us?"

"You took a while to respond, so I ordered some extra stuff in case you were still here. Wasn't sure if you liked chicken, beef, or shrimp, so I got one of each. Guy on the phone barely spoke English. When I called back to add your pork, I figured it was easier to just add to the order than try to change it." I slid a takeout container across the desk to her. "No plates. No forks. Hope you can eat with chopsticks."

"I sort of suck at chopsticks."

I thumbed toward the ceiling. "You can go upstairs and get a fork from my place, if you want. But I haven't eaten since six a.m., so you're on your own with that."

She smiled and ripped the paper off the chopsticks. "I'll deal. But no making fun of me."

It wasn't an easy task. The woman had two left chopsticks. She dropped more than she got into her mouth. But the two of us quickly established an unspoken system. Every time she dropped a piece of pork on the way to her lips, I'd smirk, and she'd squint at me. It was as much fun as tossing insults her way, but half the effort.

"So what happened with Professor Putz last night?"

She sighed and sat back in her chair. "Nothing. He asked me to go out to dinner tonight to make up for canceling on me last night."

I froze with my chopsticks halfway to my mouth. "He bailed on you again tonight?"

"Not this time. I actually bailed on him."

I shoved a shrimp in my mouth. "*Nice*. Getting even. How'd it feel?"

A smile spread across her beautiful face. "Pretty damn good, actually."

"So that's why you're all dressed up?"

She nodded. "We were supposed to go to some fancy restaurant for my belated birthday dinner. He came to my apartment to pick me up, and I overheard him talking on his cell to Rachel saying he was going over there after dinner."

"So you got jealous and canceled?"

"Actually no. I got annoyed at myself. I've spent the better part of three years taking whatever scraps I was offered from a man who's never going to see me as anything more than a friend and neighbor. I deserve better than that."

I couldn't agree more. "Damn right you do."

She sighed. "I need to move on."

I picked up a shrimp with my sticks and offered it to her. "Shrimp?"

"Okay. But put it in my mouth, or you'll have a trail of sauce all across your desk by the time I get it in."

I arched a brow. "I'll gladly put it in your mouth. Open wide."

She laughed. "You can turn something so innocent into something dirty."

"It's a gift."

I moved my offering closer, and her beautiful mouth opened so I could feed her. When her lips closed around my sticks, I felt it straight down to my cock. I imagined my own wood sliding in, being swallowed by her perfectly painted lips. The taste of the shrimp hit her tongue, and her eyes closed as she appreciated the deliciousness. At that point, I needed to readjust my pants. Again.

I swallowed, watching her swallow. "When was the last time you actually had sex?"

She coughed, almost choking on a piece of shrimp this time. "Excuse me?"

"You heard me right. Sex. When was the last time you had it?"

"You already know my history. I haven't had a relationship in almost a year."

"You meant a sexual relationship? I assumed when you said that, you meant you hadn't dated anyone consistently in that long."

"I haven't."

"You do know that not all relationships need to be more than sexual?"

"Of course I know that. But I need more than just a one-night stand."

"Like what?"

"I don't know. Off the top of my head, I need to feel safe with the person. I need to be physically attracted to them. We need to be able to get along after the act, and I need to feel like I'm not being taking advantage of—that our relationship, whatever it is, isn't one-sided. If it's purely sex, that's okay, but we both need to have that understanding."

I nodded. "Those are all fair." By that point, I'd pretty much lost my mind. Which would explain how my next thought made its way from my brain and shot right out through my lips. "How do I apply for the job?"

"The job?" She actually seemed confused. I thought I was pretty damn clear.

"Of sexual partner. I think we should have sex."

# CHAPTER TWENTY-TWO

## EMERIE

"You're insane."

"Because I think we should have sex? How does that make me insane?"

"We're pretty much opposites. You believe a relationship is the period of time people spend together before one screws the other over."

"So?"

"I believe in love and marriage and making things work."

"I'm not talking about those things. I'm talking about sex. I know it's been a while, but that's when a man and a woman—"

I cut him off. "I know what sex is."

"Good. Me too. So have it with me."

"That's crazy."

"Do you feel safe with me?"

"Safe? Yes. I guess so. I know you wouldn't let anything happen to me."

"Are you physically attracted to me?"

"You clearly know you're good looking."

"And if we were both clear on what was going on, you wouldn't feel like you were being taken advantage of." Drew tilted his chair back. "I meet all of your criteria." He winked. "Plus, I have a big bathtub. That's a bonus. Come to think of it, maybe I should be vetting you better. I'm a catch."

I couldn't help but laugh at the absurdity.

"See. Another bonus. I make you laugh."

He wasn't wrong there. Honestly, in the last two weeks, Drew Jagger had stirred a lot of things inside of me that I hadn't felt in a long time. I bit my lip. My stomach felt like a dryer with a half-empty load of laundry—bouncing around randomly as things heated up. I couldn't believe I was even considering what he'd suggested.

"How long ago was the last time you were with a woman?"

"The day before I met you."

"So only a few weeks ago. Were you dating her?"

"No. I met her while I was on vacation in Hawaii."

"Did you get to know each other before having sex?" I had no idea why I was even asking the question.

Drew set his container down on the table. "She gave me a blowjob in the bathroom less than a half-hour after we met in the restaurant bar."

I scrunched up my nose.

"Did you want me to lie to you?"

"I guess not. I think I'd have preferred that not to be your answer though."

He nodded. "You wanted to believe there was romance and an exotic setting—that it was more than it was. It was just sex between two consenting adults. There doesn't always have to be more to it."

I finished my Chinese food and leaned back, folding my hands on top of my full stomach. "While it's tempting..." I grinned. "...mostly because of that bathtub. I don't think it's a good idea. We spend too much time together for it to just be sex."

Drew's thumb rose to his mouth, and he rubbed his full bottom lip. "I could evict you."

"Then I'd definitely want to have sex with you. Because nothing puts me in the mood like being tossed out on the street," I teased.

Drew came around to my side of the desk and took my empty box and his to the garbage. I felt him come up behind me when he returned. Leaning down, his head over my shoulder, his breath tickled my neck when he spoke. "You change your mind, you know where to find me."

Even though I didn't really feel like being alone, a little while after we finished eating, I told Drew I needed to get home to do some work. His text earlier had said he had hours of work to do when he got back to the office, and I didn't want to keep him from it. Plus, I needed some time to let the discussion we'd had tonight sink in. While the entire proposal was bizarre, I couldn't honestly deny that the thought of having a sexual relationship with Drew was appealing.

⌒‿

While things returned to normal between Drew and me in the office over the next few days—and by normal I mean he ridiculed the advice he overheard me giving my patients, and I suggested he check up his ass for his missing ethics after the advice I heard him offer his clients—things between Baldwin and me remained strained. I'd heard him open and shut his door yesterday morning, and then there was a knock on my door, so I'd acted very mature and pretended I wasn't home.

I had no idea why I was avoiding him when he really hadn't done anything wrong. So the following day, when he knocked again, I took a deep breath and adulted.

"I've been worried about you," he said.

"Have you? I didn't mean to make you worry. I've just been busy with work."

"That's good, I guess. I'm glad everything is working out the way you planned with your move."

*Not everything. But whatever.*

"Yes. I'm happy with the way my practice is developing."

"Are you free for breakfast? I was hoping we could talk a bit. Catch up on everything else going on."

I was, but I lied. Looking at my watch, I saw it was seven-thirty. "I actually have an eight-thirty counseling session, and I'm not finished getting ready."

"Dinner?"

"My entire day is pretty packed." I smiled weakly. "I'll be working late to transfer my notes into the case files."

Baldwin frowned. "Lunch. We can eat in your office, if you'd like."

He wasn't going to take no for an answer. "Umm...sure."

After he left, I thought better of having Baldwin at the office for lunch and texted him I'd meet him at a nearby restaurant. Not that I was concerned Drew would be upset or anything, but there was no telling what might come out of Drew's mouth.

***

**It's not what you say, it's how you say it.**

**Today, I'd like to say** _____

**to you, and show you I mean it.**

After adding the daily quote to my whiteboard, I added it to my website and then began reviewing my case files. I had back-to-back therapy sessions this afternoon, and I wanted to be prepared in case I was late returning from lunch. Baldwin texted earlier that he'd made reservations at Seventh Street Café, a cloth-napkin-type lunch restaurant that could take a while to prepare their elaborate dishes. They didn't make burgers. They made Kobe beef burgers with fennel seeds cooked in free-range duck fat—something exotic-sounding to justify the twenty-five-dollar price tag.

Half an hour before lunch, I was surprised when Baldwin showed up at the office instead of meeting me at the restaurant as we'd planned.

"I thought we were meeting at Seventh Street Café?"

"I was in the neighborhood, so I thought I'd pick you up on the way."

I told him to come into my office so I could grab my coat and power down my laptop. Drew had been on an all-morning conference call, and of course he finished up right at that moment. He walked into my office without knowing anyone was there.

"What are you in the mood for? I was thinking dirty-water dogs. Feel like taking a walk up to—" He stopped in place when he saw Baldwin. "Didn't realize you had company."

I caught the slight tick in his jaw. He definitely wasn't fond of Baldwin.

Of course, Baldwin didn't help the cause. He responded snidely, "Yes. We have a lunch date at a place where they don't serve dirty food."

Drew looked to me, and his eyes conveyed what he didn't say out loud to Baldwin. Then he turned and went back to his office, offering only, "Enjoy your *clean food*," over his shoulder as he walked away.

I'd almost made it out of the office when Baldwin stopped to read my daily quote.

He turned to me. "Your clients like this sort of thing?"

I was defensive. "Yes. I put the same daily quote up on my website where people connect and disconnect for video-counseling sessions. Leaving people with an inspirational quote and a suggestion for giving more to their relationship is a positive reinforcement to my sessions."

"I guess that depends on what you're suggesting."

I was confused at what he didn't like about it, because I'd actually gotten the idea for daily quotes from one of his TA sessions back in college. I couldn't imagine why he seemed disturbed by my utilizing it.

As I walked out the door, I stopped to reread my quote.

*Drew.*

I was going to kill him.

He'd modified.

*Again.*

I'd written:

**It's not what you say, it's how you say it.**

**Today, I'd like to say _____**

**to you, and show you I mean it.**

He must have changed it while my door was closed. It now read:

**It's not what you do, it's who you do it to.**

**Today, I'd like to do <u>you</u>. And I mean it.**

# CHAPTER TWENTY-THREE

## EMERIE

"I have a belated birthday present," Baldwin said as we waited in the restaurant lobby for the hostess to finish seating the people ahead of us.

"You do?"

He smiled and nodded. "You have an interview for an adjunct position in two weeks. It's only teaching one class, but it will get your foot in the door."

"Oh my God, Baldwin!" Without thinking, I threw my arms around his neck and gave him a giant hug. "Thank you so much. That's the—" I was about to say *best* gift I could have asked for this year, but then I remembered what Drew had given me and corrected myself. "That's amazing. Thank you so much."

The hostess came and sat us, and we spent the next hour chatting about work and the professor I'd be interviewing with. It was nice to catch up with Baldwin—I really did enjoy his company. I realized that over the last month, my frustration because of the feelings I had for him had begun to interfere with our friendship. It was time I moved past it and enjoyed what we had for what it was.

After we finished eating, the waiter cleared our lunch plates, and Baldwin ordered an espresso. He folded his hands on the table and moved the topic of conversation away from work.

"So you're seeing the attorney you share space with?"

"No. That kiss you saw was the result of too many margaritas."

Baldwin frowned, but nodded. "Well, that's good. I'm not sure he's the type of person you should be getting too involved with."

"What does that mean?"

Yes, I was currently pissed off at Drew, and I planned to kick his ass when I returned to the office, but Baldwin wasn't going to put him down when he didn't even know him.

"He seems...I don't know. Gauche."

"He's direct. Yes. And sometimes even a little crass. But he's actually quite thoughtful once you get to know him."

Baldwin studied my face. "Well, I'm glad there's nothing between you. I'm protective of you. You know that."

Funny, in the little time I'd known Drew, I actually felt like *he* was the one who was protective of me.

Drew's door was closed when I returned to the office. I listened to make sure he wasn't on a call and then flung it wide open.

"You are such an asshole!"

"I've been told that. How was your lunch with Professor Pompous?"

"Delicious," I lied. My fancy hamburger wasn't even that good.

"Baldwin read what you wrote on my whiteboard. You need to stop screwing with me."

He grinned. "But it's so much fun to screw with you. And you won't let me *screw you*. So I have to get my rocks off somehow."

"I'm sure he thinks I'm not being professional with my clients now."

Drew shrugged. "Why didn't you tell him I wrote it?"

"He doesn't like you much already. I didn't want to make it worse."

"I don't give a shit what he thinks of me. Why do you care what he thinks of me?"

That was a very good question. One I didn't have the answer for. "I just do."

He stared at me. And then he began to rub that damn plump bottom lip with his thumb. "Wanna know what I think?"

"Do I have a choice?"

Drew walked around from behind his desk and leaned one hip against the front. "I think you like me. That's why you care what that asshole thinks."

"Right now I'm not liking you very much at all."

His eyes dropped to my chest. "Part of you is liking me." I looked down to find my nipples hard and erect. The damn things were practically poking through the silk of my blouse. *Traitors.*

I folded my arms across my chest. "It's cold in here."

Drew pushed off the desk and took a few steps closer to me. "It's not cold at all. I actually think it's warm." He grabbed at the knot on his tie and loosened it.

*Damn, why do I think that's sexy?*

My heart hammered inside of my chest.

He took another step closer. Maybe two feet separated us now. "I think your body likes me, and your head is fighting it. The two should fight it out like adults—naked in the bedroom with me."

"I think you're insane. And I'm a psychologist, so my diagnosis is probably the more accurate one."

He took another step. "So if I pulled up that skirt of yours and reached between your legs, you wouldn't be wet?"

My skin heated, and I wasn't sure if it was hearing Drew say he wanted to reach between my legs or the need I felt to have him actually do it. I couldn't look up and face him anymore, yet I also couldn't walk away. I stared at him from my eye level—he was so much taller that I watched the rise and fall of his chest. Each breath grew deeper, and mine joined his rhythm.

"Look at me, Emerie." His voice was deep and confident. Drew waited until my eyes met his before closing the gap between us with one small step. "You have three seconds to get out of my office. Otherwise you're giving me permission to do whatever I want to you."

I swallowed. My voice broke as I held his gaze. "I came in here to yell at you."

"I like it when you're angry." He paused. "One."

"You like it when I'm angry?"

"I find it turns me on. Two."

"You won't do anything at three if I tell you to stop."

He inched even closer. "Of course not. You trust me. But you won't tell me to stop." He paused. "Last chance."

I stood frozen as he counted off his last number. "Three."

Before I could object, Drew's mouth crashed down on mine. His bottom lip was so perfectly soft and plump. I'd been staring at it for weeks, and suddenly all that intense ogling took over my brain. I grabbed his tie and pulled him even closer as I sucked in that bottom lip. He responded with a groan and reached around, one hand going to each of my ass cheeks as he lifted me off the floor and squeezed hard.

My skirt pushed up as my legs wrapped around his waist. He walked a few steps until my back thudded against the wall, then pinned me to it with his hips, so he could free his hands.

*God, he knows all the tricks.* His mouth began to suck on my neck, and I heard the *whish* of his buckle being whipped through the loops.

*That noise.*

It sounded so forceful and desperate. If I hadn't already been wet, I would have been after hearing that sound.

"You have any appointments coming in today?"

"No. Just video sessions. You?"

"Thank fuck." He grabbed my shirt, one hand on each side, and ripped it open. Pearl buttons scattered across the floor. His thumbs pushed down the front of my bra, and he bent, sucking a nipple into his mouth. *Hard.*

"Oh, God." I arched my back. It hurt, but I wanted more. I grabbed for his pants, but the way he had me pinned, I couldn't reach. Yet I needed to pull something. So I tangled my fingers in his hair and pulled as he increased his suction again. Never in my life had I felt so much desire. It was so powerful, I wanted to cause him pain. Which was completely out of character for me. I liked sex sweet and loving. This was pure, unadulterated, carnal need.

My body was so on edge, so buzzing toward fevered climax, that I almost lost it when his hand moved between my legs. Pulling my panties to the side, he groaned at my wetness.

"I knew you would be soaked." Then he slipped two fingers inside of me, and I let out a loud moan.

It had been too long.

Way too long.

"Drew," I breathed a warning. If he didn't slow down, I was going to come. "Slow down."

"No fucking way," he growled. "I'll go slow after I watch you come on my fingers. I'll take my time as I lick every drop of your sweet juice from this tight little pussy. But right now, I'm not slowing down." He pushed his fingers in and out and then crooked one at just the right angle, and it sent me completely over the edge. I moaned through my release, not even ashamed that it had taken him less than five minutes to make me come.

"Jesus, Emerie. That's the sexiest thing I've ever seen."

I was just about to tell him he should go about making it happen again, when a voice echoed through the office.

"UPS. Drew, is that you?"

———

Drew had a few spare shirts hanging on the back of his office door, so I grabbed one while he went to go meet the UPS delivery guy. We'd stayed still, hoping he would go away, but he must have heard something because he started to walk up the hallway leading to our offices, which forced Drew to begrudgingly go deal with him.

Now I was frenzied, buttoning a man's dress shirt that was ten sizes too big to get myself covered—as if Drew would have let the UPS guy come back to say hello or something. Two minutes ago, I'd been higher than high, which made the fast crash hit me hard. *What am I doing?*

Sure, Drew was sexy, and I was physically attracted to him. There was no denying that. But this was a mistake. We wanted different things out of life. The fact that I enjoyed his company and spent every day with him would make it very difficult to separate sex and feelings. He was like a drug—I knew I shouldn't, but the addiction formed quickly.

I was on the bottom button when Drew came back to the office. "The UPS guy thinks I was jerking off."

"What? Why?"

"He had a package for you and asked if you were here. I didn't want him to ask for you to sign for it, so I said no, it was just me today."

"So? How does that equate to him thinking you were masturbating?"

"When he went to hand me the electronic signature pad, I noticed his eyes latched on to this." Drew pointed down. He had a considerable bulge, and you could actually see the outline of his penis pointing up through his pants. His zipper was also open and part of his shirttail was hanging out of it.

I clasped my hand over my mouth and giggled. "Oh my God." Then I took a second look at his pants.

*Oh my God.* Drew's penis was so wide and long it looked like he was carrying a whiffle ball bat.

I hadn't realized how long I'd been staring until Drew chuckled. "Stop looking at it like that, or I'm not going to be polite and let you take it a little at a time when you're sucking it in a little while."

*God, he's so crass.*

*God, I want to suck that thing.*

I shook my head and forced my eyes back up to meet Drew's. His were dancing in amusement.

"Anything you need to do before we go upstairs?"

"Upstairs?"

"To my place. I want to make sure the first time I'm inside of you, we have no interruptions."

"But...I don't think—"

Drew quieted me before I could finish my sentence by pressing his lips to mine. When we came up for air, I was dizzy. He looked me in the eyes. "Don't think. Not today. Think tomorrow. If you want this to be a one-time thing, I'll accept that. But today is happening."

My brain screamed no, but my head nodded.

He smiled. "Okay?"

"Okay."

He fished in his pocket and came up with his keys. "Take your laptop and phone. Go upstairs to my place and cancel whatever you have the rest of the day. I'll do the same and be up in fifteen minutes."

"Why can't we both do that down here?"

"Because I have a giant hard-on, and seeing you in my shirt is not going to help that at all. It's bad enough that the way you come undone when you come is already burned into my brain. I need to get things under control so I don't embarrass myself."

"Oh."

He grinned. "Yeah, oh." Then he kissed me on the lips chastely and sent me on my way with a swat on the ass. "Go."

# CHAPTER TWENTY-FOUR

## EMERIE

I didn't have anything sexy to wear, so I did the best I could. Putting off making my client calls, I first did a quick fix on my mussed hair and makeup. Luckily, I was wearing a cute black lace bra and matching G-string, so I slipped off my skirt and chose to wait for Drew wearing just his dress shirt, which I unbuttoned a bit to expose the lace of my bra. Satisfied with how I looked, I went to the living room to call up my calendar on my laptop and start canceling my patients for the afternoon.

I was looking out the window, in the middle of my last call, when I heard the front door unlock. The calm I'd allowed to seep in as I worked to reschedule my patients was suddenly chased away by a swarm of butterflies in my belly.

Tess McArdle was in the middle of a story about her recent doctor's appointment—totally unrelated to our counseling— and I thought it best not to turn around and look at Drew. I was already having a hard time keeping up with my end of the conversation now that the lock had clanked open on the front door.

I couldn't take my eyes off of Drew's reflection in the window. He set his keys down on the counter, emptied his pockets, slipped something I suspected might be a condom out of his wallet, and walked up behind me. His eyes never left the glass the entire time.

I did my best at getting Mrs. McArdle off the phone, but she wasn't taking the hint. Drew was close enough that I could feel the heat from his body at my back, but he didn't touch me. Instead, he began to undress.

First the shirt. His chest was so sculpted and beautiful. I could see all the tiny lines chiseled into his abdomen. If he looked this good in the window reflection, I couldn't even imagine how insanely gorgeous he was going to be when I looked directly at him.

Next came the shoes and socks and then...the pants. My eyes were glued to his fingers as they quickly worked the button and zipper and his slacks fell to the floor. He stepped out and kicked them to the side. I held my breath when his fingers went to the waistband of his boxer briefs and let out an audible gasp when he promptly pulled them down his legs.

"Emerie? Are you there? Are you alright?"

*Shit. Shit.* I hadn't heard a word Mrs. McArdle had said for the last minute, and she'd heard me gasp.

"Yes. I'm sorry, Mrs. McArdle," I said, completely flustered. "A...a...giant spider just crawled onto my desk and startled me."

Drew smirked at me in the reflection. He was enjoying himself. Maybe a little too much. Taking his cock in his hand, he began to stroke himself as he stared at me.

"Mrs. McArdle, I'm sorry, I really need to run. Someone is going to be coming in any moment."

Drew leaned in and kissed my neck, whispering in the ear not pressed to the phone. "Oh, someone's about to *come in* alright." He slipped his hand under the back of the shirt and palmed my ass. "I'm going to fuck you up against this window."

I clenched my thighs, but it didn't do a damn thing to stop the swelling between my legs. When his hand at my ass slipped between my thighs and rubbed my wetness from my lips up to my ass, my legs started to tremble. Was he planning on putting that enormous thing *in there*? I'd never done that before, and I wasn't so sure about starting with that giant thing.

He continued to massage me, spreading my wetness all over. By the time I finally got Mrs. McArdle off the phone, I was more lubricated than when I took care of myself and actually *used* lubricant.

I let my cell drop to the floor, not caring if it cracked in the process, and leaned back against Drew as he slipped two fingers inside of me.

"So wet and ready." His voice was so low and gravelly; I was seriously getting off on him speaking. His words. The tone. The way he wasn't asking, but telling me what he was going to do. "I love your body."

I loved the way he made me feel.

"Can...can...people see in?" I was barely coherent, but when I forced my eyes open I could see people on the street. Granted, they were far away. But still.

His fingers continued to glide in and out of me. "Does it matter? If there was a chance someone would see, would you tell me to stop right now?"

I answered honestly. "No." I wouldn't tell him to stop if we had a full audience watching, waiting to hold up signs and rate our performance. I was too far gone for that.

"Good." His fingers momentarily pulled out of me, and before I understood what was going on, Drew was ripping open my shirt. Well, technically, they were his shirt buttons pinging off the glass.

"Do you have something against buttons?"

"I have something against you wearing clothes."

Somehow he managed to remove his shirt and my bra and panties in record time, and then my warm body was up against the cold glass of the windows.

"Maybe they can see you down there." He slid a hand between my breast and the glass and pinched one of my nipples. "Maybe there's a man in one of those buildings over there." He jerked his chin to the buildings diagonally across from us, lining the other side of the park. "He's watching us with binoculars and stroking his cock, pretending he's in front of you while I'm behind you."

"Oh, God." The window was so cold, and my body was on fire.

Drew sucked along my shoulder, working his way up my neck, eventually reaching my ear. "Spread for me, Em."

I would have jumped out the window if he'd instructed me to at that point. I widened my stance, opening my legs, and Drew wrapped one arm around my waist, hitching my ass up toward him and forcing my back to arch while my breasts stayed pressed against the glass. Then he grabbed his cock, sheathed it, and dipped down to gently guide himself into me.

He pushed in and out a few times, each thrust going deeper until he was fully inside. I'd never been with a man who was so thick, and each stroke coaxed my body to wrap around him like a glove.

"Fuck. You feel so good. Your tight little pussy is squeezing me so hard. You want me to fill you up, don't you? Your body wants to suck the cum from my cock."

Jesus, I *loved* his dirty mouth. I moaned and pushed back against him, taking him even deeper. "Yes. Drew. *Please.*"

The apartment was quiet except for the noise of our wet bodies slapping against each other. It seemed to echo all around us. The exquisite sound must have made him as frenzied as it made me, because Drew began to thrust harder and deeper. Each grunt he made as he slammed into me sent my body closer to the edge. My eyes had been closed as I lost myself in the pleasure of my body, but when I opened them, they locked with Drew's in the reflection, and that pushed me over. I came long and hard, never breaking eye contact as I moaned through it.

"Fuck. You're beautiful," Drew muttered as he gave one last deep thrust, and then I felt a pulsating sensation inside of me as he spurted hot cum and told me over and over how beautiful I was.

He slowed to a languid pace after that, eventually pulling out of me so he could deal with the condom. When he returned, I was still stuck in place at the window, and he surprised me by scooping me up into his arms.

"What are you doing?"

"Taking you to bed."

I lolled my head against his shoulder. "I am exhausted."

Drew smirked. "I'm not talking about going to sleep. I'm talking about fucking you properly next time."

"Properly?" I croaked out.

"Yeah. I need about ten minutes. But I can't wait to take my time and watch your face as you come undone in my bed."

"Ten minutes?" I might have needed a few hours myself.

Drew chuckled and kissed my forehead. "We'll take a bath after round two. How does that sound?"

*Heavenly.* "You're going to withhold that bathtub if I'm too exhausted for round two?"

"Don't worry. I'll do all the work. You can just lie back, enjoy my tongue, and dream about that bath."

"And to think, I said no to all of this yesterday."

"That'll be the last time you say no to me."

"Is that so?"

"You bet your damn ass. Now that I know how good we are together, you can say no, but I won't be taking it for an answer."

~~~~~

"I left a mark." Drew cupped a handful of warm water and let it dribble down in big drops onto my protruding nipple. I was nestled between his legs as we soaked in the bathtub together.

"Where?"

"Here." He pointed to a red mark I hadn't noticed on my breast.

"That's okay. Probably no one will see it."

He stiffened. "Probably?"

"I mean it will be covered by my bra, so even if I undress for someone, like in a fitting room or at the doctor, they probably won't see it anyway."

"So you're not planning on fucking someone else before it wears off?"

I tilted my head to look up at him. "Is this more than a one-time thing?"

Drew searched my eyes. "It is."

"Okay, then. No one else will be seeing my marked skin, so we don't have to worry about it."

His jaw relaxed. "Good. Because that's not the only mark I left."

"What? Where else?"

"Here." He touched a spot on my collarbone. "Here." He pointed to a spot just below my ear. "And I'm pretty sure you're gonna find a few more on the inside of your thighs."

I laughed. "Those I definitely didn't mind. But you can't leave hickeys on my neck where patients can see them. Most of them are going through a hard time in their relationships, and they shouldn't have to stare at proof that I'm out having a good time at night."

"Got it. I'll limit my marking to your tits, thighs, pussy, and ass."

"You have a dirty mouth, you know that?"

He pinched my nipple. "You didn't seem to mind it when I was inside of you."

"Yeah, well..." I had nothing to say since he was right. I also felt my cheeks heating.

Drew chuckled. "You've ridden my face, and my saying *tits* and *pussy* still makes you blush."

"Shut up." I splashed water up at him.

Drew flicked on the jets, and I relaxed into his arms, enjoying the water massage. The whirling sound was white noise and had a calming effect on me. Although, I'd had something on my mind the last hour, and I couldn't shake it.

After a while, the jets powered down, and I got up my nerve. "Can I ask you something?"

"Your ass is pressed up against my balls. I'm guessing it's not a question I'm going to want to answer if you waited until now to ask it."

*Such a wiseass.* I asked anyway. "What happened in your marriage that you wound up divorced?"

He sighed. "You're already getting pruney. Sure you want to hear it? You might look ninety by the time I'm done unloading all the shit that went down with Alexa."

*Alexa.* I hated her already, just from her name. "Give me the short version."

"Met her my last year in college. Got pregnant after three months of sleeping together."

*He has a child?* "Wow. So you got married?"

"Yeah. Wasn't the smartest decision, in retrospect. But she seemed sweet and was going to have my baby. She'd also lived a very different lifestyle than I had growing up with money, so I wanted to provide for her and my child."

"That's very noble of you."

"I think you're confusing noble with naïve."

"Not at all. I think it's incredible that you wanted to make sure they had a good life."

"Yeah, well...long story short, she wasn't the sweet person she pretended to be in the beginning. But I kept trying for a long time."

"What finally pushed you to end it?"

Drew was quiet for a long moment. When he spoke again, his voice cracked. "It ended the night she got into an accident with my son in the car."

# CHAPTER TWENTY-FIVE

## DREW

*New Year's Eve, Three years ago*

I stared at the cross on my son's wall. It had inspired me to pray exactly a year ago. The crib I'd hung it over was gone, upgraded to a plastic toddler bed in the shape of a racecar. But I'd rehung the cross after God dropped me an early hint that I was shit out of luck wishing for my dad's health. He died three days ago.

After the service this morning, a few people had come back to our place for lunch. I was grateful they were all gone now—I needed the silence. I also wanted to have a few drinks in peace. I swirled amber liquid around in my glass.

The door creaked open, but I didn't bother to turn around. Arms wrapped around my waist from behind and hands clasped together, covering my belt buckle in the front.

"What are you doing in here? Beck is at Play Place with the sitter. He won't be back for another hour or two."

"Nothing."

"Come out to the living room. Let me rub your shoulders."

The last year between Alexa and me had been tough. It's not that we argued that much, but the novelty had long since worn off of our relationship. We had three things in common:

We both liked sex. Money—I earned it; she spent it. And our son. But when you're working ten hours a day, and then nights and weekends you're taking care of your father who is literally dying before your eyes, even sex takes a back seat.

Before my father started to decline so fast, I'd tried to take an interest in my wife's new hobbies, give us something more in common. But other than attending a play one of her classes was putting on, it wasn't easy. I ran lines with her, but she told me I didn't put enough heart into my acting. That was probably because *I wasn't a damn actor*. I went to watch her play practices, and she told me my presence made her think too much about her performance. Eventually, I gave up trying. Though the last few days, she'd been absolutely incredible.

I turned around and held my wife, kissing the top of her head. "Yeah. Let's go. My shoulders are knotted. I'd like that."

After about fifteen minutes, I'd started to relax—until Alexa brought the tension back into my neck.

"We should go to Sage's party tonight."

"I buried my father two hours ago. The only parent I had, considering my mother took off with her boyfriend when I was only a little older than our son. I'm not really in the mood for a party."

"But it's our anniversary. And it's New Year's Eve."

"Alexa, I'm not going to a fucking party tonight. Alright?"

She stopped rubbing. "You don't have to be a jerk about it."

I sat up. "A jerk? You expect me to go to a party on the day of my father's funeral? I don't think I'm the one acting like a jerk."

My wife huffed. Our five-year age difference felt more like twenty sometimes. "I need a party. The last few months have been depressing."

It wasn't like she'd helped me with my father or anything. Every weekend while I was taking care of him, she was out with her friends, usually shopping or having lunch God knows where. Her selfishness had finally gotten to me.

"Which part of the last few months was depressing? Living on Park Avenue and spending thousands on shopping every week? Or maybe it was the nanny who watched our son so you could take acting classes and go out to lunch? How about the three week-long trips you took back to Atlanta to visit your immature friends—the ones where you flew first-class and stayed at the St. Regis downtown instead of your brother's double wide in the sticks? That must have been depressing."

"My friends are not immature."

I scoffed and went to reply, but decided I'd rather have another drink than continue this conversation. Out of everything I'd said, what hurt her feelings was that *her friends were immature*? She had a warped fucking sense of priority. I walked to the kitchen, which was open to the living room where she still sat, and poured myself another drink.

"Go to the party by yourself, Alexa."

The sun was setting by the time I opened my eyes. Alexa had taken Beck to the mall to shop for yet another new dress, and I'd passed out on the couch after finishing my drink and the argument with her. Sitting up, I ran my fingers through my hair. I shouldn't have been surprised that Alexa had planned to go to a party tonight. God forbid she miss a party, especially New Year's Eve. I'd given her more credit than she deserved in the selflessness department, apparently.

My stomach growled. I couldn't remember the last time I'd actually eaten. Yesterday, maybe? Dinner at that Italian place in between the morning and afternoon wake sessions at the funeral parlor, I think. Rummaging through the refrigerator, I took out the platter we'd ordered for this morning and picked at the antipasto with my fingers. As I was stuffing my face, my cell phone started to ring, and at first, I ignored it. But after it immediately began ringing again, I reached over to check the caller ID. It was a local number—one that was very familiar. By the third ring, my brain had searched my internal phonebook and finally recalled why I knew it.

I'd dialed it off and on for the last few months, each time my father's health took a turn for the worse. Lenox Hill Hospital was calling.

The cab driver screamed at me as I bolted toward the emergency room entrance. Apparently, I'd gotten out in such a rush, I'd forgotten to close the car door.

"My wife and son were in a car accident. They were brought in by ambulance," I yelled through a round hole to the woman behind thick Plexiglas.

"Last name?"

"Jagger."

She looked up and perked one eyebrow. "Those lips, I have to ask. Any relation to Mick?"

"No."

She made a face, but pointed at a door to my left. "Room 1A. I'll buzz you back."

Blunt abdominal trauma. That's what the doctor had told us two hours ago. Alexa had needed a few stitches in her head, but Beck wasn't as lucky. His car seat had felt the full impact of the collision when a floral delivery van lost its brakes and ran a red light into moving crosstown traffic. He'd swerved to try to avoid the crash, but ended up colliding with the back driver's side of Alexa's car. Exactly where Beck had been sitting.

The doctors had assured us his injuries didn't appear to be life threatening, but an ultrasound showed there was damage to his left kidney—at least a small nick that needed to be repaired right away. I was now waiting for the nurses to bring me consent forms for surgery. Beck slept peacefully as I sat by his bedside. Alexa was getting another neurological exam in the room next to us.

After the doctor came in and told me the risks of the procedure, the nurse brought me in a stack of forms to fill out. Medical consent, privacy act, insurance authorizations, the last form was for directed blood transfusions.

The nurse explained that there wasn't time before Beck's surgery to collect blood from us, so in the off-chance he needed blood, he'd be given blood from the blood bank. However, we could donate our blood and store it for him for future use, if necessary. I filled out the form to get typed and cross-matched while we waited and asked the nurse to have Alexa sign everything next door. I didn't want to leave Beck alone in case he woke up.

The next few hours were hell while my son was in surgery. It took two hours for the assistant surgeon to come out and speak with us. He pulled a paper mask down.

"Things aren't quite as simple as we'd initially thought. The damage to your son's kidney was more extensive than the CT showed. Right now we're attempting to repair the laceration, but the tear is surrounding the vascular pedicle, which contains the arteries and veins that connect it to the aorta. I need you to understand that there's a chance we won't be able to make the repair well enough to safely leave the kidney inside your son's body. If that's the case, he'll need to undergo a partial or full nephrectomy."

He attempted to convince us that having one kidney was perfectly fine. I knew plenty of people only had one, but if we were born with two, I wanted my son to get the benefit of both, if at all possible.

Alexa and I had barely talked, other than my making sure she was okay. I was focused on Beck, and part of me blamed her for the accident. Not that it was her fault, but if she hadn't been so concerned with buying another damn dress to go out tonight, none of this would have happened.

"I saw a machine down by the elevators. You want some coffee?"

Alexa nodded.

When I returned with two coffees, the nurse was already talking to Alexa. "Oh, Mr. Jagger. Here's your blood card. It has your type on it if you should ever need it. We give it to everyone we run for blood donations."

"Thank you. Am I a compatible donor with Beck?"

"Let me see his chart." She walked to the foot of the bed where a metal chart was hanging. As she flipped through pages she said, "You're type O negative, so that means you can give blood to anyone." She stopped at a pink page. "You're lucky. It's not often a stepfather is a universal donor."

"I'm his father, not his stepfather."

The nurse hung Beck's chart back on the bed's foot rail and returned to the clipboard she'd brought in with her. A look of bewilderment crossed her face. "You're type O. Beckett is AB. " She frowned. "You're saying Beckett is your biological son?"

"Yes."

She looked to Alexa and then to me, shaking her head. "That's not possible. An O can't genetically make a child with type AB blood."

I was exhausted from one hell of a day, between burying my father and my wife and child getting into an accident. I had to have misunderstood.

"The lab made a mistake then?"

The nurse shook her head. "They're usually pretty good…" She looked back and forth between me and my wife again. "… but I'll have them come up and draw a fresh sample." After that, she practically ran out of the room.

I turned to look at my wife, whose head was hanging down. "This is a mistake in the lab, right, Alexa?"

I almost vomited when she looked up. She didn't have to say a goddamn word for me to know.

There was no mistake.

No fucking mistake!

*Beck wasn't my son.*

# CHAPTER TWENTY-SIX

# EMERIE

"You have a son?" I craned my neck back to look at Drew. We were still in the bathtub, and it wasn't easy to maneuver much sitting between his legs.

Drew nodded with his eyes closed before opening them to look at me. There was so much pain in his expression; my stomach dropped in anticipation of what was to come next. "It's a long story. How about we get out, and I'll make you something to eat while I explain?"

"Okay."

Drew got out first to get us towels. After he dried off, including a three-second rub of the towel to his hair, he wrapped it around his waist and offered me a hand.

His face was still contemplative, and I wanted to lighten the mood for him. Whatever he was going to tell me about his son clearly wasn't an easy story.

I took his hand and stepped out of the tub. "You look like you could film a shaving cream commercial right now, and I probably look like a wet rat." My hair was stuck to my face, and I was glad the mirror was fogged with steam so I couldn't get a good look at my reflection.

Drew reached around me with a plush bath towel and began to dry me off.

"You provide nice primping services," I teased as he reached down to dry one leg and then the other.

He winked. "It goes with my prodding service."

"Your prodding was pretty damn spectacular, too."

"I'm a full-service type of guy."

When he was all done drying my body (my boobs and between my legs were extra dry from all the time he spent there), Drew wrapped the towel around my chest and tucked it in at the corner. His sweet side was still on display when he tangled our fingers together for the walk from the bathroom.

In the kitchen, he pulled a stool out from under the granite island and patted the top. "Have a seat."

I swiveled around on it a few times as Drew pulled things out of the cabinets and refrigerator. Remembering what we'd done up against the glass a few hours ago, I stopped twirling and looked at the window. It was dark outside now, and I could see the lights from the city illuminated so clearly.

"Can people...can they really see inside?" A mixture of panic and embarrassment crept up my cheeks as I remembered how my breasts had been pushed up against the glass. In the moment, it had seemed exciting that someone could possibly see—added to the eroticism. But I definitely didn't want to wind up on YouTube because some creeper had filmed us through a telescope.

Drew chuckled. "No. It's one-way glass. I wouldn't put you at risk like that." He reached over my head to grab a pan and kissed my forehead on his way down with it. "Plus, I don't share things that are mine."

The first part of his response made the rational part of me breathe a sigh of relief, but the latter gave me warm fuzzies inside.

Drew was also still wearing just a towel, his wrapped around his narrow waist, and I was enjoying the view of his back muscles flexing as he chopped an onion, when I noticed a scar. It ran diagonally along the side of his torso, extending from the front to the back. The mark was faded to a lighter shade of tan than the rest of his skin—definitely not new, but something serious had happened.

"Did you have surgery?" I asked.

"Hmmm?" Drew dropped some butter into the frying pan and turned with brows drawn.

I pointed. "Your scar."

A flicker of something passed over his face. Sadness, I thought. He turned back around as he responded. "Yeah. Surgery a few years back."

Maybe I was looking too much into things, scrutinizing everything he did, but I couldn't help it. My mind was trying to put together a puzzle without knowing what the picture looked like.

Drew chopped up a bunch of other things, refusing to let me help. When he plated two gorgeous Western omelets, they looked like they could have been made at one of Baldwin's fancy restaurants.

*Baldwin.*

I couldn't waste another three years pining for a man who was never going to return my feelings. I needed to remember that Drew wasn't interested in more than sex. Getting attached and growing feelings for this man was not an option.

Yet...I couldn't help feeling some sort of connection to Drew. Like there was a reason I got ripped off and wound up sitting in his office on New Year's Eve. Stupid, I know. I had no idea what the connection between us was just yet, but I was determined to find out.

We made small talk throughout our meal, and then I cleaned up. There weren't enough dishes to run the dishwasher, so I washed while Drew dried. The two of us worked well together, and I found myself thinking it was interesting how in the office our opinions and counsel were so opposite, yet physically we were so in sync.

"You want a drink? Glass of wine or something?" he asked when the kitchen was put back together neatly.

"No, thanks. I'm too full."

He nodded. "Come on, let's go sit in the living room."

Drew moved the pillows on the couch around, putting one at the end for my head, then pointed. "Lie down."

He stood until I got myself comfortable. Then he lifted my legs and set my feet across his lap. "You ticklish?"

"Are you going to make it a challenge if I tell you I'm not?"

He flashed me a crooked smile. "No. I was going to rub your feet."

I smiled and lifted one of my feet in the air, offering it to him. "I'm not ticklish. But when you admit that to people, they find it necessary to dig their fingers into your ribs until you bruise trying to prove you're wrong."

Drew took my foot and began to rub. His fingers were strong, and when he took his thumbs and deftly rubbed at a spot on the ball of my foot—the spot where my heels placed most of my body weight—I let out a little mewl.

"Good?"

"Better than good," I sighed.

After a few minutes of his rubbing, my entire body relaxed, and Drew started to speak in a low voice. "Beck was five years old when he got into an accident with my ex-wife."

*Oh, God.*

"I'm sorry. I'm so sorry."

Drew's brow furrowed, and then he quickly seemed to realize what I thought. "Oh, shit. No. I didn't mean to make you think...he's fine. Beck's fine."

My hand went to my chest. "Jesus. You scared the crap out of me. I thought..."

"Yeah. I realize that now. Sorry. He's fine. It was scary for a while after the accident, but now you wouldn't even know he went through three surgeries."

"Three surgeries? What happened to him?"

"A delivery van creamed Alexa's car, and it crumpled into a V around the van."

"That's horrible."

"Beck's booster seat and part of the car door cut into his side, lacerating his kidney. Surgeons tried to repair it, but because of the location and size of the tear, they had to remove part of it. The day of his accident he had a partial nephrectomy on his left kidney."

"Wow. I'm sorry."

"Thank you." He took a minute and then continued. "While he was in surgery, the nurses offered to have us donate blood. I felt helpless, and I wanted to do whatever I could."

"Of course."

"Anyway, they ran a type and cross match blood test on both me and Alexa to see if we were a match to donate and store blood for Beck. Turned out neither of us was."

"I didn't realize two parents could have a child they couldn't donate blood to?"

Drew leveled me with a look. "They can't."

It took a few heartbeats for me to realize what he was saying. "You found out Beck isn't your son."

He nodded. "I was there for the delivery, so I was damn sure he was Alexa's biological child."

"I don't know what to say. That's awful. Did she know you weren't the father?"

"She knew. She won't admit it. But she knew from the start. Beck was born a few weeks early. I didn't think anything of it." He shook his head. "If it wasn't for the surgery, I might never have found out."

"God, Drew. You found out while he was in surgery. Talk about stress on top of stress."

"Yeah. It wasn't a good day. Turned out, it was one of many not-so-good days to come. The next few weeks got even worse."

"What happened?"

"Alexa and I were over before I even left the hospital that night. The truth is, we were over a long time before the accident. But Beck and I..."

Drew turned his head for a few seconds, and I watched as he swallowed. I knew he was fighting back tears. He still had my feet in his hands, but he had stopped moving. I had no idea what I was supposed to say or do, but I wanted to offer what comfort I could. So I sat up and crawled into his lap. Wrapping myself around his body, I gave him the biggest hug I could possibly give.

After a few minutes, I pulled back and spoke quietly. "You don't have to tell me any more. Another time, maybe?"

Drew gave me a small smile. "That day changed the way I felt about Alexa, but it didn't change anything I felt about Beck. He was still my son."

"Of course."

"Anyway, a few days after Beck's surgery, he sprang a fever. His wound was healing, but he seemed to be getting sicker again. They put him on IV antibiotics to treat a possible surgery-related infection, but they didn't help. The doctors ended up having to open him back up and remove the portion of the kidney they'd left in. And in the meantime, the other kidney had started to show signs of having trouble functioning. It's actually not uncommon after one kidney is removed, or partially removed, for the other to have difficulty working properly for a while."

"The poor baby. He must have been in so much pain. A car accident, surgery, starting to heal, and then more surgery."

Drew blew out a deep breath. "The days where he would get upset were actually more comforting than the days he was too weak to do anything. Looking at your child lying there and not being able to help is the worst feeling in the world."

"I can't even imagine it."

"After another week, things weren't getting much better. The infection had cleared, but the other kidney still wasn't functioning great. They started him on dialysis, which made him feel better and he got healthier, but they also started to talk about putting him on a donor list if his function testing got any lower.

"People spend years on that list waiting. And taking a five year old who feels otherwise healthy for hours of dialysis every other day was tough. So I had them test me for a match. And amazingly enough, even though I wasn't his biological father, my kidney was a good match. When he was healthy enough for more surgery, I donated one of my kidneys, which they transplanted to the left side where they'd removed the damaged kidney. That way he'd have two full kidneys, and if his other one didn't ever fully kick back in, he had double the chance of one of them working at least."

I remembered Drew's back. "That's what the scar is from?"

He nodded. "To make an already long story a little less long, the transplant was a success, and his other kidney kicked in and started functioning again a few weeks later. He's as healthy as a horse now. But it was scary as hell at the time."

The entire story was so much to take in. I had so many thoughts, but one of them was more prominent than the others.

"You're a beautiful man, Drew Jagger. And I don't mean on the outside." I leaned down and trailed a line of kisses from one end of his scar to the other.

"You only think that because I skipped the part where I packed up Alexa's shit and moved it while she wasn't home," he teased, although I could tell he wasn't joking.

"She deserved it. I would have cut holes in the crotches of all her pants, the stupid bitch."

Drew pulled his head back, his face amused. "Is that the relationship advice you would have given me if I'd shown up at your office seeking counseling?"

I thought for a minute. *What would I have done?* "I only work with couples that genuinely want to make it work. If I'd heard your story, saw the look in your eyes, I wouldn't haven taken you as a client. Because I'd basically be giving the party who wanted to make it work false hope in that case. Not to mention, it would be wrong to take money to do something I knew was never going to happen."

"Has that happened to you before? Have you had clients where one wants it to work and not the other?"

"It has. It's not uncommon, actually. I have separate sessions in the beginning so the parties can say things freely without worrying about hurting the other person's feelings. I find I get more truth in those sessions than anything else. When I first started, I had a couple that had been married for twenty-seven years—a wealthy, very social couple with two grown daughters. The man was gay and living a life he felt he was supposed to live after growing up with ultra-conservative, religious parents. It took him until he was fifty-two, but he came out of the closet to his wife and told her they should separate. He felt terrible and had been staying because he loved her, just not in the way a husband should love his wife. I wound up counseling them to separate and helping her get through it."

"Shit. Wish we'd been sharing space back then. I could have gotten her a nice settlement," Drew joked.

I shoved at his chest. "Thought you only represented men."

"How rich were they? I might have made an exception."

I laughed. "Why do you only represent men? Because of what your ex-wife did to you?"

Drew shook his head. "Nah. Just do better with men."

His answer was vague, and I had the feeling he was reluctant to answer.

I squinted. "Give me the real reason, Jagger."

He searched my eyes. "You might not want to hear it."

"Well, now I'm curious, so whether I want to hear it or not, you have to tell me."

Drew's jaw flexed. "Angry fucking."

"Pardon?"

"When I represented women who were pissed off and angry, they wanted to get even."

"So...they were bitter. That's normal in a divorce."

Drew looked embarrassed. "They wanted to get even with their husbands *with me*."

"You slept with your clients?"

"I'm not proud of it now, but yes. I was recently divorced and angry myself. Angry fucking can do a lot to help you temporarily release that rage."

"Isn't having sex with your clients against some lawyer rules or something?"

"Like I said, they weren't my finest moments."

I could tell Drew wasn't just saying he was embarrassed. He really regretted the way he'd acted, and he'd been truthful with me when he could have lied. It wasn't my place to judge his past. I'd rather judge him for the honesty he was showing me today.

"Angry sex, huh?" I tried to hide my smile.

He gave a slight nod and watched me cautiously.

"Well, I think you're a womanizing, egotistical, self-centered jerk."

Drew pulled his head back. "What the fuck? You wanted me to be honest."

"I didn't think you would *honestly* be an asshole."

He was just about to respond again when I leaned close to him and cracked a sneaky smile. "Did I make you angry?"

"Are you *trying* to make me angry?"

"I've heard angry *fucking* can do a lot to help you temporarily release that rage."

Before I knew what was happening, Drew had lifted me into the air and flipped me flat on my back on the couch.

He hovered over me. "Nice. Then I'm glad I piss you off daily. We'll need *a lot* of work on our anger issues."

# CHAPTER TWENTY-SEVEN

# DREW
*New Year's Eve, Two years ago*

Judges hate hearing cases on New Year's Eve. But I knew what my ex-wife was up to. She thought dragging me into court on our anniversary with some vague emergency motion was going to upset me. Was she really that fucking clueless? Did she think I was sitting home pining for her three months after our divorce was finalized? I'd gotten what I wanted from her out of our divorce: my freedom and liberal shared custody of our son. Whether or not he was my biological child didn't change the way I felt about him. He was my son. No paternity test was going to tell me otherwise.

The smartest thing Alexa had ever done was not fight me on shared custody. After I offered to pay a hefty monthly child support—even though technically I could have probably paid nothing—she was suddenly amicable to sharing custody. Money was all my ex-wife was ever interested in. Even while I was married to her, I think I knew the truth down deep.

I'd called her to find out what the fuck she was up to half a dozen times, but of course she didn't answer. The manipulative side of her had reared its ugly head in the days since I'd packed her bags and had them moved to a rental a few blocks away—a rental I still footed the bill for. If it weren't for Beck, I would have tossed her shit out the window when I changed the locks. But I wanted my son close to me, and he didn't deserve to live in a tenement Alexa could barely afford.

"New Year's Eve. What poor schlep are you beating up and leaving miserable to start a new year?" George, the court officer at the entrance to the family court joked as he scanned my ID. He did side work for Roman, covering surveillance stakeouts at night, and we'd become friends over the last year.

"This poor schlep. Ex-wife's still a bitch."

He nodded, having heard all about my fucked-up situation over beers with Roman one night. Handing back my ID, he asked, "You going to Roman's party tonight?"

"Looking forward to it."

"See you there. Good luck today."

Alexa and her dirtbag lawyer, Wade Garrison, were already sitting in the courtroom when I walked in. It was difficult not to laugh at her knee-length skirt and neckline that looked like it might choke her. Especially since I had a thousand photos of her out partying on weekends wearing skin-tight skirts that barely covered her ass and displaying enough cleavage to be mistaken for a hooker. They were compliments of Roman after she and I had split up—in case I needed them someday.

My ex-wife kept her face straight ahead, refusing to look at me. If there was one thing I knew about Alexa, it was that she avoided my eyes when she was being over-the-top cuntly.

The court officer called our docket number, and I made sure to go ahead of them, so I could open the gate and force eye contact with Alexa.

"You wearing that to the frat party you're going to tonight?" I whispered. "Might want to put on a better bra. Your tits are looking saggy. Probably from breastfeeding."

She glared at me. I smiled wide.

"What do we have here, folks? I read the motion and have no idea why you are standing before me today wasting my precious time," Judge Hixton said.

"I'd like to know why we're here, as well," I added.

Judge Hixton turned his attention to the other side of his courtroom. "Why don't you enlighten both of us, counselor?"

Garrison cleared his fat throat. How the hell could he talk with that collar buttoned so tight? Looked like he needed to move up from a twenty-three-inch neck to a twenty-four. "Your honor, we actually have an amended petition we'd like to submit, along with an affidavit from New York Laboratory."

The judge motioned for the court officer to collect the documents. "Have these been served on opposing counsel?"

"No, your honor. The affidavit was just received late last night. We have a set for Mr. Jagger there, as well."

The court officer distributed the documents to me, as well as Judge Hixton, and we both took a moment to read through them. I skipped the amended petition and paternity lab results and went right to the third-party affidavit. I only had to read the first half-page:

> We, Alexa Thompson Jagger and Levi Archer Bodine, have read and understand the consequences, alternatives, rights, and responsibilities regarding this affidavit and being duly sworn upon oath depose and say:

I, Alexa Thompson Jagger, am the biological mother of Becker Archer Jagger, as documented in New York Live Birth Certificate number NYC2839992.

I, Levi Archer Bodine, am the biological father of Becker Archer Jagger, the child referred to in New York Laboratory case number 80499F.

Wherefore, paternity has been established by Levi Archer Bodine with a scientific certainty of at least 99.99%.

Therefore, together we wish for a correction of the birth certificate to identify Levi Bodine as the father. We also wish to pursue full parental rights, including shared custody and visitation.

Judge Hixton's voice was sympathetic when he spoke. "Mr. Jagger, would you like a few days to respond to this motion?"

My heart was heavy with anger and sorrow. It felt like my entire world had just been ripped out from under me. I cleared my throat to fight back tears. "Please, your honor."

Everything that came after that happened in a fog. Garrison asked for temporary visitation for Bodine, which the judge declined in order to allow me time to review the legitimacy of the testing presented. A date to reconvene was set for two weeks from Tuesday, and then the gavel slammed down.

I was still standing in place after Alexa and her attorney exited the courtroom.

Levi *Archer* Bodine. The man had the same middle name as our son. Alexa had picked the fucking middle name. I'd suggested we use one of our father's names, but she'd insisted she loved the middle name Archer. *She'd always dreamed of giving her little boy the middle name Archer.*

Fucking liar.

But why was his name so goddamn familiar?

*Levi Archer Bodine.*

*Levi Archer Bodine.*

*Levi Bodine.*

I knew it from somewhere.

Eventually, the court officer came over and quietly told me I needed to leave so he could call the next case.

Stunned, I made my way through the courthouse. I passed a handful of people I knew and ignored them. I heard their voices, but couldn't make out what they were saying. It wasn't until I walked outside into the fresh, crisp air that my fog lifted. Which was perfect timing to watch Alexa get into a bright yellow Dodge Charger with the number nine painted on the side.

# CHAPTER TWENTY-EIGHT

## DREW

"Your client should be more worried about losing her medical license than a timeshare in the Virgin Islands. Her patient videotaped her bent over the examining table as he gave her a rectal exam with his dick, Alan. When we're dividing up assets, consider that video one of mine. My client spent twenty grand buying that video, but I'd say the value is a hundred times that in this room."

I was sitting in my conference room negotiating a settlement with opposing attorney Alan Avery. We'd done enough cases together for him to know I wasn't bluffing. Roman had found out a sex tape existed even before the good Dr. Appleton knew about it. And now Mr. Appleton wanted alimony and all of the marital assets.

But Alan's focus wasn't on the possible repercussions of that tape. His mind seemed somewhere else entirely. And when I turned to look over my shoulder to see what he was watching, I was pissed about more than just him wasting my time.

"She your new secretary?" he asked.

Emerie stood at the end of the hall, signing for a package from UPS. Her ass looked phenomenal in a tan, form-fitting skirt.

"No. She's a sub-tenant for a while," I said curtly.

"Married?"

"Can we get back to the settlement?" I slammed my file shut. "My client isn't giving Dr. DickUpTheAss one damn cent."

"That's ridiculous. Her husband has been mooching off her for years. She paid for all of the joint assets they have with proceeds from her medical practice."

"Yeah, well, tell her we said thank you for the parting gifts. She can earn some more. I'm sure she's a very popular proctologist."

"She's an ENT."

"Really? Video looks more like she specializes in rectal exams."

"Speaking of assholes, what crawled up yours this morning? You're in a mood."

"Let's just get this crap done. I have a busy afternoon," I grumbled.

A few minutes later, Emerie knocked on the open door. "I'm sorry to interrupt, but you have a phone call, Drew. She claims it's urgent."

"Who is it?"

Emerie was hesitant. "I don't know. She wouldn't give me her name."

"Tell her I'll call her back. It's obviously not so important if she won't even tell you her name."

Emerie locked eyes with me. "The caller has a strong Southern accent. I thought perhaps Georgia."

*Great. Fucking Alexa.*

I stood and spoke to Alan. "Excuse me for a minute."

"Take your time. Your new tenant and I can get to know each other while you're gone."

*Just perfect.*

I didn't stop the door from slamming behind me as I shut myself into my office and picked up the phone. "Drew Jagger."

"The woman who answered the phone is annoying."

I let out an irritated sigh. "What do you want, Alexa? I'm in the middle of a conference."

"I'm staying in Atlanta another two weeks."

"Like hell you are. My visitation starts on Friday, and you've already been there a week longer than the two weeks we agreed on. I haven't seen my son in more than three weeks."

"You can come here for your visit."

"I can't drop everything and fly to Atlanta every other week because you want to play with your friends. Beck needs to be home, back in school, and back to his routine."

"He also needs to get to know his *father*."

I knew exactly what she meant. *"Fuck you, Alexa. He knows his father!"*

"His *biological* father. Levi wants to get to know him. It's important."

I felt the rise of my blood pressure. "Really? If it's so important, why didn't you tell him *seven fucking years* ago when you found out you were pregnant? And why hasn't he made an attempt to know our son when he's known the truth for more than two years now? Not to mention, has he started paying support yet?"

I wasted the next ten minutes of my life in another useless argument with Alexa. For Beck's benefit, I stretched my patience as thin as it could possibly go and didn't hang up on her. I didn't trust my ex-wife to not play the only card she had left in her very worn deck: taking me back to court to reduce my visitation. Even after paternity had been proven and Levi's name replaced mine on my son's birth certificate, her redneck ex-boyfriend had never attempted to get to know Beck. We'd settled out of court on the custody arrangement, and I'd agreed to pay hefty additional alimony and child support even though I could have made a motion to stop support once paternity was disproved. But in the back of my mind, I was always waiting for the other shoe to drop—especially now that she was apparently speaking to Levi again. My son still had no idea who the man was.

Knowing how vindictive Alexa could be kept me from doing a lot of things I wanted to do to make her life miserable, like hanging up on her today.

After a minute of silence, Alexa finally got to the point she'd been calling to make. I kicked myself for taking the argument bait she'd set for me.

"If you feel that strongly about Beck coming back to New York, I suppose we could work something out."

"What do you want, Alexa?"

"Well, Levi has a big race coming up next week, and I want to be here for it."

For some reason I didn't harbor the same anger toward Levi as I did Alexa. A part of me actually felt bad for the idiot. She'd blown the sucker off, referred to him as a *grease monkey,* if I remembered correctly, in favor of snagging herself a husband with a fatter bank account. But now that the grease monkey was a sponsored driver on the NASCAR circuit, he was suddenly good enough to speak to again.

"Is there a point to this story?"

"Well, it does get loud at the races, anyway. I suppose if you wanted to fly down here and take Beck back with you for the week, I could stay down here alone before coming back to

New York. Although, I'm running a little short on cash right now, and I'd need some extra spending money to travel to see the race."

I wanted to tell her to go fuck herself, but instead I said, "I'll get tickets for me and Beck. I'll text you the time my flight gets in, and you'll bring him to the airport to meet me. You're getting a thousand cash, and don't call me for more."

"Fine."

After I hung up, I sat at my desk for another minute, trying to compose myself. That woman made me want to drink hard liquor before lunch. The extra minute or two helped just slightly, although whatever anger I'd managed to tamp down bubbled back to the surface when I returned to the conference room and found Alan still chatting with Emerie. She was laughing at something he'd just said.

"Finished so soon? Don't you have any more calls you need to make? Emerie and I were just getting to know each other."

"Maybe you should have spent the last fifteen minutes figuring out how your client is going to pay your bill when I leave her with nothing but her medical license."

"Glad to see your call has improved your mood, Jagger."

I grumbled something along the lines of *stick it up your ass* and went to sit back down.

"Drew?" Emerie said. "Before you get back to work, can I speak to you for a minute?"

I nodded and followed her into her office. She shut the door behind us. "Alan seems nice."

"He's a womanizer." I actually had no idea if he was—it just came out.

Emerie smiled. "I can see why. He's handsome, too."

I glared at her. "You want to fuck Alan?"

"Would that make you angry?"

"Are you kidding me right now? Because I just hung up with my ex-wife, and I'm already in a piss-poor mood without you telling me you're interested in the first guy who walked into the office after you got up out of my bed this morning."

Emerie walked to her desk and leaned one hip against it. "Keep that feeling. We'll put it to good use later."

I was on her in two seconds flat. My fingers pressed into her hips as I sandwiched her between my body and her desk. "Cute. You want to angry fuck? I'm more than willing to accommodate right now."

"Alan is waiting for you."

"*Alan* can listen to you scream my name while I bury my cock inside you."

The urge hit me like a brick wall, and suddenly my mouth was crushed to hers. I swallowed the sound of her gasp as one hand slid up from her hip and palmed her breast through her shirt. When her hands reached around and grabbed my ass, my other hand went to her neck so I could tilt her head to just the right angle and make her open wider for me. She smelled incredible, her skin pebbled beneath my fingers, and her hot mouth tasted so fucking good.

We were both panting when the kiss broke. Emerie looked a little stunned, and I felt a bit drugged.

"What's your schedule this afternoon?"

She thought for a moment. "Last counseling is a video session from three to four. You?"

"Be in my office at 4:01." Our kiss had smeared her lipstick. I used my thumb to wipe it from her face and then rubbed it into her bottom lip. "Put fresh lipstick on before you come. I want to fuck this mouth painted bright red."

Emerie still seemed a little shell shocked as I straightened her clothes and then my own. Looking down, there wasn't much I could do to hide the swell in my pants. Hopefully my opponent wouldn't look in the vicinity of my dick when I returned. Then again...on second thought, hopefully he would.

Once we were both smoothed out, I gave Emerie a quick kiss.

"4:01," I reminded her.

She swallowed and nodded. Just as my hand reached the door, Emerie finally spoke. "Drew?"

I turned back.

She pointed to the side of her mouth. "You have a little... lipstick. Right here."

I grinned. "Good."

---

**Drew:** *American Airlines flight 302, lands at 5:05 Friday night. Return flight is at 6:15pm. Check the gate and meet me there.*

**Alexa:** *Do they have anything a little later? Traffic from the airport will be terrible when I drive home.*

Like I give a flying fuck if she sits in traffic.

**Drew:** *No.*

I assumed I'd get some bitchy text back, but instead her name flashed on my screen with an incoming call.

Begrudgingly, I answered. "I'm not changing the flights."

My office door was halfway open, and my attention quickly diverted to Emerie slipping inside and closing it behind her. I'd lost track of time, so my eyes flashed to the top right-hand corner of my computer. 4:01.

Alexa was busy rambling on about how she'd started checking the flight schedule for the following week for *her* return flight, and the rates were too high. But I couldn't concentrate. Instead, I watched Emerie lock my office door and strut toward me. She had an impish gleam in her eye and began unbuttoning her shirt as she walked.

Reaching my chair, she put her hands on the top of the tall wingback and swiveled it to face her. I almost dropped the phone when she licked her lips and slowly lowered herself to her knees before me.

*Jesus Christ.*

Emerie got to work on unbuttoning my pants, and it wasn't until I heard Alexa's voice screeching through the phone that I remembered I was still on it.

"Are you there?" Alexa bitched.

"How much do you need?"

"Another thousand." If she only knew; I would have given her a hundred thousand just to get her off the phone so I could get my dick into Emerie's mouth in peace.

"Fine. I'll bring it. Don't call me again." I pushed *end*, tossed my phone on the desk, and looked down at the beautiful sight before me. Emerie looked up from under long lashes, and I realized her lips were painted bright red.

*Fuck yeah.*

She unzipped my pants and tugged for me to lift so she could pull them off. I happily obliged and helped her remove my boxers at the same time. My stiff cock sprang free. One of her delicate little hands wrapped around my shaft, and she gave it a few slow pumps until a small bead of precum glistened on the tip.

My eyes were glued to her as she leaned down and licked it off. Her eyes shut as she brought her tongue back inside her hot little mouth and licked her lips.

"Fuck," I groaned.

She gave me a wicked smile. "Still angry?"

"It's quickly dissipating."

I'm not sure if she was actually taking her time, or if it was my mind screwing with me, but she opened her mouth wide and everything seemed to play out in slow motion. She inched toward my cock, her tongue peeked out, and then her gloriously painted red fuck-me lips wrapped around my crown and closed. She sucked me in, taking my entire length in one deep, long, hard swallow.

"*Jesus*. Fuck, Em."

It was the oddest thing, but instead of feeling relief to have her mouth on me, knowing my release wasn't going to take long, I suddenly felt tense and uptight. I was angry to find she was good at giving head, pissed that she must have learned on some other guy.

She pulled back slowly, suctioning hard as her lips glided up my length while the flat of her tongue pressed against the throbbing vein. Then, after pulling almost all the way off, she immediately swallowed me back down. With each bob up and down, I felt a different emotion, vacillating between angry she was good at this and thanking God that she was.

She alternated between taking me deep and pumping me at the base while her slick little tongue swirled around my tip. If I'd been inside of her, the time it took me to finish would have been embarrassing. Even so, it was less than five minutes before I was holding back and having to warn her I was just about to explode.

"Em. I'm gonna..." My words were half groaned/half spoken, but she must have understood. "Em..." I gave her one final warning. But instead of moving her head away and releasing me from her mouth, she caught my gaze and held it as she took me into the back of her throat.

Fucking gorgeous. Her blue eyes looking up at me, creamy pale cheeks filled with my cock, and red lips closed over every last inch. I tangled my fingers in her hair and prayed to her name one more time as I released down her throat. She made a moaning sound as she closed her eyes and swallowed every last drop of my cum.

Unable to speak, I reached down and lifted her up, settling her onto my lap so I could bury my face in her shoulder. After my breathing calmed, I kissed her neck. "That was...incredible. It feels weird to want to say thank you after that. But shit, thank you."

She giggled. The sound made me smile like an idiot. "You're welcome."

I held her on my lap for a long time. When blood finally came back to my brain, I remembered I'd spoken to Alexa.

"Stay with me again tonight. I have to fly to Atlanta tomorrow afternoon, so I'll be leaving the office early."

"Oh? How long will you be gone?"

"Just the night. It's a long story. But I'm flying down to pick up my son and flying back with him an hour later. Alexa is staying down there for another week, and I don't want him flying alone."

"That's nice. So you'll have him for the week all to yourself then?"

Without even thinking about it, I said, "Yeah. He's gonna love you. He's a real ladies' man."

She smiled. "I'd love to stay tonight, and I can't wait to meet your son."

I'd never introduced any woman to Beck before. But for some reason, I wanted Beck to meet Emerie. Maybe it was the best blowjob I'd had in my life making me not think clearly, but I got the feeling he was *supposed* to meet her.

# CHAPTER TWENTY-NINE

## EMERIE

I woke up first. Even though I was generally the late riser, Drew was the one still sleeping at nearly seven-thirty in the morning. He lay on his stomach, the sheet tangled around his waist, leaving his taut ass on full display. Both of his arms were over his head, tucked under his pillow as he slept peacefully, facing my direction. He'd grown a five o'clock shadow and his hair was unruly—we'd only fallen asleep four hours ago—yet if it was possible, he looked even sexier than he had yesterday.

Could he have grown sexier? Possibly, but it was more likely that I'd grown to appreciate him more, to *like* him more. It was probably good that Drew's son was going to be with him for the next week. It wouldn't be hard to grow attached quickly, and the last thing I needed was to jump from a man who wasn't interested in me to a man who wasn't interested in a relationship.

My phone vibrated on the nightstand, so I reached over to grab it before it woke Drew up. After typing in my password, I found a new text had arrived.

**Baldwin:** *Casablanca tonight? I'll bring Moroccan meatballs from Marrak on Fifty-Third.*

I sighed. This was our thing. We both loved renting movies and turning them into a theme for dinner. Back in college, we'd take turns picking out the movie, and the other would have to bring food to pair with it. I'd pick *Sweet Home Alabama*, and he'd bring southern fried chicken. He'd pick *Shawshank Redemption*, and I'd bring bologna sandwiches.

Two weeks ago I would have jumped at a movie night with Baldwin, but now I felt conflicted for some reason. It wasn't like Drew and I were really dating, or even if we were, that Baldwin had any interest in me other than friendship anyway. So why did it feel wrong to say yes? Maybe because I was lying naked in bed with one man, thinking about making plans with another. That was probably what wasn't sitting right. I pushed the button on the side of my phone and decided later I'd give Baldwin's invitation more thought before I responded.

Since my bladder was calling, I decided to go to the bathroom and then make coffee before slipping out. I needed to get to my apartment for clean clothes and a quick shower before my nine o'clock appointment downstairs.

When I was done, I left a note under an empty coffee mug on the kitchen counter and headed to the subway.

Around the second stop, I realized I'd left my phone on Drew's nightstand. At least I wouldn't have far to go to get it when I got to work in a little while.

The office phone was ringing when I walked in with a few minutes to spare before my appointment arrived. I reached over the reception desk and grabbed it.

"Drew Jagger's office. How may I help you?"

"I need to speak to Drew." I'd only heard Alexa's voice once, but I knew it was her. Not too many of his clients had a southern accent and an attitude.

Over-the-top sweetness oozed from my voice. "May I say who's calling?"

"No, you may not."

*Bitch.*

I glanced over the reception desk at the phone and saw that Drew's office line was red. He was already on the phone.

I smiled as I got back on the line. "Mr. Jagger isn't available right now. Would you like to leave a message?"

She huffed. "Tell him to call Alexa." Then she hung up in my ear.

I heard Drew talking as I passed his office, so I wrote the message on my message pad and ripped off the little slip to leave on his desk before my appointment arrived. But when I went back to his office, he was hanging up the phone.

"Good morning." I smiled as I walked to him. "I just took a message while you were on the other line."

Drew leaned back in his chair with an impassive look. "I took a message for you, too."

"Oh?"

He slid my cell phone to the edge of his desk. "I thought it might be you, calling to see if you left your phone at my place, so I answered it."

There were only two people who would call me early in the morning. Since Drew was acting strangely, I figured it wasn't my mother.

"Who was it?"

The muscle in Drew's jaw flexed. "Baldwin. He wanted to know if he should order the Moroccan meatballs for tonight."

*Shit. This feels even weirder than it did this morning.* I sensed the need to explain.

"He texted this morning and asked if I wanted to rent a movie and have some dinner. I like to match food to the theme of the movie. I hadn't responded yet."

Drew's face was unreadable. "Well, he's waiting for your answer."

We stared at each other, my mind jumping all over the place, trying to figure out what Drew expected me to say or do. Luckily, the front door buzzed. I looked down at my watch, relieved that my morning appointment was a few minutes early.

Drew stood. "Is that for you?"

"I think so. I have a nine o'clock session. I'll go let them in."

"I'll get it. I have a conference call, so my door will be shut, but I don't like people to think you're alone in here."

He handed me my cell phone as he walked past. "You don't want to keep Professor Peckerhead waiting."

---

Ironically, the problem with the couple that had just left my office was they didn't say what was really on their minds. They weren't open with each other. Lauren wanted more oral sex and was embarrassed to ask for it. Her fiancé, Tim, wanted her to initiate sex more often. While Drew and I had yet to encounter any problems in the bedroom, I had no idea what he wanted from me. Here I was, counseling people that the key to any type of successful relationship is communication, yet I was hiding from Drew in my office to avoid finishing the conversation I knew wasn't done.

I sat at my desk for another half hour, feeling frustrated and angry with myself. Not to mention, Drew was the type of man who said exactly what was on his mind, so why wasn't he telling me how he felt about my having dinner with Baldwin? And why was I so hung up on what Drew thought if we were just *fucking*?

The longer I sat at my desk, the longer I stewed. I needed some clarification on what was happening between us. If I didn't get it before he left this afternoon, it was going to fester. So I decided to take the advice I was constantly dishing out. And it was better to get it over with while I was annoyed.

Standing, I took a deep breath and marched into Drew's office. He was on the phone when I walked in.

Taking one look at my face, he said, "Let me think about it. I'll give you a call back next week, okay, Frank?"

When he hung up the phone, he leaned back in his chair the same way he had this morning and nodded. "Emerie."

"Drew."

We stared at each other.

When he said nothing, I rolled my eyes. "What are we doing?"

"Right now? You're standing in my office looking a little pissed off."

I squinted. "You know what I mean."

"Not sure that I do."

"Are we..." I waved my hand back and forth between us. "...just sleeping together?"

"We spend most days together, share almost all of our meals together, and when it comes to sleeping—we don't get much of that when we're in bed together."

Drew looked amused. I wasn't.

"Are we...doing those things together exclusively?"

He stood and came around his desk. The playfulness was suddenly gone from his tone. "Are you asking me if it's okay for you to fuck someone else?"

"No!" *Yes? No? Maybe?* There wasn't anyone else I wanted to be with. Oddly, the thought of sleeping with Baldwin wasn't even appealing any longer. But I wanted to know if it would be weird if I spent time with another man.

"So what *are* you asking me?"

"I...I don't know."

Silence fell between us. I could see the wheels turning behind his eyes as he stared at me, his thumb rubbing at his bottom lip. After a minute, he pushed off his desk, and that thumb found its way to my chin and lifted.

He spoke into my eyes. "I'm not planning on sleeping with anyone else. And I expect you won't either. I thought we settled that in the bathtub yesterday."

My voice came out faint. "Okay."

"I take it this is about the message I gave you earlier?"

I nodded.

"You want to know what I think about you spending the night alone in your apartment having dinner and watching a movie with the putz?"

I nodded again.

"Alright." He looked away, seeming to contemplate his answer for a moment, and then said, "I like you. I like the way you listen to people's bullshit problems all day but still believe there's a reason to work through things. I like that you're up for anything—that you like staying in and watching old movies, or going out to a pool hall. I like the way your eyes light up when you talk about your parents. I really like the way it feels when I'm inside of you and the way you moan my name when you're about to come. I like that you made me coffee before you left this morning, and I even like that you're concerned what I'll think about you having dinner with Professor Pansyass."

He paused. "I think all that should tell you that for me, there's more here than just fucking. That being said, I'll tell you straight out that I hate the thought of you snuggling up on the couch to watch a movie with some dickhead you've been in love with for three years. But I'm not going to ask you not to spend time with him. That's a decision you need to make on your own, and I'll deal with whatever you choose because I realize my trust issues come from a place that has nothing to do with you."

I swallowed. That was a lot to take in at once. And it was way more than I'd expected him to commit to. "Okay."

"We good? Because I have four hours to do eight hours worth of work before I hop on a plane so my lazy-as-shit ex-wife can complain about the traffic getting my son to the airport while I fly nine hundred miles to pick him up and then turn right back around and fly another nine hundred miles back home. And I need at least a half hour of those four hours freed up so I can fuck you bent over your desk. Because you might have made me coffee this morning, but you didn't stay long enough for me to come inside of you, and I plan to remedy that before I head to the airport."

My head might have been spinning, but I knew one thing for sure. There was nothing I wanted more than for Drew to get his work done and make good on his plans.

I pushed up on my tippy toes and kissed his lips. "Go. What are you standing here for? You have work to get done."

# CHAPTER THIRTY

## DREW

"Look how long her legs are."

Screw biology; this boy was definitely my son. Beck was staring at a flight attendant with the longest stems I'd ever seen. She reached up to tuck some luggage in the overhead compartment above the seat in front of us and caught Beckett leaning into the aisle and staring.

"What's your name?" She smiled down at him.

"Beckett Archer Jagger."

He'd said it so proudly, I didn't have the heart to tell him it wasn't normal to recite your first, middle, and last name to strangers. The flight attendant snapped the overheard bin closed and knelt down next to him.

"Well, hello, Beckett Archer Jagger. I'm Danielle Marie Warren, and you're adorable. How old are you, sweetie?"

"I'm six-and-three-quarters."

"Six-and-three-quarters, huh? Well, I'm thirty-one-and-a-half." She winked at me and continued talking to Beck. "Only I usually round down from thirty-one-and-a-half—to twenty-seven. Can I get you something to drink, six-and-three-quarter-year-old Beckett Archer Jagger? Maybe some juice?"

He nodded. Then added, "You have legs like a giraffe."

"Beck," I scolded.

The flight attendant laughed. "It's okay. I've gotten that before. When I was your age, the kids used to make fun of me for having long legs." She pointed to her name badge, which read *Danny*. "My name is Danielle, but everyone calls me Danny for short. And when I was in elementary school, the boys used to call me Danny Long Legs. You know..." She wiggled her fingers. "...like the long-legged spider bugs? Daddy long legs."

Beckett chuckled. "My mom has a nickname for my dad."

"She does? I bet it's something better than Daddy Long Legs."

I interrupted. "Not sure we want to repeat any of the nicknames Mommy uses for Daddy these days." I looked at the flight attendant and explained, "Divorced."

She smiled and winked. "Well, how about I get you some juice before we take off? And something special for Daddy, too?"

A few minutes later, she came back carrying apple juice in a plastic cup with a lid and straw and a glass with two fingers of clear liquid over ice.

Passing them to us, she said, "We're going to be delayed a bit waiting for some weather to pass. Hope you didn't have plans for tonight." She looked at Beck and teased, "You don't have a date or anything, do you?"

He scrunched up his face like she'd just told him he had to eat all of his broccoli and beets. *Let's keep it that way for a long time, son. I haven't even figured out women yet. I'm far from ready to give you any advice.*

While neither Beckett nor I had any plans for tonight, Danny Long Legs's comment had me wondering what plans

*Emerie* had decided on for tonight. After our conversation this morning, she hadn't mentioned anything else. It might have been because the only talking we had time to do this afternoon was me whispering into her ear while she was bent over her desk with her skirt pushed up twenty minutes before I had to leave. *Come on my cock* was a hell of a lot better than any more discussions about Professor Putz.

But now it was eating at me. Was she sitting at home next to that douchebag she'd been pining over for more than three years? The asshole might act more refined than I did, but when it came down to it, we were both men, and Emerie was a beautiful woman. I'd seen the way he acted when he suspected something might be going on between the two of us. He became territorial—not jealous. Which told me a hell of a lot about how he thought. People are jealous when they want something someone else has. They're territorial when they're protecting something they already have. That fucker knew he'd had her all along.

My gut told me he was avoiding getting involved with Emerie because he wanted to have a good time—fuck his way through the faculty and his students, avoiding any real relationships. And how, exactly, did I know this about the guy when I'd only met him a few times? Because I knew the face of that type of man. I'd looked him in the mirror every day for the last two years since my goddamned divorce.

Beck had taken out his drawing pad and was drawing a giraffe. I laughed, thinking how often I doodled while on the phone. Nurture won over nature more often than not. I could totally see myself drawing a giraffe right now if that pencil had been in my hand. Although my giraffe would probably have had tits, because since I hit the age of ten, all of my doodles had pretty much incorporated tits in some way.

While during my entire childhood everything had reminded me of tits, the last week everything reminded me of Emerie. An advertisement for bright red lipstick at the airport. *Emerie's bright red lips wrapped around my cock.* The flight attendant mentioning that our plans might be ruined by the weather delay. *Emerie's plans—was she snuggled on the couch with the putz?* My son drawing a giraffe. *If I drew a giraffe, it would have tits. Emerie's tits are incredible.* All the roads in my mind had been rerouted to one destination lately.

I knocked back half of the drink in one gulp and dug my phone from my pocket.

**Drew: *What did you wind up doing tonight?***

Then I waited for the buzz to tell me Emerie had responded. And waited.

I was turning into a pussy. This was the third time I'd checked my cell phone this morning. *Nothing.* Twelve hours had passed.

After making chocolate chip pancakes that were more chip than cake, I'd asked Beck what he wanted to do. His answer was always the same: ice skating. The boy was obsessed with hockey. So I bundled the little monster up in three layers, tied the laces of our skates together, and flung a pair over each shoulder before we took off.

We made it to the lobby, and I told Beck I needed to make a quick pit stop in my office. Having still not heard from Emerie, I was starting to wonder if maybe I should worry instead of getting pissed off at what she could have been doing.

Inside my office suite, faint music was playing. It was an instrumental of some sort, and my heart sped up knowing Emerie was just down the hall. I wasn't sure if it was excitement or anger, but I heard the blood swishing through my ears as I got to her office.

The door was half open, but she didn't seem to have heard me come in, so I knocked, not wanting to scare her. Considering she jumped onto her chair, I'd say I didn't succeed.

Instinct had me raising my hands in surrender to her. Again. "It's just me."

"You scared the shit out of me."

With that, Beck, who had been standing behind me, popped out from behind my legs.

Emerie covered her mouth. "Oh my God. I'm sorry. My language."

Beck answered for me. "My dad says a lot worse."

I smiled and mussed his hair, but I needed to remember to have a conversation with him later about spilling my secrets.

Emerie climbed off her chair, walked over, and leaned down, offering her hand. "You must be Beck."

"Beckett Archer Jagger."

Emerie's lip quirked, and she glanced up at me. I shrugged.

"Well, nice to meet you, Beckett Archer Jagger. I'm Emerie Rose."

"Is Rose your middle name or your last?"

Emerie smiled and laughed. It was the same question I'd asked when we first met. "It's my last name. I don't have a middle name."

Beckett seemed to ponder that for a minute, so I cut in.

"Didn't mean to scare you. Beck and I are going ice skating. Was just worried when you didn't respond to my text last night." I locked eyes with Emerie.

She turned around and walked to her desk, lifting her broken cell phone and dangling it between her thumb and pointer. "Dropped it last night. I just picked up a new one, and I'm trying to figure out if there's a way to restore my contacts from the cloud. I don't know anyone's numbers anymore."

I let out a breath. She wasn't blowing me off. It really had been eating at me. Probably a fuck of a lot more than it should've been.

Normally, if I was interested in a woman and she didn't respond...*next*. Plenty of fish in the sea. Only with Emerie, not only had it made me anxious that she hadn't texted back, the thought of browsing my phonebook for another number didn't appeal to me at all.

"You want help with that? I break a phone every month."

She eyed the skates on my shoulders. "I don't want to keep you guys when you're on the way out for some fun."

"Beck doesn't mind. Right, buddy?"

My son was so easygoing. He shrugged. "Nope. Can I go draw at your desk, Dad?"

"Of course. Bottom right-hand drawer."

Beck took off running. He loved to sit at my big desk and draw. He could do it for hours.

I walked to the other side of Emerie's desk.

"He's adorable," she said.

"Thank you. He's a good kid." I pulled out her chair. "Sit. I'll show you how to load your new phone."

Of course, I could have sat down and done it for her in two seconds, but I preferred to lean over her shoulder and have her trapped between the desk and my body. I intentionally spoke low and let my breath tickle her neck.

"You click this folder." I put my hand over hers on the mouse and clicked. "Then this. And then use the drop-down up here and hit restore."

Watching her skin prickle with goosebumps, I leaned my head closer to her ear. "You cold?"

"No. I'm good."

I smiled to myself as I clicked through a few more screens. Then her new phone, which was already plugged into her laptop, lit up and began to restore from the cloud.

"Wow. I've been trying to figure that out for an hour now."

"How'd you break it anyway?"

"If I tell you, you have to promise not to laugh."

"But I can still make fun of you?"

"No. You can't do that either."

I stood. "Then what's the fun in hearing the story?"

Emerie laughed. "How was your trip to Atlanta, jackass?"

"Flight was delayed a few hours for weather. But it was fine. At least Alexa didn't give me a hard time."

Emerie had just given me a perfect opening. I hated that I needed to know, but screw it, I did. I attempted to at least sound casual. "How was your dinner last night?"

Emerie's brows drew down; then she realized what I was asking. "Oh. I just ordered in Chinese by myself."

"No dinner with Putz?"

She bit her lower lip and shook her head. I stepped closer. "Why not?"

"It just...didn't feel like the right thing to do."

We'd agreed we were going to be exclusive sexually, and I'd even pretty much told her I thought we had more than just great chemistry, but I couldn't very well tell her she couldn't have dinner with a guy friend. Don't get me wrong, that's exactly what I wanted to tell her—although since the thought scared even me, I figured I should keep that shit to myself.

Instead of revealing my inner pussy, I walked to her door. My eyes never left hers as I yelled to my son. "All good, Beck?"

"Yeah!" he yelled back.

"Okay. I'll just be a few minutes, buddy."

Then I quietly shut the door. "Come here?"

"What are you doing?"

"Come here."

Emerie did as I asked, coming to stand within my reach. "What?"

"I thought about you the entire plane ride home."

She swallowed. "Yeah?"

"And in the shower this morning. Had to blast the water ice cold to get my cock under control because every time I shut my eyes, I saw your ass bent over my desk."

Her eyes widened. "Your son is right in the next office."

"I know. That's why you're not bent over that desk right now, and I'm going to settle for a little taste."

She licked her lips, and deciding Beck could come look for me at any second, I was done wasting time. I cupped the back of her neck and used it to pull her close as I took her mouth in a rough kiss. My other arm hooked around her waist, and she whimpered as I tugged her body flush against mine. She smelled so damn good. A sweet fragrance mixed with her naturally sexy feminine scent was intoxicating. It took every bit of restraint I had not to turn her around and push her up against the door. When I grabbed a handful of her ass and she moaned into my mouth, I almost lost that restraint.

My dick was throbbing by the time I released her mouth. I was just about to go in for more, when I heard my son calling.

"Fuck," I grumbled, leaning my forehead against Emerie's. "I'm going to have to hide my hard-on so he doesn't ask questions I'm not ready to answer."

Luckily, I was wearing dark jeans and was able to adjust myself before going to Beck.

"What's up, buddy?"

"Can we get hot chocolate before we go skating?"

"You just had chocolate chip pancakes for breakfast. Don't you think that's enough chocolate for the morning?"

My son was smart. "But it's gonna be cold outside, and it'll keep me warm on the inside."

Emerie came to stand next to me. She smiled. "He has a good point."

"Are you going to come skating with us?" Beck asked.

"I don't think that's a good idea. I don't know how to ice skate."

"My dad can teach you. He's good at everything."

*Nice, kid.*

Emerie looked to me for help.

I shrugged. "Kid's got a point. I am good at everything."

She rolled her eyes, then spoke to Beck. "You and your dad don't need me slowing you down."

"We've never gone ice skating with anyone else. I can show you my moves."

Emerie turned to me with one brow lifted. "He's got moves, huh? Just like his father."

I lowered my voice. "Come. Let him show you his moves, and I'll show you mine later."

# CHAPTER THIRTY-ONE

## EMERIE

"I don't think it's broken." The emergency room doctor had my swollen ankle in his hand. It was already turning blue. "But we'll take an X-ray to be sure."

"Thank you."

"The nurse will be by in a few minutes to get some information, and then she'll call for the X-ray technician."

"Okay." I turned to Drew. "This is all your fault."

"My fault?"

"Yes. You were making me go too fast."

"Too fast? A grandmother pushing a bucket on the ice lapped us. You shouldn't have let go of my hand."

"I got scared."

We'd ice skated for more than two hours, and I still couldn't seem to get the hang of it. Because I was so unsteady on my feet, my ankles were constantly wobbling back and forth, which caused my skate to loosen. The last time I fell, there'd been no ankle support, and I twisted the damn thing. It hurt, but I hadn't thought it was broken.

Drew, however, took one look at the swelling and decided we needed a visit to the ER. There was no talking him out of it. His buddy, Roman, had met us in front of the hospital and took Beck back to his place so Drew could stay with me.

The nurse came by with a clipboard. "I need to ask you some questions. Your husband can stay if you want, but he'll need to step out when the technician comes to shoot the X-ray."

"He's not..." I motioned between Drew and me. "We're not married."

The nurse smiled. Not at me, but at Drew. She also batted her eyelashes.

*Really?*

"Well, then I'll need to ask you to step outside," she told him. "I'll come get you after I finish asking your..."

She waited for Drew to fill in the blank.

"Girlfriend."

"Oh. Yes. I'll come get you when I finish with your girlfriend."

Was I imagining it or had she been fishing to see if we were together? Drew kissed me on the forehead and said he'd be back. As soon as he left, the nurse started rattling off medical questions. Only then did it hit me that Drew had just called me his girlfriend.

———

"I can walk."

Drew had just scooped me up for the tenth time. He'd carried me from the rink to the cab, from the cab into the hospital, from the hospital into the cab, and from the cab all the way up to his apartment where he proceeded to set me up on the couch with my foot elevated. *Just as the doctor instructed.*

Now, he'd just had food delivered, and he was carrying me to the table.

"Doctor said not to put weight on it."

"It's fine. It's just a sprain. The boot will stop me from putting too much weight on it anyway."

Beck pulled out the chair as his father approached with me cradled in his arms. Roman, who had been taking containers of food out of the cardboard delivery box, looked at us funny. Today was my first time meeting him, and he probably thought I was a drama queen.

"I'm so embarrassed. I swear I'm not usually this big of a klutz."

Roman continued to take in the scene before him, watching as Drew set me down and proceeded to scoop food onto the plate in front of me. I got the feeling Roman was a man who didn't miss much.

"You're fine. Florence Nightingale here shouldn't have let you fall."

Drew growled. "I didn't let her fall. She let go of my hand."

I winked at Roman, letting him know we were on the same page, then deadpanned. "He let me fall."

"Bullshit." Drew froze with a tray of ziti in his hand. He'd already shoveled way too much onto my plate. He looked to me and then to Roman. "I didn't drop her, but I'm going to drop you if you keep starting shit."

"Watch your language," I said.

Roman just chuckled.

Dinner was far from peaceful. First Drew and I disagreed over politics, and then Roman, Drew, and Beck had a heated discussion about who was going to make it to the playoffs in hockey this season. It was loud, and we occasionally talked over each other, but I couldn't remember the last time I'd enjoyed a meal so much.

After we finished, Drew insisted I couldn't help cleanup and toted me back to the living room. Roman, who Drew had instructed to help clean up, cracked a beer and joined me instead.

"Want a beer?"

"No, thanks." I slouched down on the couch and folded my hands over my stomach. "I'm too full from the twenty pounds of pasta and chicken parmigiana Drew piled on my plate."

Roman took a draw on his beer, watching me over the top. "You two fight a lot?"

I smiled. "We actually do."

"That's his tell."

Confusion must have been apparent on my face, because Roman set his beer bottle on his knee and elaborated. "We met in sixth grade. I stole his girlfriend—"

I interrupted. "The way Drew tells the story, he stole *your* girlfriend before you bonded over the chicken pox."

"He told you about that?"

I nodded. "He did. It was an oddly sweet story. He told it with reverence."

"Anyway, the two of us have been fighting since sixth grade. But he's also my best friend. Him and his old man were closer than any father and son I'd ever met. They fought daily. It's not a coincidence that he argues for a living, too." Roman sipped from his beer and seemed to ponder his next words. "Wanna know how I knew it wasn't going to work out with Alexa?"

"How?"

"They never argued. Not until the end when she started to show her true colors as the selfish bitch she always was.

And that's a different type of fighting than Drew does when he loves."

"We're not—"

Roman leaned back into the couch with an easy smile. "I know. I can see that neither of you have figured it out yet. Talk to me in a month or two."

⁀

"There's night construction on 49th, you should try 51st."

"Jesus Christ, you're a pain in the ass," Drew mumbled as he made a sharp left turn.

We'd argued for a half-hour over my going home. He wanted me to stay at his place so he could help me get around. But with his son there, it wasn't the right thing to do. Eventually he gave in, but we waited until after Beck went to sleep. Then Roman had stayed so Drew could drive me home.

When we arrived at my building, I made a half-assed attempt at arguing against him carrying me, then gave up. Wrapping my arms around his neck, I leaned in to enjoy it.

"You might want to think about cutting back on the burgers," Drew teased.

"Watch it. Any fat jokes and I'll be cutting back on *all* meat."

"You're full of shit. You like my meat way too much."

"You're so full of yourself."

"Maybe. But you're going to be full of me in about five minutes, too."

The elevator door opened. "We don't have time for that. You need to get back so Roman can get home."

"Screw Roman." One of the hands cradling me slipped down to my ass and squeezed hard. "I've had your ass in my hands all day. We're getting naked."

"What if I don't invite you in?"

"Good point. Maybe I should fuck you right here in the elevator then." He pointed his chin up to a small camera in the corner of the car. "Someone might be watching. Give 'em a good show."

I'd been leaning my head against Drew's chest, so I tilted it back to look up at him. His eyes were filled with heat. If we didn't get up to the privacy of my apartment, there was a chance someone really might be getting a show. But why weren't we moving yet?

"Did you push my floor?"

"Fuck," Drew chuckled and leaned forward to push the button on the elevator panel. Just before the doors slid together, an arm stopped them from closing.

Of course, it had to be Baldwin.

He looked at me in Drew's arms and then saw the boot strapped up my leg. "Emerie? What happened?"

I felt the grip around me tighten.

"I fell ice skating. It's just a sprain."

Baldwin eyed Drew.

*What the hell? Does he need verification?*

"She's been checked out. It's not broken," Drew said curtly. His jaw was set so tightly, I could see the muscle flexing.

The elevator door closed, and the inside of the car became worse than awkward. It felt...suffocating. The two men stood side by side. I suddenly wished I'd argued more about being carried. By the time we got to the third floor, I was certain there wasn't much oxygen left in the quiet car. Baldwin extended his arm to let us get out first.

I attempted to find my keys in my purse, but it was difficult in my current position. When Drew stopped in front of my door, I said, "Would you mind putting me down so I can find my keys?"

He lowered me gently, keeping his arm around me to reduce the weight on my foot.

Baldwin stopped at my door. "Is there anything I can do to help?"

I opened my mouth to respond, but Drew beat me to it.

"I'll take care of whatever she needs."

Baldwin pretty much ignored him. "I can drop you at the office in the morning and pick you up."

"I have a car," Drew muttered as he took the keys from my hand and unlocked the door.

"It's not necessary for you to come out of your way. We're leaving from the same place, and I can route myself to drop you on my way to the university."

I ignored the eyes burning into me and turned to Baldwin. "That would be great. Thank you. Or I can take a cab. I don't want Drew having to come all this way uptown in the morning, especially dragging his son with him."

"Then it's settled. Text me in the morning if you need help getting ready or anything."

"Thank you."

Baldwin gave Drew a nod and then *finally* went to his apartment. The entire encounter had probably lasted the sum total of three minutes, but it felt like hours.

Inside, I flicked on the lights and busied myself taking off my coat. Drew was quiet, and I sensed a comment coming. After a minute, I started to relax and think maybe it was all in my head, that I had misjudged the situation and the awkwardness was only felt by me.

I was wrong.

"That guy's an asshole."

"What did he do?"

Drew must have taken my question as defending Baldwin. His entire demeanor changed. "Do you want to fuck him?"

"What? No! Where the hell did that come from?"

He ran a hand through his hair. "I gotta go. I don't want Beck to wake up and me not be back yet."

While I could understand that, five minutes ago he hadn't been planning on rushing back. Drew had just gone from desperate to be with me to desperate to get away from me in under five minutes flat.

"What just happened here?"

"Do you want me to take that brace off of you or do anything before I leave?"

Frustrated, I snapped at him. "No. Just go."

I pressed my head against the door after shutting it behind him. My mind was spinning, but the same question kept running through it:

*Do I want to sleep with Baldwin?*

# CHAPTER THIRTY-TWO

## DREW

The next morning, I debated going over to Emerie's place a half-dozen times before deciding I'd just make it worse if I showed up. I didn't want her to think my apology was a cover because I didn't want Putz driving her to work. Of course, I didn't want the dickhead to drive her. But around two o'clock this morning, after beating up my pillow, I'd finally come to my senses.

My acting like a jerk had nothing to do with Emerie. Between a cheating ex-wife and my daily dose of clients who'd been burned or had burned their spouse, I wasn't exactly the most trusting person. I still didn't think I was wrong about Baldwin—the guy was a dickhead, and my gut told me something would eventually go down once he realized Emerie wasn't waiting on the sidelines for him anymore. But that wasn't on her either.

It was almost ten by the time she finally showed up at the office. Beck only had a half-day of school, so I was hoping she didn't have a morning appointment she needed to jump right into. I'd been on high alert listening for her to come in, so she was barely inside when I got to the reception area.

And the dickhead was with her. His arm wrapped around her waist, he was attempting to assist her in walking. I could see from her face that the entire thing made her uncomfortable.

"Morning."

"Good morning." Emerie forced a pensive smile. "I told Baldwin he didn't need to walk me inside. But he insisted."

I managed to reply with a hint of sincerity. "You need help. Doctor said no weight on that ankle."

Testing my resolve, I backed off and let him walk her all the way to her office as I returned to mine. I'd be lying if I said I didn't eavesdrop though. He asked her what time he should pick her up, and Emerie said she had plans after work and would get a ride.

Once Putz was gone, I took a deep breath and walked into her office. She was setting up her laptop in the docking station.

"You have a patient now?"

"Nope." She didn't look up.

"So we can talk?"

She looked up at me. "Oh. You're in the mood to talk now?"

I deserved that. "Maybe I should start off with an apology right away."

Her face softened, but she folded her arms across her chest, trying to be a tougher sell. "That would be good."

"I'm sorry about the way I acted last night."

"You mean accusing me of wanting to screw another man after we'd already agreed we were going to be sleeping together exclusively?"

"Yes. That."

Emerie sighed. "I'm not that type of person, Drew. Even if I wanted to sleep with someone else, I wouldn't while I'd given someone a commitment."

She'd just unintentionally hit my sore spot. I'd spent half the night and morning taking ownership of the fact that I had trust issues—those were easy to blame on other people. *It was Alexa's fault. My work has killed my faith in the human race.* But when it came down to it, I liked this woman— maybe more than I should after such a short time—and it scared the crap out of me. She'd spent the last few years of her life waiting for some other guy to notice her, and I wasn't sure what would happen when he finally did.

Sure, I was jealous. But I was also fucking scared. And I definitely didn't like feeling that way.

I walked over to her, not so much because I felt like I needed to be close to say what I needed to say, but because I hated to be on the other side of the room when I could be near her.

It was especially chilly outside today, and her cheeks were pink, matching the tip of her nose. I cupped her cold face into my hands and leaned down and planted a soft kiss on her lips.

Then I pulled back so we were at eye level. "I'm sorry for being a jealous jerk. I'd planned to tell you why it wasn't my fault I was jealous—that my history and job made me this way—and maybe that's part of it. But it's not all of it. To be honest, the truth didn't hit me until a few minutes ago."

"And what's that?"

"I need to hear where your head is with that guy. You followed him halfway across the country a few months ago. I know you had strong feelings for him. And if you say you'd tell me if you wanted out of this exclusive thing, I believe you. But what I need to know is, if he told you today he had feelings for you, would you be telling me you wanted out?"

Emerie stilled, a flash of something flickering across her face before our eyes locked. "Why don't you sit?"

# CHAPTER THIRTY-THREE

## EMERIE

*Practice what you preach.*

That was a tall order when Drew Jagger stared at you, waiting for an answer. He wanted to know what would happen if the man I'd been crazy about for the last few years, the man I'd moved to New York to take a chance on, suddenly decided he wanted to be with me. It was a question I'd been asking myself since both men left me alone with my thoughts last night.

I owed it to Drew to be honest. Heck, I owed it to myself.

"I've had feelings for Baldwin for so long, I don't remember what it feels like to not have them."

Drew leaned on the edge of my desk, his legs spread in a stance that was so inherently male and dominant—something so simple, yet it reminded me that what I was about to say was true.

"But whatever I've felt for Baldwin is very different than whatever is going on between us."

Drew's eyes flashed, and I had to squeeze my thighs to stop myself from getting excited about him growing angry. There was no doubt that pissing each other off was some kind of screwed-up foreplay for us, but this wasn't the time for that.

"Baldwin is smart and courteous. We share a passion for psychology and sociology. He doesn't use foul language, he takes me to fancy restaurants, and he's never once raised his voice to me."

Drew was brooding. "There better be a fucking *but* coming soon."

My lip twitched. I needed to get through the hard part before I gave him his but. "There is. But I want to be completely honest."

The look in his eyes told me to get to the point. He nodded for me to continue.

"I'd be lying if I said I didn't have feelings for Baldwin. *But* then there's you. You confuse the hell out of me, and I have no idea where whatever is going on between us is going to land, but there's one thing I'm sure of."

"What's that?"

"When I look at you, it makes me realize why it would have never worked out with him."

His eyes softened. "I suck at trust."

"I know."

"I'm still gonna yell, and I use *fuck* as a noun, adjective, and verb."

I smirked. "I've learned there are times when your language *really* works for me."

Drew reached out and ran two fingers over my chin, down my neck, and along my collarbone before moving them into my cleavage. "Oh yeah?"

That was all it took. The deep rasp of his *oh yeah* and a simple touch. I couldn't explain why I felt things for Drew any more than I could explain the taste of water. Yet somehow, he had become a necessity for me, and I was in no way ready to take on a drought.

I whispered, "Where's Beck?"

Drew's eyes followed his fingers as they dipped into my sweater. "School. Don't have to pick him up for another hour."

My body prickled at the thought of how we could spend that hour. "Any clients before then?"

He began to unbutton the small pearl buttons that ran down the front of my sweater. "Nope. You?"

I shook my head.

Whatever patience Drew had been practicing went out the window after that. In the next minute, he lifted me from my chair, tore off my panties, and propped me atop my desk, facing the chair with my skirt bunched up around my waist. All while being careful of my air-casted leg.

Then he sat in the chair, facing my exposed pussy, and loosened his tie.

"What are you doing?"

"Showing you I'm sorry. Spread wider."

*Oh my.*

I opened my legs for him and shivered at the way he looked at me down there. When he licked his lips, pulled his chair closer, and tugged until my ass was at the edge of the desk, I was already halfway to orgasm, and he hadn't even laid a finger on me yet.

"I might not like to eat at fancy restaurants, but you'll always be fed, and I'll eat you until you're the one screaming obscenities."

*That* totally worked for me.

Things were different after our talk this morning. There was an intimacy, a bond of some sort, that hadn't been there before. Drew picked up Beck from school and brought back lunch for all of us before the two of them left for the library then ice skating again. I loved that Drew made his afternoons with his son part work and part play for both of them. Beck did story time on the children's rug while Drew worked on a case in the adjoining room. When they were done, Beck read books to Drew, and then the reward was ice skating.

I had an afternoon full of patients, and even at almost six-thirty in the evening, I felt a renewed hopefulness that there was a solution for every couple's problems. My optimism had spilled over into my sessions in a good way.

I was packing up my laptop when I heard the front door open and then little feet flying toward my office.

"We got all the stuff for movie night!" Beck yelled. His chubby cheeks were red from the cold, and he was bundled like a little snowman.

"Oh, really? What are you planning on watching?

Beck held up two fingers. "We got *two* movies. One is for dinner food and the other is for dessert."

I didn't quite understand what he meant, but his excitement was contagious. "That sounds great. Which movie will you watch first?"

Drew appeared behind his son. "He made me drop him off at the curb instead of going under to the parking garage so he could run in and tell you first."

Beck smiled so wide, I could almost count his tiny little teeth. He held up a CD jewel case. "For dinner, we got *Cloudy with a Chance of Meatballs*." Then he pointed up to his dad, who held up a takeout bag.

"Mamma Theresa's makes the best meatballs in the city."

Beck nodded fast, then held up a second jewel case. "And for dessert we got *Snow White and the Seven Dwarfs*."

Beck pointed up to his father. It was like they were doing a little skit.

Drew held up another bag. "Gooseberry pie from The French Pastry."

I smiled. "What is gooseberry pie anyway?"

Drew shrugged. "Hell if I know. But we had to go to three bakeries to find it, and the thing cost twenty-six bucks, so it better taste good."

Beck added, "I'm going to have mine with vanilla ice cream. That's not part of your movie party though."

"*My* movie party?"

"Dad said you liked movie theme parties. Can you come?"

Another little piece of the wall I'd built around my heart because I was afraid to fall for this man chipped off.

Drew watched me, assessing my reaction. I couldn't have hidden it if I wanted to.

My hand went to my chest. "You are the sweetest. I can't believe you made a movie theme night for me. I'd love to come."

Anxious to get started, Beck took off yelling down the hall, "I'll get the elevator."

"Don't get in it until I'm there," Drew warned.

I finished packing up my stuff and went to the doorway. Pushing up on my tippy toes, I gave him a soft kiss on the lips. "Thank you."

He winked. "You got it."

Drew scooped me up—because I apparently wasn't allowed to walk until this air cast was off—and walked toward the elevator.

Lowering his voice, he said, "Think I'm gonna like this dinner and a movie theme thing—finally put my porn collection to good use."

# CHAPTER THIRTY-FOUR

## EMERIE

The rest of the week was just as amazing as movie night. Spending time at home with Drew and Beck showed me so much more about the man than I would have learned on dozens of dates. Come to think of it, that should be part of the dating ritual. On the second or third date, the man should have to bring a child, perhaps a niece or nephew if he doesn't have children of his own, so you can see the relationship he has with them. It would cut to the bottom line better than six months of dating.

Whether we had breakfast or dinner together each day, Drew always managed to carve out time for all three of us together and for the two of them alone. It was starting to feel like my own little family. But in the back of my mind, I realized things wouldn't always be this way. Alexa would be returning tomorrow, and I wasn't sure what that would add. I was definitely curious about her.

This afternoon I would be watching Beck alone for a few hours while Drew had a deposition he couldn't reschedule. He'd planned on asking one of the assistant teachers from Beck's school who sometimes watched him, but I insisted I could handle it.

Drew had a stash of movies that we could watch upstairs in his apartment, and I'd bought some old-school Jiffy Pop popcorn to make on the stove. Babysitting would be a piece of cake.

Or so I thought.

Then I had to call Drew's cell phone and interrupt his deposition ten minutes after it started. To tell him we needed to go to the hospital.

"I'm so sorry." It was the millionth time I'd said it. We were in a small curtained room in the same ER we'd sat in for my twisted ankle not even one full week ago. Only this time, Beck was being treated.

"Things happen. It was an accident. Now he knows better than to touch the stove."

"*I* should have known better." Beck and I had made the Jiffy Pop together. He'd never seen popcorn made that way. His big chocolate eyes grew like saucers watching the silver foil inflate with each pop of the kernels. When the popping had slowed, and the foil looked about to burst, I'd slid the silvery pan from the heat onto a cool burner and poked a hole in the top to allow steam to escape. When Beck went to sift through the movie cabinet, I thought nothing of going to the bathroom. I was out of the room less than three minutes, thinking how nice the afternoon was as I washed my hands... when the screaming began.

The poor little guy had gone back to the stove and, unaware that part of the flat top burner was still hot since it was no longer orange, tried to hop up to watch the steam coming out of the top of the Jiffy Pop. He'd unknowingly placed his entire hand on the still-hot burner.

"His mother's kitchen has gas. I should have explained that the top stays hot to him when I got the new stove a year ago. It's not your fault. It's mine."

Beck shrugged. The boy was a trooper. "It doesn't even really hurt that much anymore."

The doctor said it was a simple first-degree burn and applied Silvadene lotion, then wrapped Beck's hand with gauze on the inside and an ace bandage around the outside.

I put my hand on Beck's knee. "I'm so sorry, honey. I should have told you it stayed hot even when the color changed."

A little while later, a nurse came in and gave us dressing instructions, a tube of cream, and some gauze to use the next day so we didn't have to get to the store right away. Even though everyone treated it like it was a common occurrence, I still felt like shit.

The first time Drew left me alone with his son, I'd broken him.

———

"I look like a boxer!" Beck announced on the way home from the hospital. "Dad, can you wrap my other hand? And maybe get this stuff in red?" He pointed to the ace bandage.

"Sure, buddy."

The two of them were back to their normal selves, but I still felt horrible. Drew reached over and put his hand on my knee as he drove. "People are going to start looking at me funny with you two."

I furrowed my brow.

"You're in an air cast, and he's got a hand wrapped."

covered my mouth. "Oh my God. Imagine—they look at ɪny, when both injuries are completely my fault."

Drew's voice lowered. "Seriously, I see you sitting there trying all sorts of guilt on for size. It was an accident. It could have been me making the popcorn, and the exact same thing would have happened."

"But it didn't."

"Stop beating yourself up. Two months ago he had a black eye from running into the dresser while his mother was watching him. He's a little boy. They do shit without thinking and get hurt."

"Oh, no."

"What?"

"I hadn't even thought of his mother. She's going to hate me."

"Don't worry about her. There wasn't much of a shot of her liking you anyway."

*Great. Just great.*

# CHAPTER THIRTY-FIVE

## EMERIE

"Who are you?"

It only took three words to know the woman who walked into the office the next morning was a *bitch*.

Skin-tight jeans, brown leather high-heel boots on long, thin legs, and a tiny little waist in a top that that showed skin even though it was the end of January and freezing in New York City. I didn't want to look any higher. I wanted to go home and change into something less professional and more sexy. There was no doubt in my mind who she was.

Dreading it, I skimmed the rest of the way up and was met with a face as nice as the body. *Of course.*

"I'm Emerie Rose. And you are?"

"Alexa Jagger. Drew's *wife*."

Drew suddenly appeared next to me in the lobby. "*Ex*-wife." His narrowed eyes matched his curt response.

Alexa rolled her eyes. "Whatever. We need to talk."

"Make an appointment. I'm busy this morning."

She completely ignored Drew and brushed past him, strutting her way to his office.

The two of us remained standing in the lobby for a moment.

I spoke softly. "Well, she's lovely."

Drew took a deep breath. "You might want to put earplugs in."

*"We're going!"*

"You're not taking him on the road to follow a bunch of race car drivers around the country and home schooling him! Go, if you want to go, but Beck is staying here."

"What is he going to do here with you? You work sixty hours a week."

"I make it work. At least here he has his school, his routine, his home."

"You don't make it work. You dump him on a babysitter. I've heard more about the new sitter this morning than you. And apparently she's not even competent to watch him since his hand is burned."

*Shit.*

The yelling quieted, and I knew Drew was trying to get himself under control. I pictured his jaw clenching and flexing as he breathed in fire and attempted to push out ice.

When he finally spoke, his tone was more than angry; it teetered on lethal. "You have no idea what you're talking about. I don't ship my son off to a babysitter. He was with me or my girlfriend the entire time, and he was well cared for."

*"Girlfriend?"* Alexa spat. "You're bringing my son around your fuck of the month now?"

*"Our* son." Drew growled. "And she *isn't* a fuck of the month. Unlike you, I've never introduced Beck to anyone I was seeing casually. All the times he's mentioned random men being around, I've kept my mouth shut and trusted you

were being careful and respectful around him. And I expect the same in return for Emerie."

"Emerie? The woman I met in the lobby? You're fucking the hired help?"

"We're sharing space. She's a psychologist, not the hired help. And what the fuck would it matter to you if she swept the floor here? At least she *has* a job. You should try it. It might make you appreciate the thousand-dollar boots you're wearing right now."

"I'm raising our son. It's a full-time job."

"Funny how he's *our* son when I'm footing the bill for that full-time job. But *yours* when you want to take him on a NASCAR tour of redneck country."

"I'm taking him," she snapped

"You're not taking him."

"I don't think it's something you want to fight about. Beck should get to know his father and spend time with him."

I braced myself for the roar I knew was coming.

"*He is spending time with his father!*"

"I meant his biological father."

"That wasn't my choice. You made sure of that. God knows *I wouldn't have fucking married you had I known you were a whore carrying another man's child!*"

"Screw you!"

"Get out, Alexa. Just get the fuck out."

Even though I knew it was coming, I jumped when she whipped open Drew's office door, and it slammed against the wall. Alexa left a wake of stomps and crashes behind her.

I waited in my office for a few minutes, unsure whether I should give Drew time to cool off or attempt to comfort him. Eventually, when I heard nothing but silence, I decided to check on him.

Drew's chair was pushed back from his desk, and he sat with his elbows on his knees and his head in his hands.

"You okay?" I asked softly.

He didn't look up when he answered. His voice was hoarse. "Yeah."

I took a few hesitant steps into his office. "What can I do?"

Drew shook his head a few times, then looked up. "Can you make me that little boy's *real* father?" My heart clenched in my chest when I saw his defeated expression. His eyes were red and filled with unshed tears, and I felt the pain I could see on his face.

I knelt before him. "You are his *real* father, Drew."

Even though he was listening to me, I wasn't getting through. So I decided to share a story I'd never told anyone.

"When I was nineteen, I decided I wanted to know who my birth mother was. I have no idea why; nothing had gone wrong. I was just curious, I think. Anyway, my adoption was open, so the information was there if I wanted it. Not wanting to hurt my parents' feelings, I decided not to tell them and got the information on my own."

Drew was paying attention now, so I continued. "One Saturday, I told my parents I was going to a friend's house and instead drove four hours across the state to the address where my birth mother lived. I sat outside her house and waited until she came out. Then I followed her to where she worked at a diner. After a couple more hours, I got up the nerve to actually go inside. I'd watched through the window, so I knew what section she was serving and requested a table near the window so she would be my waitress."

Even though Drew was the one hurting, he reached out and squeezed my shoulder for encouragement. "What happened?"

"She came over to take my order, and I bumbled every word that came out of my mouth. But I managed to order toast and tea while I stared at her." I paused, thinking back to that day. "She had red hair."

Drew stroked my cheek.

"Anyway, while she was taking an order at the table next to me, my phone rang, and I saw it was my mother. I let it go to voicemail because I thought maybe she'd found out what I was doing somehow and was angry. But when I listened to her message, she'd just wanted to check in on me and see if everything was alright. She said I'd seemed a little down the day before. Needless to say, I felt guilty as hell. When the waitress—my birth mother—came to deliver my toast a few minutes later, I was crying. She looked right at me and never even asked if I was okay. Couldn't wait to dump the toast on the table and disappear."

I sighed. "I took one more look at the woman who had given birth to me and realized my mother was the woman who'd left me the voicemail. I was biologically connected to that waitress, and she didn't feel anything different for me than a complete stranger. Because that's what I was...a complete stranger. I threw a twenty on the table and never looked back."

I caught Drew's eyes. "Being a parent is a choice, not a right. I really didn't understand why my parents celebrated Gotcha Day until then. You're Beck's dad, no different than Martin Rose is mine. Anyone can become a father, but it takes a real dad to love and raise a child as his own."

"Come here." Drew lifted me from the floor onto his lap. He pushed a lock of hair behind my ear. His previously angry and sad eyes had warmed. "Where'd you come from?"

"I broke in and showed you my ass, remember?"

He laughed, and I felt a little of the tension dissipate when he wrapped me in his arms and kissed the top of my head. "Thank you. I needed that."

I was thrilled to have soothed him. Because Drew had been with Beck all week, this was actually the first afternoon we'd had alone in as long.

"I don't have an appointment for another two hours, if there's *anything else* you need."

Drew was standing with me cradled in his arms practically before I finished the sentence. I yelped at the sudden motion. Expecting him to have me spread-eagled right there on his desk, I was surprised when he began marching toward the office door.

"No desk sex?" I asked.

"The desk is for fucking. I want to make love to you."

# CHAPTER THIRTY-SIX

## DREW

*I could get used to this.*

I'd just gotten out of the shower and walked into the kitchen. Emerie was standing at the stove wearing one of my dress shirts, which hung to her knees, and making something that smelled almost as good as she did. Music was playing, and I hung back in the doorway and watched as she swayed from side, singing some song I didn't recognize.

As if sensing me, after a minute she turned and smiled. "Breakfast is almost done."

I nodded but stayed put another minute, enjoying watching her. Five days ago, after Alexa had stomped in and started in on me about wanting to take Beck on a road trip, I'd assumed my week would be shit—as was typical after one of our arguments. But Emerie had a way of calming me, making me focus on the positive. It might also have helped that she'd been in my bed every night to help me alleviate any stress, and that I'd woken this morning to her head beneath the covers and her tongue licking me like I was a lollipop.

She smiled and winked with a blush. "Go sit. My turn to feed you."

*Yeah. There's a distinct possibility I could get used to this.*

---

"What time is your first appointment?" I asked. We'd finished breakfast, then I'd fucked her on the kitchen counter before cleaning up the dishes while she got ready. Now she was brushing some shit onto her eyelashes as she leaned in to the mirror.

"Ten. But I need to run to my apartment first. You?"

"No appointments until this afternoon, but I have to draft a motion and get it over to family court by then. What do you need from your apartment?"

"Clothes. Unless you think I can get away with a belt and heels with this?" She gestured to my dress shirt, which hung open, and she had nothing on underneath it. Loving the easy access, I cupped one tit in my hand before reaching down and kissing her perky nipple.

"Why don't you keep some clothes here for the nights you stay over, so you don't have to run home commando in your clothes from the day before?" Even though the statement came without much thought, it didn't freak me out after I'd put it out there. Odd.

Emerie looked up at me. "Are you offering me a drawer?"

I shrugged. "Take half the closet, if you want. I don't like the idea of you running around the city with your skirt and no underwear on in the mornings—even though I don't really get why you can't just turn them inside out and wear 'em again."

She crinkled up her nose. "That's a guy thing."

After she finished putting on the makeup she kept in her purse, she got dressed and went back to her apartment. I called Alexa and left a message that I'd be by to pick Beck up for the weekend about five tonight.

Grateful that her voicemail had answered instead of her, I went downstairs to get some work done, still in my good mood—only to be greeted by a process server waiting at my door. I was a divorce lawyer; it wasn't unusual to be served first thing in the morning. It was unusual for the service to be from an Atlanta court.

———

I'd just finished reading the same paragraph in the motion for the fifth time.

> *Changes have occurred since the last custody judgment that necessitate a modification in the child visitation order. The changes were unknown at the time of the final decree and justify a revision to the custody arrangement.*

It was the next part that had me sitting in my chair, rather than heading to Alexa's apartment, because I feared what I was capable of after reading the rest.

> *Annexed hereto, paternity has been established for Levi Archer Bodine and not the defendant granted visitation in the final decree of custody.*

> *The petitioner requests a modification from equal shared custody to allow the*

*defendant visitation every other weekend for a period of eight hours. The increased visitation of the petitioner is to allow time for the introduction of the biological father to the minor subject child.*

*Further, the defendant's shared custody should be reduced based upon recent incidents of child neglect. Namely, the defendant has engaged in conduct which put the subject child at risk by exposing the child to known criminals. As a direct result of that conduct, the subject child has been injured.*

*Wherefore, the petitioner has reason to be concerned about the safety of the minor subject child and requests an immediate modification of the custody decree.*

The annexed documentation in support of the petition included a copy of the purported criminal's most recent arrest and an emergency room report. The criminal was Emerie, and of course, it was only a partial copy of the charges of indecent exposure. There was no mention that she'd been a teenager or that the charge was reduced last month. In addition to that crock of shit, there was a copy of the emergency room report bearing the diagnosis of accidental burn, along with an affidavit from a nurse that verified Beck was brought in with his father and the woman who had been watching him at the time of the injury: *Emerie Rose.*

After the third time I reached voicemail, I couldn't take it anymore and headed to Alexa's in person. It wasn't the smartest idea, considering the mood I was in, but I needed to have it out with her. I had only one thing to lord over this woman, but I had lots of it: money. I wasn't above paying her to cut this shit out. *Again*. This little game was retaliation for telling her she couldn't take Beck on a two-week tour following the NASCAR circuit. She needed to show me who was in control. I knew my ex-wife; she was cunning and all about making sure she had the upper hand. Our fight, and likely seeing Emerie, had left her feeling that I needed to be put in my place.

The first knock on her apartment door went unanswered and only served to piss me off and make me knock louder. After two impatient minutes, I took out my key. When I'd kicked Alexa out and rented her this place, I'd kept a key for myself. There'd never been an occasion to use it, but I was done with her avoiding me.

The lock was jammed, but after a minute of jiggling the key around, I felt some sense of relief hearing the loud clank as it slid open. Not wanting to get smacked in the head with a pan, I cracked the door open and yelled.

"Alexa?"

No answer.

A second time. "Alexa?"

The hallway was quiet, and there wasn't a sound coming from inside the apartment. Deciding it was safe, I pushed the door open.

And my heart stopped when I saw what was inside.

# CHAPTER THIRTY-SEVEN

# EMERIE

Something was going on.

Office doors had been slamming for the entire last half of my telephone counseling session. In the past ten minutes, yelling had started as well. One voice was a very pissed-off Drew, and the other was Roman, who'd recently arrived. He frequently did investigations for Drew, but whatever was happening seemed way more personal than just a case.

After apologizing again to my patients—lying and telling them I was going to have a word with the construction crew about their language—I hung up and started toward my closed office door. I stopped upon hearing my name.

"Emerie? What the hell has she got to do with this?"

"Alexa basically told the court that I'm sleeping with an ex-con."

"An ex-con? What'd she do? Get a parking ticket?"

"It's a long story, but she was arrested for indecency last month."

"What?"

"Happened when she was a teenager. It was an appearance ticket for skinny dipping that turned into a warrant because she hadn't paid it. It's a misdemeanor...nothing more serious than a parking ticket. But, of course, Alexa is making it out to be something more. The petition calls her an ex-con with a penchant for indecent exposure. And she also added in that it was the same ex-con who recently caused Beck to get burned."

"*Fuck.*"

"Yeah. Fuck. That's not the worst part. I could talk my way out of that in a New York court with the shit the judges hear here every day. But she filed the change of custody motion in Atlanta."

"How can she do that when you both live here?"

"I just came from her apartment. She's gone. Doorman said she left yesterday and gave a forwarding address. Her place is empty. *She fucking moved!*"

---

Drew wasn't a heavy drinker. He had the occasional glass of whiskey or a beer or two, but slamming them back wasn't something I'd seen him do.

*Until tonight.*

Even though he'd assured me that none of it was my fault, I still felt guilty as the catalyst for making him look like an unfit parent.

We sat in Drew's apartment; both of us had cleared our afternoon schedules. I'd promised Roman that Drew would be at the airport for their flight tomorrow morning. The two of them were flying down to Atlanta to attempt to talk to Alexa, and I was really glad Drew wasn't going alone. He couldn't even say his ex-wife's name without growling.

Closing the door behind Roman, I locked the top lock, picked up Drew's drink from the kitchen counter and dumped

VI KEELAND

the rest down the drain. Then I went to the couch where he lay with one arm covering his eyes. His legs were longer than the couch, and his feet dangled over the end. I unlaced his shoes and began to take them off.

"You trying to get me naked?" Drew slurred. "Fuck the shoes. Take off my pants."

I smiled. Even loaded, the man was still himself. "It's almost eleven o'clock. Your flight is in ten hours. I figure you need to get some sleep. The morning may not be too kind to your head."

His large shoes clomped to the floor as I slipped them off, followed by his socks.

"I can't lose my son."

My heart broke, hearing the anguish in his cracked voice.

"You won't. If you can't buy her off, you'll convince a judge that your son needs you and belongs with you."

"There's not much justice in our justice system. People like me twist it into a game every day."

I didn't know how to respond to that. I just wanted to do whatever I could to make him feel better. So I slipped off my own shoes, crawled up on the couch, and wrapped my arms around him, snuggling against his chest.

"I'm sorry this is happening. It's so clear how much you love that little boy. A judge has to see that."

He squeezed me in response, and a few minutes later, after I thought he'd drifted off to sleep, he spoke again, his words barely a whisper.

"You want kids, Oklahoma?"

"I do. I'd love to have a few and maybe adopt, too."

"You're going to be a good mom someday."

"We couldn't find her. The address she left for forwarding was her brother's place. Guy's a loser. Got to his place at two o'clock, and he was still sleeping," Drew's chuckle rumbled over the phone line. "Well, he was until he was suddenly dangling in the air from Roman's hands."

"You broke in?"

"Didn't have to. Front door wasn't even locked. Trust me, he doesn't need to. Roaches don't even want to go inside that place."

"Did he tell you where Alexa was?"

"He didn't know."

"He's lying for his sister?"

"Don't think so. He would have given her up. His skinny little junky ass was so afraid of Roman, he pissed himself. Plus, I know the guy. He would have tried to sell me where she was for enough to buy his next fix if he'd had any clue. Guy would sell his mother for twenty bucks."

"So what do you do now?"

"I got to the courthouse before they closed and filed an emergency restraining order asking the judge to force her to go back to New York. Our custody agreement doesn't allow either one of us to take Beck out of state without permission from the other. They'll add the motion to the calendar with her change of custody demand for the day after tomorrow. If we can't find her by Thursday, she'll have to at least show up for court then."

"Is there anything I can do?"

"Nah. Thanks, babe. Just hearing your voice is good for me."

I smiled. "Maybe later tonight I'll call you and this voice will have some dirty things to say."

"Yeah?"

I bit my lip. "I'm a team player. I want to help any way I can."

"I'll get rid of Roman for a while later. He likes to sit at the bar and nurse a few whiskies at the end of the day. Don't think I'll be doing that for a long time after last night. Much rather hear you come while you tell me how much you miss my cock."

"You got it. I'm going home soon."

"Okay, babe. Call me later when you're settled in."

"Drew?"

"Yeah."

"Just so you know, I miss you and your cock."

He groaned my name. "Hurry up home."

I'd never had phone sex, and I was really looking forward to calling Drew. So much so that I'd put on a cute little silky shorts-and-camisole set and some perfume for the occasion. It was a little after ten, so I figured he'd probably be settling in for the night, too. Picking up my cell, I dialed his number and smiled when he answered with a gruff voice.

"You naked?"

"No, but I can be."

My hand was on the kitchen light switch, ready to turn it off and take my cell phone to bed with me, when there was a knock at my door. Drew heard it, too.

"Someone there?"

"I think so. Hang on a second." I walked to the door and peeked through the peephole even though I knew who it was without looking. It wasn't like I had many friends in the city, much less ones who would just drop by.

"Can I call you back in a few minutes?"

"Do I want to know who it is?"

"Probably not. Give me a few minutes to get rid of him."

After I ended the call, I grabbed a sweater from the closet and pulled it on before opening the door.

"Baldwin? Is everything alright?"

"Yes, fine. I just wanted to check on you. I knocked last night, but you weren't home. So I tried this morning, and you still weren't here, and then you didn't answer my texts today. I was beginning to get worried."

My feelings for Baldwin had been so jumbled, I'd forgotten he was a good friend to me for a few years.

"I'm sorry. I didn't mean to make you worry. I'm fine. Everything is fine. Just a crazy day yesterday, followed by a hectic one today."

He didn't seem convinced, so I decided to be honest.

"I've started seeing someone; I stayed over at his place last night."

"Oh." He gave me a sad smile that seemed forced. "Well, I'm glad you're okay."

When I didn't offer to have him come in, his eyes roamed over my face like he was looking for something. I waited in awkward silence, clutching my sweater shut as I stood there.

Eventually, Baldwin gave me a curt nod, and his eyes dropped to my bare legs. "Is it the lawyer?"

For some reason, it rubbed me wrong that he called him *the lawyer* and not by his name. "Drew. Yes."

He looked into my eyes. "Are you happy?"

I didn't even have to think about the answer. "I am."

Baldwin's eyes closed briefly, and he gave me another silent nod. "Maybe we can get coffee this weekend and catch up?"

I smiled. "Sure."

Coffee at Starbucks was probably the best way to reset our friendship. The reset was entirely on my end, because Baldwin had never really been interested in me the way I'd been in him. But now that I was seeing someone, it wouldn't feel right to go out with him for dinner. Maybe someday in the future, when more time had passed between the feelings I had for Baldwin and the start of a new relationship, but right now it would just feel wrong.

After we said goodnight, I took a minute to regroup my thoughts before going to the bedroom to call Drew back. It had been a long time since my feelings for Baldwin had grown. I couldn't turn them off completely, but something had definitely changed. Even though I knew part of me would miss the unrestrained comfortableness I'd enjoyed with Baldwin when there was nothing holding me back, I realized it was more important for me to respect the boundaries I knew Drew would want me to have—like not inviting a man into my apartment this late while I was in my cute little pajamas.

Feeling content, I turned off all the lights and slipped into bed as I dialed Drew's number on my cell.

"Hey," I said.

"Visitor gone?" Wariness had crept into Drew's confident voice.

"It was Baldwin. He wanted to check on me. Apparently he knocked last night and this morning and was worried because I didn't answer his texts today either."

"What'd you tell him?"

"I told him I'd slept at my boyfriend's and had been busy, but everything was fine."

"Your boyfriend, huh? Is that what I am?" There was relief in his voice.

"Do you prefer to be called something else?"

"I don't know. What else you got?"

"Hmm...let's see...how about man who gives me many orgasms?"

"That sounds like my Indian name."

I laughed. "How about landlord with benefits or Captain Prolactinator?"

"Call me whatever you want to Professor Putz, as long as he knows you're mine."

*Mine.* I liked the sound of that. I wasn't sure how it had happened. Knowing us, it had started to blossom in the middle of a fight and flowered while I was bent over his desk, but regardless of how we got here, somehow we had. And I realized there was nowhere else I'd rather be.

"Are you alone?"

"Roman's down at the bar. Bartender is a woman. Don't think he'll miss my company."

"Okay, good." I reached over to my end table and opened the drawer. "Did you hear that?"

"Don't tell me he's knocking again."

Slipping my vibrator out of the drawer, I decided Drew needed a little distraction from the last two horrible days. I switched it on and held it close to my cell for a few seconds before lowering it down my body.

"Is that—"

"My vibrator. It's been lonely the last few weeks."

Drew growled. "Fuck. I wish I was there to watch you."

"I think I'd like that. Maybe when you get back."

"Not maybe. I'm coming straight to your place from the plane."

His reaction fueled me. I rubbed the vibrator on my clit and spoke as my voice strained.

"How about you come a different way first?"

# CHAPTER THIRTY-EIGHT

## DREW

"She's got balls," Roman not so quietly whispered to me as Alexa smiled our way while strolling into court with her lawyer, Atticus Carlyle.

My hands clenched into tight fists. After coming up empty for a day and a half looking for her, I don't know why I was surprised she'd picked that asshole. I hated that fucking guy almost as much as he hated me. He was the quintessential good ol' southern boy—thick drawl, bow tie, and worked God into his opening and closing arguments. He was also the one attorney who'd ever made me lose it in the courtroom. And we happened to be assigned the judge who'd hit me with sanctions as a result of that unraveling. It was starting to feel like nothing was a coincidence.

Needing to keep whatever semblance of calm I had left, I couldn't even look at the other side of the court. Judge Walliford took the bench, and the uniformed clerk called our docket number. He spent a few minutes reading with his glasses at the tip of his nose and then looked up.

"Well, well, well, lookie what we have here. Seems the three of us have done this little dance before *(be-fo-wah),* haven't we?

"Yes, your honor," I said.

"Sure have, your ahn-na. Good to see you again," opposing counsel drawled.

Walliford shuffled some papers and removed his glasses, then leaned back in his chair.

"Mr. Jagger, why do you think this case should be heard in a New York City courtroom instead of here in Atlanta? Do you not trust the wheels of justice to turn at the same speed as you northerners like things done?"

How the hell was I supposed to answer that? I'd filed a motion for a change in venue based on residency. I cleared my throat. "No, your honor. I'm sure this court would do a fine job in any case presented before it, but since the plaintiff and I are both residents of New York, I believe the proper jurisdiction would be New York County. According to our agreement—"

Carlyle butted in. "Your ahn-na, my client is a resident of the good state of Georgia. She was born and raised here. During her short-lived marriage to Mr. Jagger, she was a temporary resident of New York for a period of time, but she's recently bought a house in Fulton County, and *this* is the state of her residence." He held up some papers and continued. "I have here a copy of the deed to her new home, her Atlanta driver's license, and a copy of the lease where she was *temporarily* staying in New York. You'll see the lease was not even in Ms. Jagger's name."

"That's crap. The lease was in my name because I was paying for it. She's lived there for two years." I knew before I finished that I'd made a huge mistake with my outburst.

Judge Walliford wagged his finger. "I will not tolerate that language in my courtroom. You northerners might find it acceptable to communicate that way, but this is not a smoky bar or some slick city street. You will respect this bench. I'm warning you, Mr. Jagger. After your behavior last time you were in this room, you're on a very short leash."

And *that* was the best part of my day. Judge Walliford denied my motion to change venues to New York and ordered a full trial on the change in custody petition Alexa had filed—to begin two weeks from Monday. The only thing he did in my favor was enforce our current custody schedule, where I had Beck Friday, Saturday, and Sunday nights, as well as Wednesday for dinner. Although he ordered my visitation to take place in, you guessed it, *the great state of Georgia.*

I waited until we were outside of the building before even attempting to approach Alexa. The last thing I needed was for her to scream that I was harassing her and have Walliford lock me up.

I gritted my teeth. "Alexa, can I speak to you, please?"

Carlyle took her elbow. "I don't think that's a good idea, Alexa."

I ignored him, looking my ex-wife in the eye. "You owe me at least this much. It's been more than two years since I found out, and it still goddamn hurts. But I've never let Beck see or feel anything different than what he is to me. No matter what some fucking blood test says, he's my son." She looked away. "Look at me, Alexa. *Look at me.*" When she finally met my eyes, I continued. "You know me. Will I give up even if I lose in two weeks?"

Her lawyer stepped in. "Are you threatening my client?"

I continued to hold Alexa's eyes. "No. I'm asking her to put our son first and not drag this out."

She took a deep breath. "He's not your son. Let's go, Mr. Carlyle."

Thank God Roman was standing next to me. He wrapped his arms around my chest so I couldn't go after her, even as she walked away.

Before the flight home, I attempted unsuccessfully to sync my calendar so I could spend a few hours shuffling my schedule in order to spend Monday, Tuesday, and half the day Wednesday in New York, then be back in Atlanta for dinner with Beck on Wednesday night. I'd then stay in Atlanta and work remotely Thursday through Friday before I picked up Beck again for the weekend. It wasn't going to be easy to cram an entire week's worth of client appointments, depositions, and court appearances into two and a half days, but what choice did I have? My son needed to come first. He was already confused by the sudden move and not being able to spend his weekends at Daddy's place. I also had little doubt that if I missed a single visitation, Judge Walliford would hear about it. I didn't need to give him any more ammunition to use against me.

Even though my son was my priority, I had another focus now that I was back on New York soil. I hadn't been sure I'd be able to catch the last flight home from Atlanta, so I didn't mention to Emerie that there was a chance I'd be back tonight. It was late, almost midnight, but I gave the cabbie her address instead of mine anyway.

For the six days I'd been gone, we'd talked every night—and most nights ended with my jerking off to the hum of her vibrator. It had helped take the edge off, but at the same time also made me hungry for the real thing.

The inside of her apartment building was quiet. I made my way up in the elevator without anyone questioning me, since her building had no doorman. I hated that, though. She needed a safer place to live—any asshole could be knocking on her door. Come to think of it, one was about to. Setting my bags down to knock, I glanced over at the apartment next door.

*Yeah. She definitely needs a safer place to live.*

After two rounds of knocking—the second one so loud I thought I might wake a neighbor or two—a sleepy-looking Emerie came to the door.

Since she'd been asleep, her contacts were out, and she had her glasses on. *God, I love her in those things.*

"Hey. What are you—"

I didn't give her a chance to finish, didn't even say hello. At least not in so many words anyway. Instead, I helped myself inside, walking her backward as I not-so-gently took her face in my hands and kissed her. I kissed her hard and long, kicking the door closed behind me before lifting her so her legs could wrap around my waist. It felt incredible—like the cure for the perpetual suck-ass feeling I'd had for the last week.

When I slipped my hand under her sexy little sleep shorts and grabbed a handful of her backside, she moaned into my mouth, and I had the urge to put her down so I could fist pump. But that would have meant moving my already fully erect cock away from the warmth between her spread legs, and there was no damn way that was happening. So instead, I somehow made my way to the couch without tripping and unceremoniously dropped her on it before covering her with my body.

"I've fucking missed you." My voice was raw.

Emerie's eyes were hooded and happy. "I guessed that much from your hello."

I started to suck on her neck as my hands moved to take down her shorts and underwear at the same time. "Did you miss me?"

Her fingernails dug into my back as I nipped my way from her neck to her ear. "Yes," she breathed. "I did. A lot."

I bit down on her earlobe as I stroked two fingers up and down her pussy. "How much. Are you wet for me?" I already knew the answer, of course, but I waited for her to tell me.

"Yes."

I rubbed her clit with my thumb. "Yes what?"

"Yes, I'm wet for you."

"Tell me your *pussy* is wet for me. I want to hear you say it." I was already unbuckling my pants. Who knew how dexterous I was—somehow managing to undress both of us with one hand while sucking on her neck, her ear, her lips, and the other hand rubbing her wet pussy.

"My...pussy is wet for you."

God, there was nothing sexier than hearing Emerie say she was hot for me. The last week of hell was a distant memory, and all I could think about was being inside of her.

"I missed you so much," I told her again, because even though I'd already said it, it was just so goddamn true.

And I needed to be inside of her. She was going to have to take a big, fat IOU on the foreplay this time—although from the sound of her panting, the feel of her wet heat, she didn't seem to mind. I pushed in slowly, my body shaking to keep under control. When I was fully seated, I would have sworn that frayed nerve endings had come alive for the first time in years. Her tight pussy enveloped my cock, and her legs wrapped around my waist, clenching me even tighter.

*Jesus, I don't remember the last time it felt this good.*

I started to move, mostly because I needed to feel that tight vise milking me as I slid in and out, and I realized I wasn't going to last very long. It was just too incredible. Emerie opened her eyes as I pulled out, and our gazes locked. Taking both her hands, I twined our fingers together and lifted them over her head. I wanted to kiss her, but I couldn't stop looking at her long enough. The way she panted with every thrust down and made a little moaning sound with every stroke back was mesmerizing to watch.

Her hips joined in, rocking in unison with mine. Up and down, in and out.

"Oh, God, Drew. Right there. Don't stop."

Miraculously, I managed to hold back long enough for her to come. I watched it transform her face—her head tilted to the side, her eyes rolled closed, her full lips parted, and it was the most beautiful thing I'd ever seen.

When she'd started to come down, I picked up my speed, thrusts coming harder and faster, chasing her orgasm as my own pushed to the brink. Just as I was about to explode, I realized why it had felt so different, why every nerve was suddenly awakened for the first time.

I hadn't put on a condom. *Shit*. I was going to have to pull…

"Em, I didn't—" I attempted to explain why I was about to ruin her ending, but I was running out of words as fast as I was endurance. "No condom."

She looked me in the eyes. "It's okay. I'm on the pill. Come inside of me. *Please*."

There was nothing I wanted more than that—to pour myself into her. My body ached for it with animalistic need, but as I let go, it also felt like I was giving her something I'd been holding back on a much deeper level.

For the first time since the night I met Alexa and she told me she was on the pill, I took a chance on trusting someone.

Only, for some reason, it didn't feel like a chance with Emerie.
It just felt right.

# CHAPTER THIRTY-NINE

## EMERIE

I felt the bed dip as Drew got up. "Where are you going?"

"I was trying not to wake you." He walked around to my side and kissed my forehead. "It's early. Go back to sleep."

"What time is it?"

"Five-thirty."

I leaned up on my elbows in the dark. "Why are you up so early?"

"Need to get into the office and figure out how I'm cramming the six days of work I have booked into five already, into only two days a week for a while."

"I take it you haven't looked at your calendar in a day or two?"

"Tried to, but the damn thing was locked and wouldn't sync up."

I settled back into the bed and pulled the cover up. "Your first appointment isn't until ten. I didn't think you were back until this morning, or I would have started today earlier. Everything is rescheduled for the next two weeks for you. They're long days, but I was able to get all of your in-person meetings into two days each week. I converted one in-person meeting to a telephone conference, and you have that from

Atlanta on Thursday next week. But everything else is all set. I also reworked my schedule the opposite way, so I'm light on the days you're here and full the days you're gone. That way I can help out with whatever secretarial stuff you need done to keep your day moving."

Drew was quiet for a minute, and I started to worry maybe I'd overstepped and I shouldn't have gone into his calendar. But I'd wanted to do what I could to help. The bedroom was dark, and I heard the rustle of his clothes—although I wasn't sure if they were coming off or going on until he climbed back into bed. I felt his warm body press up against my side. He was still silent, so I turned to face him.

"Did I overstep?"

He stroked my cheek. "No, babe. You didn't overstep."

"You're being so quiet. I thought maybe I'd upset you."

"Just thinking."

"About what?"

"How much right now I feel like I'm home, and I haven't set foot in my apartment in a week."

That quite possibly could've been the sweetest thing anyone's ever said to me. He was also right. I'd been jittery all week and hadn't realized until now that I'd settled the minute I looked through the peephole last night.

"I know what you mean. You make me feel calm. At peace, I guess it is."

"Yeah?" His hand slid down my cheek, and his thumb rubbed the hollow of my neck.

"Yeah."

"I'm glad." He kissed the top of my nose. "You know what I'm thinking now?"

"What's that?"

"How I should thank you for fixing my schedule. Whether

I should use my mouth to eat you for breakfast or turn you over and take you from behind while I finger your ass."

I giggled. "You're really crass. You went from sweet to pig in ten seconds flat."

His hand at my neck dropped to my breast where his finger grazed over it and then pinched...hard. "You like my crass mouth."

Deciding he was right, I didn't fight the truth. "What were my choices again?"

I heard the smile in his words. "Mouth or all fours?"

I swallowed. "Why only one? You don't have to be at the office until ten."

"You want some more coffee?" It was after six p.m., and Drew still had another client coming in and a dozen phone calls to return.

"I'd love some. Thank you."

I made his coffee just the way he liked it and brought it into his office. He was reading something with a blue back that I'd signed for an hour ago.

"Thanks," he said without looking up.

"You seem to be thanking me a lot today."

"Just wait until you see what I have up my sleeve for tonight," he replied.

I knew he was busy, so I didn't want to take up too much of his time screwing around. He stopped me as I got to the door.

"My place tonight? You can sleep in while I get an early start tomorrow, or take a bath if you want. My new slave-driver of a secretary has me booked starting at seven a.m."

"Are you sure you wouldn't get a better night's sleep if I stayed home? You need your rest with all the traveling and stress you have going on."

Drew let the packet of papers he was reading from drop to the desk. "Come here."

I walked back to stand in front of his desk.

"Closer."

When I stepped around to where he sat, he surprised me by yanking me down onto his lap. "Four hours of sleep next to you is better than eight in an empty bed."

"You better watch it, Jagger. You're losing your sour and turning sweet on me."

"I've been sweet on you since the first night you attempted to kick my ass. Now go. Go get your stuff. You don't need to stick around here if you're done, and we're supposed to get snow later tonight."

I left to do as Drew had instructed—pack an overnight bag and head back.

The entire trip to my place, I couldn't stop thinking about him. Drew was the kind of man who didn't make it easy to get past his exterior, but when you did, it was worth the fight he'd put up to keep you out. Over the last week, it felt like our relationship had really turned a corner.

I even called my parents while I was packing my bag and decided to tell them about the new man in my life—something I rarely did. Of late—say, I don't know, the last three years—it had been because there *was* no new man, but I also knew my mother would worry about me. She'd worry I was going to get hurt, or worry I'd unknowingly picked a serial killer to date—because, of course, everyone who lived in a big city had the potential to be a closet serial killer. So I was careful how much I divulged.

"That's wonderful, honey. How did you meet?"

*Uh...he broke into my office and then bailed me out of jail the next day. Best first date ever.*

"He's actually the landlord for my new office."

"And he's a nice young man?"

*We didn't fight...today.*

"Yes, Mom. He's very nice."

"What does he do for a living?"

*Well, he thrives on misogynistic tendencies he developed because of his lying, cheating ex-wife, and attempts to extricate men from their failed marriages by leaving women penniless.*

"He's an attorney. Family law."

"An *attorney*. Very nice. And family law. That's a noble profession. When do we get to meet this fellow?"

"I'm not sure, Mom. He's so busy with work right now."

*And fighting for custody of his son...who isn't technically his son because his bitch of an ex-wife saw him as her meal ticket when she got pregnant with another man's baby.*

She sighed. "Well, just make sure he has the right values. Money and a handsome face often cause temporary blindness."

"Yes, Mom."

We talked a little while longer and then, I have no idea where it came from, but I asked her a question that fell out of my mouth.

"How did you know Dad was the right one for you?"

"I stopped using the word *I* when I looked into the future."

"What do you mean?"

"Before I met your father, all of my plans were just that— *my* plans. But after I met him, even after only a few weeks,

I stopped seeing the future as mine and started seeing it as *ours*. I didn't even notice it for a while, but when I talked about things that were coming up—Saturday nights, holidays, whatever—I eventually realized I'd started saying *we*, not *I*."

I stopped at the grocery store on the way back to the office and picked up some things to make dinner. Drew was going to be living in a hotel in Atlanta and working long hours when he was here, so I figured he'd appreciate a home-cooked meal. He came in as I was taking the lasagna out of the oven.

"Smells good in here."

"Hope you like lasagna."

"It's my second-favorite meal."

"What's your first?"

He came up behind me, brushed my hair to one side, and kissed my neck. His word vibrated against my skin. "You."

"Control yourself. You need to enjoy a homemade meal when you can. Your next few weeks are going to be busy."

I opened the drawer to the right of the stove to get a spatula and found two matchbox cars and an old flip phone in with the cooking implements.

"I wondered where you kept the toy cars."

Drew chuckled. "When I tell Beck to clean up, he just shoves shit in drawers. Last year I found crayons in the spoon section of the utensil drawer. He'd taken the spoons and thrown them all in the garbage. When I asked him why, he shrugged and said we didn't need them because we could scoop things better with our hands but nothing else made color on paper."

I smiled. "He has a point."

Drew reached into the drawer and took out the flip phone. "Remember when we first met, and I looked through the pictures on your phone?"

"Yes. You told me the best way to get to know someone is to look at their cell phone pictures when they least expect it. Then after I let you look through mine, I found out yours was empty." I exaggerated a sigh. "Jackass."

Drew opened the flip phone, pressed some buttons, and offered it to me. "I'm gonna go wash up and change before dinner. This is Beck's cell. It doesn't have service, but he likes to use it to take pictures. Every time I start to doubt whether I'm doing the right thing by staying in his life, if I'm confusing things by not backing off and letting his biological father step in, I scroll through those pics. Take a look."

Drew went to the bedroom, and I poured myself a glass of wine and sat down at the dining room table to look through the pictures.

The first photo was of Drew shaving. He stood in the bathroom wearing nothing but a towel wrapped around his waist. There was shaving cream on the left side of his face, and he held the razor near his chin after shaving one line down. The other cheek was already cleanly shaven. Off to the side, in the reflection of the mirror, I could see Beck holding the camera with one hand, and the other held a spatula covered in shaving cream up to his face, which was also half cleared of white foam.

The next photo was of Beck standing in a stream. It looked like it could be upstate somewhere. It was probably taken a year ago, given how much Beck's face had matured. He wore waders and smiled huge for the camera as he held up a small fish he must have just plucked from the stream.

I kept scrolling—photos of Beck and his dad ice skating, a shot of them sitting together on the subway, one of Drew reading *Harold and the Purple Crayon* in Beck's bed, them riding bikes with Roman in Central Park, one that I had to turn the phone upside down to realize I was looking at the picture right side up—it was Beck taking the photo of the two of them while on Drew's shoulders. He'd leaned over to snap the shot of their faces.

Photo after photo revealed their life together and showed just how much Drew *was* Beck's father, no matter what a lab test said.

The very last photo surprised me. I hadn't even known Beck had a phone at the time it was taken, much less that he had snapped a picture. It was the afternoon we'd gone ice skating—prior to my falling and injuring my ankle. Beck must have been standing on one side of the rink, while Drew and I were on the other, and I attempted to skate. My legs were spread wide—something I couldn't seem to stop that day— and I was laughing on my way to falling into an ungracious split. Drew had one arm wrapped around my waist, trying to hoist me back up, and was looking down at me while he too was laughing. We looked so happy—almost...like we were falling in love.

My heart swelled in my chest. Drew was right. The best way to get to know someone was to steal glances at their pictures. He looked through the pictures and saw the love of a father and son—a reminder of why he needed to fight. I saw a good man, one fiercely passionate about the things he loved and who would do anything to protect them. Rubbing my finger across the screen as I stared at the picture of us, of me falling, I realized I'd fallen in more ways than one that day.

I had to blink back tears to keep my emotions from getting the best of me, and decided I should get up and cut the lasagna to busy myself.

Still preoccupied, I wasn't thinking and grabbed the side of the hot lasagna pan to turn it so I could cut.

"Damn it." I shook my hand and flipped on the kitchen faucet to run cold water over the mild burn. *I'm batting a thousand around this stove.*

Of course, Drew appeared at that moment. "What happened?"

"I touched the hot pan. It's not bad, just stings a little."

Drew took my hand out of the stream of running cold water, inspected it, and returned it when he was done.

"I'll serve. Go sit. I don't want to end up in the ER for a third time already this year."

We spent the entire dinner catching up, since we hadn't exactly spoken too much last night or this morning—unless you counted communicating with our bodies. Drew filled me in on his custody-trial strategy, and I told him about some new clients I'd taken on. The entire thing felt bizarrely domestic and natural. After we were done eating, Drew loaded the dishwasher while I cleaned the counters and table.

"Where was that picture taken of Beck fishing? He looked so adorable in his little waders."

"Upstate. Roman has a cabin in the mountains up in New Paltz. It's rustic, but has a big old clawfoot bathtub you'd like. We should go up in the spring."

"I'd love that."

A few hours later, we were brushing our teeth and getting ready for bed when Drew said, "Tess called today."

"Who?"

"My secretary. She said her doctor thinks she can come back part time in two weeks. Her recovery after the hip surgery is better than expected, and moving around is good as part of her physical therapy."

"That's great." In the whirlwind of the last month, I hadn't really been looking for a new office. The first week I'd called one real estate agent, who'd shown me closet space in areas I didn't want to be for more than twice my budget. I'd taken a break after that. Although at the moment, the thought of what I could get for my money wasn't half as depressing as the thought of not seeing Drew everyday anymore.

"I'm sorry. I need to get back to looking for new space."

Drew's brow furrowed. "What are you talking about?"

I rinsed my mouth and spoke to Drew in the mirror. "Our deal. You let me stay while your secretary was out in exchange for answering the phones and helping out until I found a new place."

He turned me around with his hands on my shoulders. "You're not going anywhere."

"I can't afford to pay my share of what the rent must be for your office."

"We'll work something out."

"But—"

He silenced me with a kiss, but kept his face close to mine. "We'll figure it out. Let us just get through dealing with this shit in Atlanta, and then we'll sit down and talk about it, if you want. Okay?"

I didn't want to add any more stress to what he was already feeling, so I nodded. "Okay."

It wasn't until we'd gotten into bed, and I ran the entire day through my mind, that I connected some of the dots from the last few hours.

*"Roman has a cabin in the mountains up in New Paltz. We should go up in the spring."*

*"We'll figure it out. Let us just get through dealing with this shit in Atlanta..."*

*"How did you know Dad was the right one for you?"*

*"I stopped using the word I when I looked into the future."*

Drew was settling into *we* as much as I was, whether he was aware of it or not.

When he slipped into bed next to me, I wrapped my arms around him tight. Maybe, just maybe, neither one of us had found the right one before now...because we hadn't met each other yet.

# CHAPTER FORTY

## DREW

It had been the longest three weeks of my life.

The bailiff called the court into session. Judge Walliford took his sweet-ass time—I'm sure he'd call it *proper southern time*—to walk to the bench. Then he sat and rifled through a bunch of papers. Roman sat in the first row of the gallery right behind me, and he leaned forward to squeeze my shoulder for reassurance as I waited to find out how much my visitation was going to take a hit. I knew it was coming. I just had no idea how bad it would be.

The last time I was this nervous, this on edge about what was going to happen to the rest of my life, was the day I married Alexa. And we know how that fucking turned out. I looked over at my for-once-conservatively-dressed ex-wife. She, of course, stared straight ahead, not returning my stare. That woman was a piece of work.

Finally, Walliford finished shuffling papers around and cleared his throat before diving into a bunch of formalities for the record. "Docket numb-ah *179920-16. Jagger vs. Jagger*. Petition for reduction in custody. Cross motion to compel relocation and enforce the previous signed custody agreement."

Then he finally looked up. "Be-fo-wah I git started with my decisions, I'd like to take a moment to say that this was not an easy case. I had to consider the rights of both parties present in this courtroom, the rights of a biological father who was robbed of years of bonding with his son, as well as what is in the best interest of the boy."

He looked straight at Alexa. "Ms. Jagger, I hold you largely accountable for the mess we have here today. If you had one inkling of a doubt that your husband might not be the boy's father, you had a duty to get to the truth when that blessed child was born."

For the first time, I felt a sudden pang of hope. Walliford had never shown his hand, and I'd assumed he'd fallen for the southern charm Alexa had been laying on thick since day one. What came out of his mouth next shocked the shit out of me even more.

"Mr. Jagger, I'd like to commend you on your devotion to young Beckett. It's clear that you love and care for the child no differently than if things had turned out differently with the results of the paternity test some years ago."

Inwardly, I jumped into the air and fist pumped, but somehow I managed to feign humility.

"Thank you, your honor. That means a lot coming from you."

"Right. Well, that being said, let's get to the business at hand today. On Ms. Jagger's petition for a change in custody, I find no circumstances that warrant a modification. The order setting the visitation of Andrew M. Jagger is hereby affirmed without change."

He looked at Alexa. "Ms. Jagger, the fact that your petition to increase custody was in order to allow Mr. Bodine to start to have visitation with your son is a step in the right direction. However, it has not gone unnoticed that Mr. Bodine has not once made an appearance during these proceedings. To be quite frank, his lack of interest and participation makes me question his priorities and interest in his son's life. Regardless, he is the boy's father, and I'm going to grant Mr. Bodine some visitation. However, this time will come out of *your* time with your son, not Mr. Jagger's time. This court hereby grants Levi Bodine's petition for custody in the amount of eight hours per week. After a relationship is established, and Mr. Bodine has proven to this court his desire to be involved in his son's life, I'll consider additional visitation. However, this likely will also come from your time, Ms. Jagger."

I stood before the court utterly dumbfounded. Mentally, I was busting through the yellow tape at the finish line with my hands held high as I finished the almost-four-week-long marathon I'd been running. I just couldn't believe I'd won.

Behind me, Roman let out a triumphant *yes*, and I stood there stunned, feeling like it was a dream and any second I was going to wake up to have the nightmare of reality hit me.

Then Judge Walliford finished. "Lastly, on Mr. Jagger's cross motion to compel Alexa and Beckett Jagger's relocation to their home in New York City, that motion is denied."

Wait. *What?* "Your honor, if I am retaining my visitation, how can you deny my motion for my son's return home?"

"Isn't that obvious, Mr. Jagger? Your son is going to be here in the great state of Georgia. You might want to think about relocating." He banged his gavel and stood to leave the courtroom.

"This is bullshit! I have a practice in New York. Alexa doesn't even have a job here."

Walliford froze mid-step. "That'll be one thousand dollars for using that language and tone in my courtroom. You don't like my decision, take it up with the court of appeals."

I held the bathroom wall to keep myself upright long enough to take a piss, then stumbled from the bathroom back to my barstool. Tie and jacket God knows where, zipper still open, shirt half tucked in and half hanging out—I looked as trashed as I felt.

"I'll have another on the rocks." I slid my highball glass toward the bartender. He looked at Roman, then at me. "You gotta ask my father's permission or something? Just give me the damn drink."

Did I mention I'm an even bigger dick than usual when I'm drunk?

My cell phone jumped around on top of the bar. Emerie. It was the third time she'd called. Also the third time I didn't answer.

"Not gonna answer that again?" Roman asked.

I slurred, "Whassssthepoint?"

"How about to let the lady have a good night's sleep tonight? God knows you're gonna have one when you pass out by five p.m, you selfish prick." Roman drew on his beer and set it down on the bar. "She loves you. You'll work it out."

"Work what out? It's over."

"What are you talking about? Don't be an asshole. It's the first woman I've ever really seen you fall for. How long we been friends?"

"Too long apparently, if you're going to start lecturing me."

"What did I tell you in the back of the church right before you married Alexa?"

In the condition I was in, most of my life was blurry, but that morning was always crystal clear. I'd thought about Roman offering me his keys to split on more than one occasion since. "*Car is in the back if you want to bail,*" he'd said. When I'd reminded him Alexa was carrying my baby, and I was doing the right thing, he'd said, "*Fuck the right thing.*"

The bartender brought my drink, and since I was still able to remember a portion of my life I had no desire to recollect, I promptly sucked back half the glass.

Then I turned to look at Roman—well, two Romans. "You never did say I told you so."

He shook his head. "Nope. Won't say it if you don't take my advice and figure shit out with Emerie either. Not much on rubbing bad choices in people's faces."

"Sometimes the choice is made for you by circumstance."

Roman chuckled. "That's crap, and you know it." He paused. "Remember Nancy Irvine?"

It took me a minute to reach back into the depths of my alcohol-marinated brain. "Chicken pox girl?"

He tilted his beer in my direction. "That's the one."

"What about her?"

"Remember the pact we made never to go for the same girl?"

"Yeah."

"Well, after you move to Atlanta and leave Emerie heartbroken because you're too stupid to try to figure out how to make it work, I'll be there to comfort her—among other things. Payback's a bitch."

"Fuck you."

"What do you care? She's just pussy to keep you busy. Not worth your trouble."

As if on cue, my phone lit up with Emerie's name, indicating a text had arrived. I grabbed it and my drink from the bar and stood.

Wobbling on my feet, I leaned in to my friend. "Fuck you."

Then I stormed off to find the hotel elevator.

# CHAPTER FORTY-ONE

## DREW

If I could have just cracked open my skull and let a few of the little trapped drummers out, I might have had a chance of getting up off my couch.

It was a fucking miracle I'd gotten onto the plane at all. Would never have happened had it not been for Roman, who dragged my hung-over ass from that hotel room this morning at six a.m.

Now it was noon. I'd been home for more than an hour, and I finally grew a set of balls and responded to Emerie.

I *texted* back.

Yeah. *Balls*. Sure.

And I lied.

It wasn't the first time. Certainly wouldn't be the last.

**Drew: *Sorry about last night. Was sick as a dog. Food poisoning. Bad sushi, I think.***

The little dots started jumping around immediately.

**Emerie: *Just glad you're okay. I was worried. What happened in court?***

Admitting the truth would mean dealing with it, and I wasn't ready yet.

**Drew:** *Judge adjourned handing down his decision until next week.*

**Emerie:** *Sigh. Okay. Well, maybe that's good. He's really giving it attention.*

I couldn't be a dick when she was trying so hard to remain positive.

**Drew:** *Maybe.*

**Emerie:** *When are you coming back?*

That was when I started to feel like a real shithead. It was one thing to hold off telling her about the decision. In my head I could justify that as avoiding hurting her, but sitting upstairs lying to her when she was probably downstairs answering my phone...that was just being a coward.

That realization didn't make me any less of an asshole though.

**Drew:** *Probably get the last flight out tonight. It'll be late by the time I'm back.*

**Emerie:** *Can't wait to see you.*

I finally said something that wasn't a lie.

**Drew:** *Yeah. Me too.*

There was a mirror in the lobby that reflected the hallway leading back to the private offices. I halted when I caught sight of Emerie—so fucking beautiful. So sweet and honest and everything good. My palms began to sweat as I stood there watching her. Her door was closed, and she was writing something on the whiteboard, probably something positive about making things work that would make me feel like an even bigger scumbag when I read it.

I'd spent the last twenty-four hours thinking of how it should go down, what would hurt her the least. There was no reason to tell her what had happened in court. She believed relationships could endure anything if two people worked at it. There was no doubt in my mind she'd want to try staying together while we'd be separated by almost nine hundred miles. At first, it might even seem to work. But eventually shit would start to fall apart. It always does. We probably wouldn't even realize how bad things had gotten until it blew up in our faces. Emerie had just settled into her life in New York, letting her live it was the right thing to do.

So all I could seem to come up with was getting it over with quickly. Don't drag this shit out and try to do the long-distance thing—because that will just waste more of her time. She wasted three years of her life hanging on to that asshole Baldwin; I wasn't about to lead her on like that. Fast and complete detachment—like ripping off a Band-Aid. The sting hurts like a motherfucker, but then when you let the fresh air in, you go from covering up a wound to healing.

She capped the marker and took a step back, reading whatever she'd just written. A slow smile spread across her face, and the headache I'd finally just gotten rid of rushed back with a vengeance.

I took a deep breath and headed to my office.

Emerie stepped out of hers just as I was about to pass.

"Hey, sleepyhead." She wrapped her arms around my neck. "Too bad you didn't take a little longer. I was about to go upstairs to wake you." She kissed me on the lips and added, "Naked."

"Emerie..." I cleared my throat because my voice was pathetically cracking. "We need to—" I never got to finish my sentence, because before I could even add the word *talk*, both our phones started ringing, and the UPS guy yelled from the lobby. Instead of ignoring it, I jumped at the reprieve like the no-balls jerk I was.

Then, after the UPS guy left, the building super came to talk to me about some work they were going to do where they'd need to cut the water for about two hours tomorrow. By the time I'd extricated myself from that conversation, my client had showed up twenty minutes early for his appointment. I couldn't very well make him wait in the lobby while I dumped my girlfriend, so my conversation with Emerie was going to be delayed for at least an hour.

But one appointment ran into the next, and one hour ran into two, and suddenly it was almost seven o'clock at night. Emerie had done nothing but smile and look happy to have me back all day. She'd even ordered me lunch and sat in the lobby bullshitting with one of my clients for ten minutes so I could gobble down the food. Now all of my excuses were gone, and the office was quiet.

I stared out my window, drinking the coffee that had magically appeared on my desk a half-hour ago, when Emerie came into my office. I knew this because of the click-clack of her heels, not because I turned around.

She came up behind me and wrapped her hands around my waist. "Crazy day."

"Yeah. Thanks for everything. For lunch, coffee, answering the phones and door all day. Everything."

She leaned her head against my back. "Of course. We're a good team. Don't you think?"

I closed my eyes. Damn. *Just rip the Band-Aid off, Drew, you pussy. Rip it the fuck off.* I swallowed and turned around to face her.

"Emerie...I'm not cut out to be on a team."

She laughed, probably not yet fully understanding what I was saying. Then she looked up and saw my somber face. Her smile wilted.

"What are you talking about? You're a great team player. I pick up where you need me to, and you do the same for me."

*Rip the fucking Band-Aid off. Fast.*

"No, Emerie. That's what an employee does for their employer. We're not a team."

She looked like she'd been hit with a physical blow. Her plump bottom lip quivered for a half a second, and then she regrouped—her entire demeanor changing. Arms that had been casually at her side folded into a protective stance over her chest, and she straightened her spine. The fucked-up thing was, for a brief second, I got *turned on* watching her jump into fight mode. After all, arguing was how we'd started this mess to begin with. But it was definitely not the time or place to think with my dick.

"Every relationship goes through periods where one person needs to lean on the other more. There will come a day when I'll need to lean on you."

The relationship counselor in her kicked in, and I realized I needed to be blunt. So rather than ripping off the Band-Aid, I sliced open a new wound.

"I don't want you to lean on me, Emerie. I need to end things between us."

She took a step back, so I stepped up to the plate again and slammed home. "My son is my priority, and there isn't room for anything else in my life."

Emerie's voice was a whisper. "I understand."

"I'm sorry." Force of habit, I reached out to touch her shoulder, give her comfort, but she backed away like my hand was fire.

Looking down, she said, "I left your messages on the desk, and your first appointment was moved up to seven-thirty."

There was so much I should have said, but all I did was nod. Which she didn't even see.

Emerie walked to the door of my office, and all I wanted to do was take back the last five minutes—rewind time and tell her I didn't just want to be her teammate, I wanted to be her whole fucking team. But instead I stood there and watched her walk away. Because it would only be harder a month from now or a year from now—*long-distance relationships don't fucking work*. One of us would be a hell of a lot worse off when time passed and someone cheated.

Emerie disappeared into her office and came back out a moment later wearing her coat with her laptop and purse slung over her shoulder. She gently pulled her office door closed—so gently, I almost didn't even hear her leaving. Maybe that was the point. But I did, and when I looked up to catch one last glimpse of her, I saw that she was crying. I had to grip the chair in front of me in order to keep myself from going after her.

Then she was gone.

And as I stood in place for the next hour with shit whirling through my mind, all I could think was—who was I trying to protect here?

Her...or *me*.

# CHAPTER FORTY-TWO

## DREW

I didn't think it was possible to get any more miserable than I'd been the last week. Alexa and I had fought for an hour when I picked up Beck, and then she started in right where she'd left off when I brought him back two days later. My son hadn't felt well all weekend and wanted to know why we couldn't go home to my place anymore. I didn't know what to tell him, and the longer I left shit in limbo, the harder it was getting.

To make matters worse, my flight back to New York was delayed for six hours, and the last decent night's sleep I'd had was the night before the judge handed down his decision. Even the flight attendant asked me if I was feeling okay. The truth of the matter was, I wasn't feeling okay—I was fucking miserable trying to figure out my move to Atlanta. Although that wasn't the *real* reason for my recent hatred of life.

By the time my flight landed at JFK, it was midnight. I was so exhausted from lack of sleep, I thought I might actually pass out tonight, finally get some desperately needed shut-eye. But then I made the mistake of stopping in the office, just to look around.

It was quiet. I didn't expect Emerie to be here this late. She'd avoided me at all costs before I left for Atlanta anyway—coming to the office only to meet her in-person appointments and leaving immediately after. I presumed she was doing the rest of her working from home. Plus, having access to my schedule, she'd have known I was due back earlier in the evening, so I was certain she'd be staying away.

I dropped my bags at the reception desk and walked through the eerily silent office. Emerie's door was closed, and I tried my hardest to pass it by, but I just couldn't do it. Even though I was relatively certain no one was in there, I knocked first, then slowly creaked the door open. It was dark, but the hall light illuminated enough for me to see inside. Although I was sure the darkness had me imagining things. So I flipped the light on. My heart leaped into my throat as I froze and stared.

Empty.

The office was fucking *empty*.

I blinked a few times, hoping my eyes were playing tricks on me, but nope—she was gone. For good this time.

"I need you to tail someone for me."

"Good fucking morning to you, too, sunshine." Roman plopped down into the guest chair on the other side of my desk.

When I'd texted him at six this morning, he was already on his way to my place. Since I hadn't slept all night and decided to make productive use of my insomnia, I told him to meet me in the office.

"There's nothing good about it." I tossed the file in my hand on the desk and rubbed my eyes.

"You look like shit, man." Roman leaned back in his chair and lifted his boot-covered feet onto my desk, crossing them at the ankles. Normally, I'd knock them off, but I didn't care enough this morning.

"All the traveling has caught up to me."

"Yeah, that's the reason."

"What's that supposed to mean?"

"Nothing. What do you need?"

"I want you to tail Emerie for me."

"What the fuck for? Isn't she across the hall from you half the day?"

"She moved out."

"When did that happen?"

"Sometime over the last few days, I assume. Got back at midnight, and her office was cleared out."

"Guess that explains you looking like you haven't slept in two days."

"I just need to know if she found a new place to rent. I found a small house to lease down in Atlanta. Dave Monroe is going to join me part time here, taking over some of the work that my clients won't care if I don't handle personally. Between that and working remotely, I'm thinking I can come back twice a month for a few days instead of the back and forth every week. There's no reason she can't stay here. It would be easy to avoid me."

"So you're really doing it? Going to leave your practice and move to Atlanta?"

"What choice do I have? I'll appeal, but there's no guarantee it'll change anything. Beck feels the limbo I'm in. I can't live in a hotel room—he'll never settle without being able to have his own place to sleep and keep his things. He needs to feel like he's at home, that I'm there if he needs me—

school events, doctor's appointments. He just made a pee-wee hockey team. What would I do when his games were on days I was in New York every week? Plus, I can't go back and forth fifty two times a year, cramming forty hours of work in two days. It's tough after a while."

"How long is the lease at the house you found?"

"A year." My shoulders slumped. "Figure it'll take nine months before I even get a date for oral arguments on my custody appeal."

"You sign it yet?"

"Not yet. Meeting with the landlord when I go back down at the end of the week."

"Good. Give me a few more days."

"For what?"

"I got a guy down in Atlanta working on something for me."

"Do I even want to know?"

Roman smiled. "Fuck no. Then you can't be implicated."

It was the first time I'd laughed since...I wasn't sure when. That was Roman—a man with a plan who always had my back.

"Well, whatever it is, thanks."

"So what do you want done on Emerie? Just tail her? How about a hint on what I'm looking for?"

"I just need to know she's okay. See if she found office space and if it's in a safe neighborhood."

Roman raised a brow. "So you don't want me to find out if she's fucking someone?"

I clenched my jaw so hard I nearly cracked a tooth. "No. If you find that out, don't even tell me that shit. Especially if it's that asshole Baldwin—because he'll just screw her over."

"Like you?"

"What the hell does that mean? I didn't screw her over. *I* got screwed over. I'm doing what's best for her."

Roman stood. "Not gonna fight with you, buddy. I'll tail her if that's what you want. But maybe you should ask yourself if what's best for Emerie might be letting her make her own decision on how to handle your relationship."

# CHAPTER FORTY-THREE

## EMERIE

"You were amazing," Baldwin said from the doorway.

I looked up from packing my lecture materials. "How long have you been standing there?"

"I caught the last five minutes."

"You're being kind. I was a nervous wreck."

He smiled. "It gets easier. But seriously, it didn't show."

Two days ago Baldwin had called to say one of the department's TAs had to leave unexpectedly and asked if I wanted to fill in. It would practically assure me the adjunct faculty position I was interviewing for tomorrow, so I agreed, even though I had zero desire to do anything these days. Getting out of bed was an effort.

After I finished packing, I walked to the door. "Are you heading to a class?"

"Nope. Just finished grading papers and wanted to check in on you. How about some lunch? There's a great little bistro a few blocks away that makes the best ahi tuna salad."

For the last month, I'd been avoiding Baldwin out of deference to Drew, but there was no reason to do that anymore. Even though I wasn't much in the mood for company, I knew locking myself in my apartment and being sad wasn't really healthy.

"Sure. I'd love to."

Baldwin and I ate lunch outside next to the heat lamps since it was a beautiful afternoon. At one point, I got up to go the ladies' room, and I spotted a man sitting in a car parked half a block down. The car was at my back while I was eating, so I had no idea how long it had been there, but I could have sworn the man inside was Roman. After we finished lunch, I looked for the car again, but it was already gone.

Later in the day, after running my afternoon errands, I went home to do an online counseling session. I couldn't even open the front door all the way because my apartment was crammed with office furniture. It probably wasn't the smartest idea to leave before finding new space, but I just couldn't stay there anymore. Even when Drew wasn't around, all I could think about was him. I'd thought ridding myself of having to see the desk we'd had sex on and the copy room we'd first met in would help me think about him less. Unfortunately, my thoughts traveled with me instead of staying behind at the office.

While I was setting up my laptop so my patients wouldn't see the crazy room full of office furniture, a knock came at my door. I hated that I got my hopes up, thinking maybe it was Drew. I was confused when I saw Roman through my peephole.

I opened the door. "Roman?"

He stood gripping the top of the doorway. "I've been instructed to tail you."

"I thought I saw you at the restaurant today."

"Can I come in? I won't take up much of your time."

"Ummm...sure. Of course. But I should warn you, the place is a mess. I moved my office into my tiny apartment and have no place to put anything, so it's basically taken over my living room." I opened the door as wide as I could, and Roman came in. "Can I get you something to drink?"

He held up his hand. "I'm good."

There were piles of files all over the couch. I started to collect them to make room for him to sit.

"Do you want to have a seat? Get comfortable so you can tell me why you're following me?"

He chuckled. "Sure."

I sat down on my office chair across from him and waited for him to begin.

"Drew asked me to tail you. He claims he wants to make sure your new office is in a safe neighborhood."

"And what if it wasn't? What's he going to do with that information?"

Roman shrugged. "Shit don't always make sense when a man's in love."

"In love? Did you miss the part where he dumped me?"

"Never thought I'd say this about my best friend. Known the man since elementary school, and he's always had balls of steel, but he's afraid."

"Of what?"

"Of falling in love. Mother cheated on his father and took off when he was a kid. Wife lied to him about the kid she was pregnant with being his, then continued to screw the baby daddy after they were married. He fell in love with that little boy, then she took being a father away from him. Also gets reminded day in and day out at work how few relationships make it—especially ones where the couples don't spend time together. Finally found some good in his life with you. I hate to see him throw that away because he's too afraid to take a chance. Did he even tell you the judge let Alexa stay in Atlanta, and he's moving there?"

"No."

There was an ache in my chest. The way he'd ended things made a little more sense now. A part of me could understand why Drew would be skeptical that things could work between us. His past had pretty much taught him that when you fall in love, it gets taken away. But that didn't excuse what he'd done. Whether he was justified or not didn't change the fact that he hadn't even tried to fight for us. He hadn't even told me what was happening.

"I'm sorry for what he's going through, Roman. None of it is fair to him. But even if it were true that he still cared about me, what could I do about it? I can't make him unafraid. He didn't even want to try. That tells me I wasn't worth the risk to him. I need to be worth more than that."

Roman nodded. "I get it. It's just...I saw you with that professor today at lunch."

"Baldwin and I are friends. Yes, we have history—or I should say *I* have a history of feelings for Baldwin. But I fell in love with Drew, and that taught me that the feelings I thought I had for Baldwin weren't ever really love. Because it was never like this with Baldwin—what I have for Drew is at a different level."

Roman smiled. "You said *have*, not had."

"Of course. I can't turn off feelings just because I was hurt. It's going to take effort to move on from Drew."

"Do me a favor? Don't start trying too hard yet. I'm still holding out hope my friend is going to pull his head out of his ass."

# CHAPTER FORTY-FOUR

## DREW

I don't sweat.

I've stood up in court and flown by the seat of my pants when a witness changed his testimony and a judge was staring down his nose at me—nothing. Yet somehow, today I had to blot my forehead, and the paper napkin stuck to my sweaty palms.

Why did I have to do this today? I wasn't ready. *Beck* wasn't ready. But that wouldn't stop my ex-wife. She'd threatened to tell Beck when I returned him later tonight if I didn't, and though she wasn't a woman of her word, I was certain she'd make good on this threat.

It was the second time in as many weeks that I was channeling my father. *Rip the Band-Aid off* was his favorite cliché. I only hoped my son's face didn't look anything like Emerie's did when I broke things off.

I turned to Beck, who was belly laughing watching cartoons, and looked at my watch. *Shit.* I was out of time to stall.

"Beck? Buddy? I need to talk to you about something before you go back to Mommy's tonight. Do you think you can turn off the TV?"

He turned to me, such a sweet, easygoing boy. "Okay, Daddy."

After he got up and grabbed the remote from the desk, he sat back down and turned, giving me his full attention. My mouth was suddenly dry, making it hard to speak. There was no easy way to break this to a kid, no matter how I padded it.

"Is everything okay? You look like I do before I barf." Beck stood. "Do you want me to get you a bucket like you do for me when I barf?"

I laughed nervously. "No, buddy. I don't need a bucket." *At least I don't think I do.* "Sit down. It's about me being your daddy."

His face fell. "Are you not going to be my daddy anymore? Is that why you won't take me home to your house?"

I might need that bucket after all. "Oh, God. Nothing like that at all. I'm never going to stop being your daddy. But..." Fuck it, here it goes. "But some kids are lucky and have more than two parents."

His eyes lit up. "Are you going to marry Emerie?"

*Jesus.* That hurt on so many levels. "I don't think that's going to happen, Beck. No."

He was getting excited and went off track. "Because Mikayla from school has a stepmom. Her parents are divorced like you and Mommy, and now she has *two* mommies."

"No. Well, yes. No. Sort of. The thing is...*I'm* actually your stepdad."

"So I have two dads?" He scrunched up his nose.

"You do. When you were born, your mom and I were married. I didn't know you weren't my..." I felt the words start to bubble in my throat and had to clear it a few times to fight off showing how upset I was. I needed Beck to know what I was telling him would have no effect on our relationship, and my crying wouldn't send the right message.

I started again. "I didn't know you weren't...my son, biologically, until years after you were born."

"If you're not my blogical dad, then who is?"

"It's a man named Levi. Mom says you've met him already a few times."

His eyes lit up. "The race car driver?"

I was emotionally conflicted. While it sucked for me that he was excited about that asshole being related to him, if it made it easier for him to accept the news, I was all for that.

"Yes. The race car driver."

"He drives a cool car! It's got a hood scoop, and it's loud."

I forced a smile. "Your mom is going to have you start to get to know Levi. But it doesn't mean that anything is going to change between you and me."

He thought about everything I'd said for a moment, then asked, "Do you still love me?"

Beck might be almost seven and starting to get too cool to hold my hand as he walked into school, but all bets were off now. I hoisted him onto my lap and spoke directly into his eyes. "I love you more than anything in this world."

"So you're not leaving me because I have a new dad?"

"No, Beck. I'd never leave you. People don't leave when they love someone. They stick around forever. That's why I'm moving to Atlanta. Your mom brought you down here, and I go where you go."

"Did my blogical dad not love me, and that's why we lived in New York?"

Jesus. He had some tough questions.

"I know it's confusing, but Levi didn't know you were his son when you were born. So he didn't get a chance to know you. Now that he knows, he's gonna love you too, I'm sure."

I realized it was time I sat down and had a talk with Levi to make sure my son would be the priority he needed to be. If he was going to be part of his life, he'd better not be a disappointment.

"Will he live here, too?"

"I'm not sure, buddy."

"But you said people don't leave when they love someone. So he'll only leave if he doesn't love me?"

God, I was fucking this up royally.

"Sometimes you have to leave physically when you love someone, like maybe for work, but you figure out other ways to still be with them every day. When I said people don't leave when they love someone, I didn't mean they had to be there in person every single day. You just have to get more creative to find ways to be together when you can't be there in person. Like you and I did the last month when I had to go back to New York to work."

"Like FaceTiming with Mom's iPhone?"

"Exactly."

"Like Snapchatting?"

"I'm not up on that one. But if you say so."

Beck nodded and was silent for a while.

It was a lot to take in, especially for a kid his age. To this day, *I* could barely process it.

"You have any questions, bud?"

"Do I still get to call you Dad?"

My heart dropped. "Yes, you definitely do. I'm always going to be your dad."

"What will I call Levi then?" The thought of my son calling another man Dad was physically painful. But my own pain didn't matter.

"I'm sure you, Mom, and Levi will figure that out eventually."

A few minutes later, Beck asked if he could turn his

cartoons back on. He seemed no worse for the wear. I, on the other hand, felt like I'd just done ten rounds in a heavyweight fight with my hands tied behind my back. I was mentally and physically exhausted.

That night, after I dropped Beck back with Alexa, I laid in my bed at the hotel, replaying our conversation over and over. It was important to me that I stood behind the things I'd said to my son today. Kids learned more from what parents did than what they said. I needed to show him I was here for the long haul, especially because I couldn't control what Levi and Alexa did.

As I attempted to fall sleep, one thing kept nagging at the back of my mind and wouldn't let me settle. It was something I'd said. While I believed the words to be true, if I was being honest with myself, I wasn't exactly living up to my own edict. And it had nothing to do with my son.

*People don't leave when they love someone. They stick around forever.*

The following morning, my unsettled feeling had sprouted. The root had been there for the last few weeks, but since my talk with Beck, it had grown like a vine and taken up residence in my stomach, my head. And it had coiled around my heart so tightly I could barely breathe.

I had to drag myself out of bed so I could get to the airport for my flight. In the back of the cab, I checked my departure time and fidgeted. I knew myself, how I could obsess over shit, and I *needed* to know. Finally giving in, I texted Roman at five in the morning.

**Drew: *Is she seeing someone?***

As always, he responded within a few minutes. He was the only person I knew who required less sleep than I did.

**Roman:** *Thought I wasn't supposed to tell you that part.*

**Drew:** *Just tell me.*

**Roman:** *You sure you can handle it?*

*Jesus Christ.* I wasn't actually so sure I could. If he was asking, it wasn't good.

**Drew:** *Tell me.*

**Roman:** *The neighbor is moving in on her. Sent her some flowers—huge thing of yellow roses. Also took her out to lunch the other day at some fancy place with a big price tag and stupid, tiny food.*

*Fuck.*

**Drew:** *Anything else?*

**Roman:** *Started tailing him a bit. Took some woman to dinner last night. Tall. Great legs. Halfway through dinner it looked like they had an argument. She pulled some dramatic shit, standing and throwing the napkin on the table, then stormed off. Think he might have dumped her.*

The unsettled feeling in my gut was there for a goddamn reason. I was going to lose her forever if I didn't get my head out of my ass. Pulling up to the airport, I typed one last text to my friend before exiting the cab.

**Drew:** *Thanks, Roman.*

He immediately typed back.

**Roman:** *Go get her. About fucking time.*

⁓

I was almost as nervous as I'd been yesterday when I had to break the news to Beck. But there was also something different about the way I felt. *Determined.* No matter what it took, I was going to make Emerie forgive me and give me another chance. I'd fucked up—I could place blame on a million experiences in my life, but the truth of the matter was *I'd fucked up.* And I was about to start fixing it.

There was an out of order sign in front of two of the elevators in her building. I stood in front of the lone functioning one, tapping my foot as I watched the numbers come down over the doors. It stuck on nine for thirty seconds, then stopped at eight for just as long. *I don't have time for this.* I'd already wasted enough time. Looking around, I saw the sign for the stairs and broke into a jog. My heart pounded as I took them two at a time up to the third floor.

Then I was standing in front of Emerie's door, and it dawned on me for the first time that I had no idea what I was going to say. Two hours on the plane, and I hadn't come up with an opening statement. Good thing I'm a fly-by-the-seat-of-my-pants kind of guy when it comes to oral arguments.

I took a deep breath, steadied myself, and knocked.

When the door opened, I realized how completely unprepared I was.

Because it was Baldwin staring at me from inside.

# CHAPTER FORTY-FIVE

## DREW

"Where's Emerie?"

"She's getting dressed. We have a breakfast meeting at the college to attend this morning. Not that it's any of your business."

Professor Putz was still standing inside, and I was the one out in the hall. The symbolism ate at me. I brushed past him and went into Emerie's apartment.

"Sure, come on in," he mumbled, sarcastically.

I turned to face him, folding my hands across my chest. "Now leave."

"I beg your pardon?"

"I need to speak to Emerie alone, so I would appreciate it if you would disappear."

He shook his head. "No."

My brows lifted. I didn't think the peckerhead had it in him. If it were any other time, I might've been impressed with his tenacity. But right now, it just annoyed the shit out of me.

I took a step forward. "You can either leave on your own, or I'll help you leave. Either way, you're leaving. What's it gonna be?"

Finding I wasn't playing around, he took the smart route and opened the door. "Tell Emerie I'll see her at school later."

"Yeah. I'll be sure to give her the message." I gave the door a shove, slamming it closed on his heels.

Turning around, I found Emerie's living room cluttered with office furniture. The place barely had enough room for a couch and chair before. Now it was also filled with a desk, office chairs, file cabinets, computer equipment, and everything else from her office.

The door to her bedroom creaked, and Emerie walked out, looking down as she scrolled through something on her phone.

"I pulled up the psychology department bios on the college's website. Tell me again who we're meeting? I'm so bad with names."

My answer stopped her in her tracks. "It's just me and you."

Emerie's head whipped up, and she blinked a few times as if she were imagining the man standing in her living room.

"Drew. What are you doing here?" She looked beyond me. "And where's Baldwin?"

"Gone."

"Gone where?"

I looked down at my feet for a minute, then caught her in my gaze. There was a crushing sensation in my chest as I found the same sadness that loomed inside of me behind her eyes.

My voice was low and hoarse. "Do you love him?"

She stared at me for long seconds, the wheels in her head turning. I held my breath the entire time. Finally, she shook her head.

*Thank God.*

That was all I needed to hear. Anything and everything else we could work out. I could make her forgive me, she could learn to trust me again, but I couldn't make her not be in love with another man. She was still standing in her bedroom doorway, and suddenly there was way too much space between us. I stalked over to her, not giving a shit if it was a caveman move. The overwhelming urge to touch her outweighed any need for etiquette.

She didn't move. With every step I took, my heartbeat grew faster. She still didn't move when I reached out, cupped her face in my hands, and slowly brushed my lips against hers, testing the waters. Taking that as a green light, or at least not a bright red flashing one, I went back for more. Planting my lips over her mouth, soft went out the window, and I kissed her hard. She opened, moaning as I pulled her flush against me. The sound shot right to my dick, and the hard kiss quickly elevated to a frenzy. She smelled amazing, tasted as sweet as I remembered, and the feel of her body pressed to mine was better than I'd ever experienced.

God, I was such a fucking idiot. How could I have ever walked away from this?

The kiss went on for a long time. When it broke, it didn't take long for her doubt and fear to creep back in—not to mention anger.

"You can't just show up—"

My lips crashed down on hers, cutting her off. This time, she tried to fight me. She gave one weak shove to my chest, which only made me wrap my arms around her tighter. Eventually, her fight went limp, and she gave in again. When our kiss broke, I left my lips inches from hers as a reminder that I'd be on her in less than a heartbeat if she started again.

"Just give me a minute before you rip into me, okay?"

"Sixty seconds," she said.

The corner of my lip twitched. *God, I missed that mouth.* And not just the feel of her soft lips and submissive tongue—I missed her sass. Brushing two fingers across her cheek, I gave it to her straight. My voice was raw as I laid it all at her feet.

"I love you."

A hopeful smile rose on her beautiful face. But then she remembered. She remembered what I'd done to her the last few weeks, and her smile fell.

"You have a funny way of showing it. You love me, so you dumped me?"

"The judge didn't change my visitation schedule with Beck, but he allowed Alexa to stay in Atlanta. I have to move."

"I know all about it. Roman told me."

"Roman?"

"Yes, Roman."

"What the fuck?"

"Don't you *what the fuck* me. At least Roman had the courtesy to fill me in on *why* you were acting like an asshole."

"I was scared."

"So was I. But I didn't walk away."

I looked down. "I know. I could give you a million excuses about why I did what I did, try to justify myself. But all those reasons lead back to one thing." I paused and then spoke into her eyes. "I was afraid."

"And now? Now you're not afraid anymore?"

I shook my head. "I finally realized I was more afraid of losing you than I was of taking a chance and getting hurt. Guess you can say I grew a pair of balls."

She softened. It looked like she wanted to believe me, but was skeptical. I couldn't say I blamed her.

"How do I know they're not going to shrivel up and disappear again?" Her voice cracked. "You really hurt me, Drew."

"I'm so sorry. And I know right now my word isn't worth much to you. But I swear to God, Em, if you give me another chance, I won't fuck things up this time."

Her eyes welled up. "You'll be living in Atlanta, and I'll be here every day—some days working at the college with Baldwin. How would it even work?"

"However you need it to work. We'll take turns. One week you'll come to Atlanta; one week I'll come to New York. Or every other if that's too much on you. And we'll do a fuck of a lot of sexting and FaceTiming. I don't have it all planned yet, but we'll figure it out. It won't be easy, but it'll be worth it. I love you, Emerie. I'd go three hundred and sixty-four days thirsty if it meant I got to drink you in for just one."

A tear slid down her cheek, and I caught it with my thumb. "Please tell me these are happy tears, Em."

"I don't think a long-distance relationship will work."

"We'll make it work. Please. Please give me another chance."

She shook her head rapidly. "No."

"But—" I attempted to change her mind, but this time she silenced me.

Emerie pressed her lips to mine.

The kiss was filled with so many crazy emotions that I could feel them pulsing through my veins and into our connection. When we finally broke, she was panting, and I was in a fucking panic. *She's saying goodbye.*

"It won't work long distance."

"Em, we'll make it work."

"No. I'm going with you to Atlanta."

"We'll figure it—wait...what?" I stared at her, incredulous. "Repeat that."

"I said I'm going with you to Atlanta."

"What about the job you applied for at the college? Your patients?"

"I'm a TA for the rest of this semester. I just interviewed for the guest adjunct position. They may not even hire me. The semester ends in three months. We'll commute back and forth until then. With a little experience on my resume, maybe I'll have an easier time finding a part-time adjunct job down there. And most of my clients are portable—they were doing video-counseling sessions before. Maybe I'll even keep a few and come back and forth while you keep your clients here. You need to be near your son, and I want to get to know him, too. He's part of you."

"You're serious? You almost gave me a heart attack saying long distance wasn't going to work."

She smiled. "Good. Serves you right after what you've put me through the last few weeks."

Without warning, I lifted her into the air. She yelped, but the smile on her face told me she was happy. Her legs wrapped around my waist, arms wrapped around my neck, and I squeezed her so hard, I worried I might hurt her.

"God, I fucking love you."

"You better."

"I do."

I took her mouth in another kiss and walked with her in my arms until I could find a clear surface to set her down on. That surface happened to be the kitchen counter, which also happened to be the perfect height. My dick was already hard, feeling her heat through my pants.

Somehow we managed to rip each other's clothes off while keeping connected the entire time. I sucked beneath her earlobe, and my fingers explored the crack of her ass while she unbuckled my pants. When my pants fell to the ground, I slipped down my underwear, and my cock bobbed against my stomach.

Looking between us, I said, "We missed you."

She laughed. "I missed you both, too."

I needed to be inside her so bad. "The foreplay is going to be short, but I'll make it up to you on the back end. It'll be postplay instead." I reached down and grabbed my cock, lowering it to half-mast so I could use it to rub her wetness all over her. She was slick and ready, and I was impatient as hell, so I pushed inside. Emerie looked down between us, watching my cock disappear inside of her as I slowly pushed in.

When I was fully seated, I lifted her chin. "Watching you watch me put my cock inside of you is the sexiest thing I've ever seen in my life."

She smiled. "I'm glad, because I really liked watching it."

I stroked her cheek with my thumb. "On second thought, this smile right here, this might be the sexiest thing I've ever seen in my life."

I began to move, slowly at first, gliding in and out. Something was different about this time, like all the barriers between us had been removed, and I was finally free to love her.

I kissed her lips gently. "I love you."

She searched my eyes. "I love you, too, Drew. I didn't know it until I felt the real thing, but I'm not sure I was ever really in love before I met you."

It felt like she'd given me a crown. In that moment, I was a fucking king. I wasn't sure what I'd done to deserve her, but I was greedy enough not to care. She was mine to keep, and I planned on keeping her forever this time.

Even though it had been only a few weeks since the last time I was inside of her, that was way too long. I tried to go slow, but when she tightened her legs around me and her pussy clenched, fisting my cock, I knew I wasn't going to last long. She liked it when I talked during sex, so I whispered everything I wanted to do to her in her ear—how I couldn't wait to rub my face in her pussy, how I wanted to come all over her tits, and how later I was going to bend her over the counter she was sitting on and take her from behind, finishing all over ass cheeks that would be hot and red from my hand stinging them.

She moaned loudly, yelling my name and begging for me to go harder. I sped up my pace, and after I felt her body spasm all around me, I came long and hard inside of her. There was no way the neighbors didn't hear our spectacular finish—and I certainly hoped *one in particular* had enjoyed hearing it.

After our breathing calmed, I wiped a stray hair from her cheek and looked into her sated blue eyes. "So, you're really moving to Atlanta with me?

"I am."

"I found a little house with a yard that's available to rent. Maybe you can come see it, and we can decide if we want something bigger."

"I've been living in this shoebox for six months—anything will seem bigger."

"It's got three bedrooms, a big bathtub, and the landlord told me I could repaint it if I want to."

"Are you saying you'll allow me to add color to your life?"

"I'm saying you already have. You're the red in my black and white world."

## EMERIE
*One year later*

"Did you get it?"

Roman reached into his jacket pocket and pulled out an envelope. "Right here." He shook his head. "Still can't believe you pulled this shit off."

I spotted Drew coming down the hall. "Put it away. Here he comes."

Roman slipped the envelope back into his pocket and pulled out a flask instead. Twisting off the cap, he offered it to me. "Swig?"

"No, thanks."

Drew walked in as Roman put the beat-up, old metal flask to his lips. "You still carry that thing around with you?"

"Never know when you'll need a shot of Hennessy, my friend."

I was surprised Drew hadn't started doing shots after the last few days. I'd pretty much driven him crazy getting ready for tonight. My parents would be arriving in the next few minutes, and a half dozen of Beck's friends were coming, too. Even though we'd lived in Atlanta for nearly a year now, it was really the first time we'd be having company. Well, except for

Roman—who didn't count as a guest. He was always family to Drew, and over the last year, he'd become my family, too. He was the annoying brother I'd always wanted.

Sometimes when he'd visit, I'd find him on the couch playing video games with Drew at two in the morning. Other times, he'd make Drew miss his flight when he had business in New York because he'd dragged him out on a stakeout. But all the time, he was there for us. Most people got scars from the chicken pox. Drew got a treasured friend for life. Somehow that made sense with those two.

Beck came barreling in from the yard. His clothes were drenched, and brown water dripped from his little head. "I watered the garden!"

"Ummm...did you water the garden, or did the garden water you?" I pointed to the bathroom. "Go take a bath before everyone gets here."

"Can I just go in the pool naked?" He jumped up and down, holding his hands in the praying position.

"No, you can't go in the pool naked. The neighbors will see you."

Beck pouted and slumped his shoulders before turning to drag his feet en route to the bathroom.

"Roman and I are going to pick up beer," Drew announced. "Need anything while I'm out? Pick up the cake you ordered?"

"My parents are swinging by the bakery on their way here. It's a tradition that they pay for the cake. Don't ask," I lied.

Drew kissed me on the cheek. "Whatever you want." Then he whispered. "By the way, you didn't seem to mind if the neighbors saw *you* when you were naked in the pool the other night."

I suppose he had a point. Although in my defense, we'd just had Beck for three weeks while his mother was on her honeymoon in Bali, I'd had a glass of wine, and Drew had just come back from the gym so his muscles were particularly bulgy. Plus, it was dark out, and hell—have I mentioned that his muscles were particularly bulgy?

Ten minutes later, I'd just finished prepping the melon ball salad when the doorbell rang.

My smiling parents greeted me with arms in the air. "Happy Gotcha Day!"

After coming inside to go to the bathroom, I stood watching the party in the yard from the kitchen window for a few minutes. Everything was going great. My parents were talking to Drew's new law partner and his wife, Roman was flirting with the single mom of one of Beck's best friends—I might have mentioned the other's single status to each them ahead of time—and Beck was climbing in the treehouse he and his father had spent four months building after we moved here.

And today was Gotcha Day. My parents were here, and this year was going to be even more special than ever.

From the yard, Drew caught me watching and excused himself from conversation with one of his new friends. He slipped into the house and came up behind me, wrapping his arms around my waist and joining me to gaze out the window.

"What are we looking at?"

"My life."

"Yeah?" He turned me around and gave me a sweet kiss. "Now I'm looking at mine, too."

My heart sighed. "I love it when you sweet-talk me."

"Last night you loved it when I dirty-talked you."

I wrapped my arms around his neck. "Maybe I just love you."

"I am pretty awesome."

Rolling my eyes, I laughed. "Egomaniac."

Drew kissed me on the forehead. "Your parents are anxious to have cake. I think your mom has a sweet tooth."

My parents had started bugging me about the cake the minute they walked in. Only not for the reason Drew thought. The sun had started to set, and it was probably an hour past the time I should have been serving cake—but I was stalling. A sudden case of nerves had hit me, after more than six months of anxiously waiting for this time to get here.

"I promised Beck he could help carry the cake. Why don't you make a pot of coffee, and I'll go grab him?"

I found Beck, and he raced to the house when I told him it was time. He smiled from ear to ear, and it brought back so many memories of the excitement of my first Gotcha Day.

Seeing his son's excited face, Drew said, "That must be some cake."

"It's in my room. Uncle Roman said he put it under my pillow because he's better than a fairy," Beck yelled over his shoulder, already halfway down the hall.

Drew's brow furrowed; I extended my hand to him without explanation. "Come on."

Beck's room was bright yellow. We'd let him pick the color when I moved down to Atlanta permanently after the semester ended. True to his word, Drew didn't complain about all the color I added to the house. Each room was brighter than the next—except our room, which I'd painted a muted gray. I'd picked it because when I'd asked Drew what color he might like in our bedroom, he'd told me I was all the color he needed. So I figured I'd give him what he liked in the bedroom—since that was the place he always gave me what I liked.

Beck stood next to his bed with the envelope behind his back. He looked like he might burst with the excitement, his smile was so wide.

I nodded to him. "Go ahead."

Beck whipped the envelope out from behind his back and shoved it at his dad. "Happy Gotcha Day."

Hesitantly, Drew took the thick, white envelope, then looked at me. "It's for me? But it's your day, babe."

I shook my head. "Open it."

Drew slid the documents out of the envelope and unfolded them. He was an attorney, so it wouldn't have taken long for him to figure it out even if the caption of the order hadn't said it all. He stilled as he read the heading, then looked up at me in shock.

I nodded.

Receiving confirmation of what was clearly written on the top of the paper, Drew quickly rifled through the dozen stapled pages to get to the last one. I knew what he was looking for—all the signatures to see that it was official. And there it was in black and white, just the way he liked things. The signatures of Justice Raymond Clapman and Levi Archer Bodine.

When he looked back up at me, his eyes were filled with tears. "How the..."

"Happy Gotcha Day, Dad. You got *me* for Gotcha Day! Now you and Emerie can celebrate the same day!"

Of course, it was only a formality. Drew had always been Beck's father in both his and Beck's hearts, no different than I was with my parents. But sometimes, making things official ties up the bow on what is already the greatest gift. Later I'd tell Drew that we'd be paying additional child support for the next dozen or so years—although I knew he wouldn't care one bit.

When I'd agreed to take over Levi's child support payments in exchange for him signing the adoption papers, I'd always intended to pay the support from my earnings anyway. It would be my way of supporting the child who'd become mine too over the last year.

Turned out Levi wasn't much interested in being a father to Beck. He also wasn't much interested in Alexa cramping his style by coming to his races. Apparently, all of the other women he was sleeping with didn't like it much either. Less than two weeks after Alexa had made Drew break the news to his son that he had a different biological father, Levi dumped her. He'd wanted nothing to do with getting to know Beck. His only connection was the huge chunk of his paychecks Alexa made sure the state collected as child support after he'd pissed her off.

So, a few months back, while Drew was in New York on business and the NASCAR races were in Georgia—Roman and I took a little daytrip to talk to Levi. My plan of buying him off was certainly better than the one Roman had concocted—which involved a friend of a friend in the Atlanta police department setting Levi up for a DWI arrest, then threatening to ruin his livelihood as a driver if he didn't sign over his parental rights.

I figured it was a long shot that he'd sign adoption papers in exchange for taking over his support—but I had nothing to lose and everything to gain for Drew. And sometimes long shots paid off. Now that Alexa had found some new meal ticket to hitch herself to, she didn't object to the adoption.

Deep down, she knew it was the right thing, and ultimately, she didn't care as long as she got her monthly support check and had a man by her side.

Drew stared down at the papers in disbelief. I thought maybe he was trying to hold back tears, but when a drop splattered on the papers, I realized he was crying, not holding them back. Opening his arms wide, he hooked one around me and one around his son and hauled us against his body. Then he let it all go. His shoulders shook, and his body vibrated as he silently sobbed.

I couldn't help but join in. It was a beautiful moment—one that reminded me so much of my own Gotcha Day and my parents' tears. I hadn't understood what all the fuss was about then, but today so much became clear.

After we dried our eyes, Beck asked if we could have the cake.

"Go ahead, bud. Why don't you go get the cake and take it outside. Emerie and I will meet you out there in a few minutes."

"Okay, Dad." Beck raced from his room, leaving just the two of us.

Drew stared at me with an astonished look on his face. "I can't believe you did this. No one has ever done anything so meaningful for me in my entire life."

I started to get choked up again. "Roman helped."

Drew pushed my hair behind my ear. "I'm sure he did. But it's you who gave me everything I could ever ask for."

I squeezed his hand. "That's only fair, because you've given me the same."

He let go of my hand and took a step back. "I haven't given you everything yet. But I intend to, if you'll let me."

What came next happened in slow motion. Drew dug in his front pocket and came up with a small black box before dropping down to one knee.

"I've been carrying this thing in my pocket every day for the last week, trying to figure out how to give it to you. I wanted it to be special—I thought today might be the day, but I was waiting for the perfect moment. I can't think of a more perfect one, can you?"

One hand flew to my mouth as I looked down at him. "You're right. It's perfect."

Drew squeezed my other hand. "Emerie Rose, since the day you broke into my office, vandalized it, and showed me your ass, I've felt like a piece of me was missing when I wasn't around you. You're the color in my black and white world. Before I met you, I didn't understand why things never worked out with anyone else. But I finally understand it now; it's because they weren't you. So, please tell me you'll marry me, because you've already given me everything else. The only thing missing from my life is you having my last name."

It felt like I was in a dream. Tears spilled down my cheeks. "Is this real? Is this really happening right now?"

"This is as real as it gets, babe. You, me, Beck...maybe one in your belly and another we adopt someday. We're already a family. You officially gave me Beck today. Now make it official and give me you, too. Say yes."

"Yes! Yes! Yes!" I got so excited, I tackled Drew, knocking him back from where he was kneeling, and we both wound up on the floor.

We stayed down there for a while as my future husband kissed away my tears. "Your proposal was so sweet. Dare I say romantic? I didn't think you had it in you, Jagger."

He rolled us so he was on top. "I had it in me. But you're going to have it in you as soon as I can get these people the hell out of here."

I smiled. "There's the pervert I know and love."

"Just want you to be happy, babe." He paused. "And naked."

And I would be. Because somewhere between the fighting and the clothes-ripping angry sex, I'd fallen madly in love with an unexpected man at the most inconvenient time. And it turned out to be exactly what we both needed.

# THE END

# ACKNOWLEDGEMENTS

First and foremost, thank you to my readers—never in my wildest dreams could I have imagined where this journey would take me when I started writing. Your support and excitement for my books is a gift that I cherish. Thank you for allowing me to tell you my stories and be part of your escape!

To Penelope – I could fill this book with the thank you notes you deserve, but I'll sum it up as best I can. My life is an adventure with you in it, and I can't imagine it without you. Thank you for the constant help and support, but most of all for your friendship.

To Julie – You define strength. Thank you for always being there for me.

To Luna – You bring my books to life! Thank you so much for the amazing friendship and support and for keeping Vi's Violets exciting with your beautiful teasers and passion for reading. I can't wait to meet you this year!

To Sommer – Thank you for allowing me to drive you nuts...again.

To my agent, Kimberly Brower – For being so much more than my agent. I can't wait to see what new adventures the next year takes us on.

To Elaine and Jessica – Thank you for tuning up my story so that it runs smoothly!

To Lisa at TRSOR and Dani at Inkslinger – Thank you for organizing everything that went into releasing this book.

To all of the incredible bloggers – Thank you so much for everything you do. I am sincerely grateful for the time you so generously give to read my work, write reviews, create teasers, and help share your love of books! I am honored to call you my supporters and friends. Thank you! Thank you! Thank you!

Much love
Vi

# OTHER BOOKS BY VI KEELAND

Life on Stage series (2 standalone books)
Beat
Throb

MMA Fighter series (3 standalone books)
Worth the Fight
Worth the Chance
Worth Forgiving

The Cole Series (2 book serial)
Belong to You
Made for You

Standalone novels
Bossman
The Baller
Playboy Pilot (Co-written with Penelope Ward)
Stuck-Up Suit (Co-written with Penelope Ward)
Cocky Bastard (Co-written with Penelope Ward)
Left Behind (A Young Adult Novel)
First Thing I See